The
Enduring
Echo
of
Words
Unsaid

Villa Campanile Press

Our lives are determined by the words we choose, whether spoken or unsaid. Sometimes in life, when something goes without saying, that is all the more reason to say it.

Prologue

A year ago, during the waning days of 2016, I knew how I was going to die; I just didn't know when. No, I didn't have a serious illness or cancer, just an obvious character flaw and an aching need for it to be over. My death was going to be sudden, dramatic, and glorious; my one grand act in an otherwise subdued life. You see, I knew I was going to die in a violent, high-speed collision on a rural road, exactly two miles from my home outside of Boulder, Colorado. How could I have known this? Because every day as I drove to work, I came upon a long uphill stretch of rural blacktop, and, at least once a week, I accelerated to ninety miles per hour and climbed that hill in the other lane, the one for oncoming traffic. Few vehicles traveled the road—on many days, I didn't pass a single one—but I knew, eventually, I'd smash into an unsuspecting pickup or sedan or eighteen-wheeler at the crest of that hill, and my life would be over. It might be the next time, the next week, or it might take a decade. What had started one day as a foolhardy dare had somehow turned into an irrational quest.

Considering my antics on my hill, most would probably think my life was miserable by traditional standards, but that was far from the truth. Though I'd dropped out of community college during my second semester, I'd done well for myself. I had all the trappings of success: a wife and children, my own company, a brimming brokerage account, a home in the mountains, and a garage stocked with premium vehicles. From the outside looking in, my life looked great, but I was empty on the inside, and I was broken.

In my early twenties, I partied too much and worked dead-end jobs, everything from bartender to pizza cook to warehouse worker to waiter to cashier at an all-night convenience store. In thin times, I even sold pot and assorted pharmaceuticals to my friends to keep a roof over my head and gas in my car. I lived in rented homes with many roommates and rarely had twenty dollars in the pockets of my unwashed pants. I didn't own anything but a rusty scrapheap of a car and my free time, but that was enough for me. At what was usually a jumping-off age, I was in free fall.

During that time, I remember my father, Raymond Bryant, a prominent trial lawyer who was never able to hide his disappointment in his only son, once said to me, "You'll never get anywhere in life if you keep *flitting* around like you do." The word means as it sounds, but I looked it up in the dictionary anyway. It suggests a transient nature and instability, someone without roots, substance, or prospects. A worthless person. A ne'er-do-well who never commits to anything. His words always weighted my spirit and lingered like self-doubts in the back of my mind.

As my pickup truck sped towards the crest of my hill, I felt a rush of euphoric anticipation. I'd convinced myself that the meaning of life and what comes next would be revealed to me in a brilliant epiphany at the moment of impact. In that instant, I'd meet the Creator of this beautiful, life-sustaining planet, everything that occupies and inhabits it, and everything that surrounds it. I'd learn the Grand Plan. As part of my head-on collision, I envisioned an arched launch through the windshield like a cliff diver's glide off a rocky ledge in an exotic locale, so I never fastened my seatbelt, and I'd disconnected the airbags. In my mind, it was all so graceful.

When I reached the crest, my truck (and my spirits) lifted momentarily from the road as it topped the hill and then returned to the pavement with a thud. No violent jolt and riotous collision resulted, and no sounds of shattering glass and crumpling metal ensued; once again, the westbound lane was unoccupied. My foot relaxed its pressure against the gas pedal as I steered my vehicle back into the proper lane. On the other side of the hill, exhilarated and full of adrenaline, I always wondered if I'd truly experience my brilliant epiphany or if my dead father would appear instead and say, "What the hell were you thinking?"

Five days after my twenty-seventh birthday, I started working with an entrepreneur who was building his own home on a wooded, seventy-acre parcel south of town. In his early forties, he'd made an uncountable fortune from boutique hotels in Denver, Aspen, and Telluride, and he wanted his own mountain retreat. A deliberate man who oozed competence, the entrepreneur was skilled in carpentry and homebuilding, and he hired me to provide muscle, setup, and cleanup when needed. Since my sophomore year of high school, I'd destroyed plenty of brain cells during my excessive partying, but my physical abilities were still largely intact.

I worked alongside the entrepreneur for two years and helped him build a stunning home. Along the way, I learned a lot about the art and craft of homebuilding, and I also recognized an opportunity for me to build homes in rural areas near Boulder. My first projects were modest homes and small cabins, but I quickly moved up to grander, more luxurious homes that became the mainstay of my company's business. In less than five years, I went from pitching clients for projects to having clients pursue me to build their homes. By my mid-thirties, I'd become a successful homebuilder with a bankable reputation.

My home was typical of the homes I built. It was stone and cedar construction on seven beautiful acres, five bedrooms, seven bathrooms, and just over 4,500 square feet of living space, with magnificent windows that provided panoramic views of the twinkling lights of Boulder, and a four-car garage for the extra vehicles needed for mountain life. It was a modern home with the latest electronic gadgets, convenient features, and luxury appointments, and one that made the success of its owners obvious. In many ways, the homes I built elevated the lives of the owners.

At the age of thirty-five, I met and married a wonderful woman named Abigail, who was four years younger than me. Abby taught third graders at the local elementary school, and we had three children of our own, a son and daughter we'd conceived, as well as our oldest son,

Matthew, from her previous relationship. Matt was only two years old when I met him, and I was the only father he'd ever known. Together, we were a relatively happy family with good, full, busy lives.

So, why did I accelerate and change lanes when I reached my hill? Why was I in desperate need of an epiphany? Why was I seeking a violent conclusion to my not-so-horrible life? Those were complicated questions that I thought about a lot.

I couldn't say life had been cruel to me or dealt me an unbearable hardship. On the contrary, I had good genes, a good mind, good health, and a good family. My lot in life was better than most; I had many reasons to be grateful. And still, despite my good fortune, I got little satisfaction or fulfillment from any of it. Basically, I trudged through my days feeling empty and aching. I'd never spoken to a mental health professional, but I suspected my emptiness was rooted in the fact that my success happened after my father died, which made it feel unacknowledged and illegitimate. Ours was a complicated relationship where his high standards and my inadequacies caused stress for both of us. We couldn't be in the same room together. We never talked; we always argued.

"What will you do without a college education?" my father asked one afternoon in his home office.

"I'll find work," I answered, always keeping my answers brief to shorten our exchanges.

"Without an education, you'll be looking for work your whole life."

"I'll be okay," I said smugly.

"Are you content working for minimum wage?"

"I get by."

He scowled. "When I was your age, Alex, I was third in my law school class."

"I'm not you, Ray."

"I know you're not me, but you've got to make something of your life."

Though I tried to keep our argument brief, our words grew angrier and more punctuated with expletives as it dragged on. About twenty minutes into it, both of us shouting at each other, my father suddenly grasped his chest and collapsed, suffering a massive heart attack right in front of me. He died before the paramedics reached the house. I was twenty-three at the time, and that miserable afternoon haunted me like I'd actually broken his heart with my poor choices.

Fortunately for me, the year of 2017 turned into a personal journey that I never could've anticipated. The challenges of that year taught me to understand and accept myself as never before and create stronger bonds with the people in my life. It was my hardest year by far, but it also produced my most profound growth and a feeling of peace and contentment I'd never imagined. As part of my journey, I healed the wounds left over from my relationship with my father, confronted my shortcomings with my own family, and, most importantly, took my foot off the accelerator and returned to my lane.

Chapter One

Typical of clear winter nights in our home, the billions of sparkling stars in the front window seemed to meld with the city lights at the horizon and transform Boulder into a celestial body on a cold, cold evening in early January 2017. Also typical in our home, Abby shone in the evenings as our family gathered—though generally not for long—recounting the small victories, minor mishaps, and pressing concerns of another day over dinner. But not on this night. As soon as I entered our living room, I noticed that her curly blonde locks were mussed, and her quick glance my way seemed bewildered. A chilly, westerly wind was slicing through the conifers outside, but normally, Abby would have fixed her hair once inside. And as a third-grade teacher, she was typically cool, collected, and aware of all in her charge, but she seemed flustered and even frazzled. Instead of taking my usual seat at the kitchen island, I watched from across the room as she handed a plate of fish sticks and fries to our oldest, seventeen-year-old Matthew, a senior at Boulder High School.

"Take these to your room and play some video games," she told him. Her tone was off also.

Matt hesitated. He squinted as he tried to decipher her unusual instructions. Normally, he'd try to sneak away and retreat to his bedroom while his mother tried to keep the family together. Even he, a not-so-bright teenager who struggled to maintain a C-average in school, sensed something was amiss. Finally, Matt shrugged his shoulders, mumbled, "Okay," then turned and left the kitchen.

"Good night, Matt," I called out from across the room, knowing I wouldn't see him again that evening.

He glanced my way as he walked but didn't speak. Matt said very little to his mother and even less to me. He was at that age.

Concerned and a little apprehensive, I walked slowly toward my wife. Something was wrong, very wrong. I assumed our other children, Christi and Nate, were already in their bedrooms, but I waited until I reached her to ask.

"Are you okay?"

"I don't know," she said, looking down at her hand while fidgeting with her ring.

"Did something happen at school?"

"No, it isn't that."

"Is Matt smoking pot again?"

"No, Matt is good."

"Well, what is it?"

Abby's eyes pooled with tears, causing me to stop breathing and wait on her words. A strong and confident woman, Abby didn't cry often. In fact, sadness in any form was unusual for her. Slowly, she raised her eyes to meet mine in a look that conveyed repentance. "Matt's father isn't dead," she said.

My head rocked backward. "You told me he died of an overdose before Matt was even born."

"I lied," she said, "but you have to understand that he was dead to me."

"That's a pretty big lie."

"I know. I'm sorry."

"That's two big lies in three months."

"I said I'm sorry," she repeated, her brow wrinkled, tone biting. "Let's focus on Matt."

We'd arrived at a scary precipice, where our next words could be disastrous, words neither of us wanted to speak or hear, words that would only serve as a push at exactly the wrong moment. Even a slight nudge from either of us might send us over the edge. In her eyes, I saw fear. I felt that same fear inside of me. For both our sakes, I decided to back away from the edge.

"Does he want to meet Matt?" I asked.

Her face contorted. "It's more complicated than that."

"Well, tell me."

"He is alive and on death row in a state penitentiary in Texas."

"What?"

"He is alive…"

"I heard you," I snapped, surpassing the previously hushed level of our voices.

"Shh," she said, "we can't let the kids hear us."

Tears and mascara were now streaming down Abby's pale cheeks. She wiped her face with a napkin and took a deep breath. Needing a moment, I stepped away and walked in a circle around the kitchen island as I tried to gather my thoughts. I'd never been cool under pressure, but I was overwhelmed by her news.

"Why are you telling me this now?" I finally asked.

"Because the State of Texas has set his execution date."

"Oh my God."

"Yeah."

"Matt thinks I'm his biological father."

"Yeah. He does."

"We never planned to tell him otherwise."

"I know."

"What's the date?"

"August 23rd."

I let that date hang in the air, as I tried to catch my breath. It was all too much to absorb. I built homes for a living—exhausting, sometimes back-breaking work—and yet, I couldn't remember the last time I felt this drained. Leaning on the counter for support, Abby looked equally exhausted, like a woman on the verge of collapse.

"What's his name?" I asked.

"Donny Reed."

Abby had told me his name years ago, back when we'd first met, but I'd put it out of my mind. It wasn't something I wanted to think about.

9

Donny Reed was Matt's biological father, but I'd made the choice to simply ignore that fact. For Abby and me, we'd always had an unspoken pact to pretend that Donny never existed, to simply go forward with me as his stand-in, and never give him billing. Since Matt hadn't met him or even suspected he existed, we thought it okay to ignore the biological reality that I wasn't his father. After all these years, when she spoke his name, it felt like she'd resurrected a ghost.

"What did he do?" I followed up.

"He murdered a woman while robbing a convenience store."

Donny was on death row, so the fact that he'd murdered someone shouldn't have shocked me, but it did. In my mind, there was no way to reconcile Abby's connection to him. It was inexplicable. None of the adjectives used to describe death row inmates would ever be used to describe Abby. She was virtuous.

"Are you okay?" I asked. "Do you feel like you should contact him or write a letter?"

Her brow V'd. She rallied her energy to blast her ex. "Oh, hell no," she said. "He was a no-good methhead who ran off when I got pregnant."

"Okay," I said, feeling rebuked. "No letter then."

It had been eighteen years since she last saw Donny, and she was clearly angered by his reemergence in her life. Her past, like a mangy, rabid dog, had followed her home that night.

"More than anything else," Abby added, "I feel ashamed. If your child's father is going to be executed, that's a pretty good sign you haven't always made the best choices."

"You chose me."

"Well, the jury is still out on that one."

We chuckled. For me, it was a nervous, exhausted release of tension; I wasn't in a laughing mood. In fact, this might've been the least funny conversation I'd ever had. Both at a loss for words, we stared at one another for a long while.

"What are your thoughts?" Abby asked.

"Are you kidding me? I don't know what to think. I am absolutely blown away."

"We've got a big dilemma here."

"A big fucking dilemma, all right," I said with added emphasis. "I don't know what to do."

"Should we tell Matt about his biological father?"

"No way, we can't. I barely have a relationship with him as it is. Once he finds out I'm not his real father, things will only get worse."

Abby smirked. "You're his father, Alex. Don't be stupid."

* * *

I slept very little that night. Mostly, I stared out the window at the moon as thoughts about Matt, Abby, and the rest of my family surged through my mind. I also thought about Donny Reed and what he'd done that was so horrific that the State of Texas planned to snuff out his life. And finally, I thought about my father because no analysis of my problems or failures in life could ever happen without resurrecting him. While he was alive, he'd been my personal judge, jury, and executioner.

I didn't connect with Matt, but I certainly related to him. He reminded me of myself at his age. The muddled look on his face took me back to high school and well into my twenties. At six feet two inches tall and more than two hundred ten pounds, Matt was large for his age, so much so that he played offensive tackle for the varsity football team in his sophomore year. But he didn't return to the team for the next season as his interests narrowed, and he withdrew into himself and his room. Before I reached my teens, I'd also distanced myself from everyone, and I'd spent a lot of time alone in my room. Much like Matt, I seldom expressed my thoughts and feelings and built a metaphoric moat around my world, one intended to keep everyone away. Fortunately, as I reached my twenties, I outgrew my loner ways, and I could only hope Matt would do the same.

The opposite of Matt and me, Abby drew people to her and embraced them. She emitted light and warmth and energy, so naturally, people wanted to be around her. Like everyone else she encountered, the moment I met her, I was drawn to her. I wanted to be near her. Her curly blond hair, light blue eyes, and bright smile were both alluring and comforting at the same time. She had a way of putting people at ease. On several occasions, I'd witnessed Abby at work in her classroom and observed the wonderful effect she had on children. She shone so brightly that she somehow lit a small light in each of them, causing them to giggle and smile and laugh and glow from within. Her students were, quite simply, in awe of her. Thinking about Abby in her classroom also made me think about how important it was for children to have the Abbys of the world in their lives. Recognizing that my kids had Abby was a real comfort to me. She was a great mother. I also wished I'd had an Abby in my life when I was young.

Abby once told me, "When you think kind thoughts, say them. Don't keep the good stuff inside." She truly lived by that credo.

Our daughter, Christi, a freshman in high school, was just like her mother and even more so. Along with her warm and kind persona, she couldn't keep anything inside her. In the evenings, Christi always dominated the dinner conversation, rambling on and on about her friends and her day. At her age, every detail of her day was significant and required scrutiny. If a boy glanced her way in the lunchroom, we'd surely hear about it that evening. If a teacher assigned too much homework, we heard about it in syllabus detail. Christi liked to talk so much that she joined the debate team, which meant Abby and I had to travel all over the state to hear our daughter talk some more. Abby and I often laughed about that ironic addition to our parental duties on our drives to her competitions. Fortunately, Christi was good at structuring an argument and usually won her debates.

Our twelve-year-old, Nate, was a technology geek and the gifted one in the family. From an early age, it was obvious that my father's brilliant mind had skipped a generation and re-emerged in our lineage in Nate. Before he'd even started school, Nate mastered reading, math, computers, and piano like they were second nature to him. At night, Nate's room lit up like a boardwalk arcade and was often as noisy, with some of the same annoying sound effects blaring from the speakers. The subject matter on his large screens was wide-ranging, everything from video games to concert performances to college lectures to skateboard competitions to master classes. Passing his room, I often thought that the internet was being put to good use, for once, as a brilliant mind had access to limitless information and possibilities. Sure, he was still a kid and often distracted by video games set in ancient tombs or on medieval battlefields, but, at other times, he pursued data and knowledge with a voracious appetite. Abby often reminded me that Nate needed academic challenges and would probably also need to attend an elite college. Intellectually, I knew he'd surpass me before he reached high school.

During my sleepless night, I mostly wondered if I'd shortchanged my family, and Matt most particularly, by failing to connect in a meaningful way with them the same way my father had failed to connect with me. I wondered if I'd treated Matt, my stepchild, differently than my biological children. Was it merely a coincidence that he struggled while our other children thrived, or had I somehow failed him? Should we tell Matt I'm not his biological father? If we do, how will he take the news? I had so many questions but none of the answers. At that late hour, only one thing was clear to me: The events of the prior evening had created a lot of unrest in my mind.

Frustrated by my inability to sleep, I retrieved my phone from the nightstand, noticed the ungodly hour illuminated on the screen, 3:17 a.m., and then searched the internet for "Donny Reed Execution." I selected the first search result that appeared, titled, "Execution Date Set for Reed."

Huntsville, Texas. Officials at the Texas State Penitentiary in Huntsville announced today that convicted murderer, Donald Clark Reed, will be executed on August 23, 2017. In accordance with his sentence and Texas law, at or around 6 p.m., Reed will be given an injection of chemicals in lethal quantities sufficient to cause his death. It will be the ninth execution by the state in the calendar year. On May 9, 2001, at approximately 10:37 p.m., Donny Reed entered the Quick Stop Market & Gas in Abilene, Texas, and ordered the store's owner, Mary Jo Donovan, seventy-eight years old at the time, to hand over the cash. Security video showed that Donovan complied by removing the cash from the register, placing it in a paper bag, and handing it across the counter to Reed. Despite her compliance, Reed raised his gun and shot Donovan in the face, killing her instantly. With seven children and twenty grandchildren, Donovan was such a sympathetic victim that Reed was labeled, "The Grandma Killer." At his trial, Reed's attorney, J. William Scott, argued that Reed was high on methamphetamine during the crime and was therefore incapable of forming the requisite intent to commit murder. That defense failed to sway the Texas jury, and Reed was sentenced to death. When the judge asked if Reed wanted to make a statement at sentencing, he defiantly answered, "No one has ever given me a break in my whole life, and I don't expect one from you, Judge. Just gimme the damn needle."

Chapter Two

On the following Monday, as I grabbed my laptop and keys from the kitchen island, Abby grabbed a brown bag lunch from the refrigerator. She jotted a quick note on the bag with a black marker as she always did. Sometimes it was a short, sweet, love note. Other times, it was a quote she'd read. Often, it was a smiley face with Xs and Os beside it. She did the same on the kids' lunches. Two or three days a week, Abby packed lunch for me. Otherwise, I'd return home for lunch or, occasionally, drive into town.

"Go easy today," she said as she handed the bag to me. "You look tired."

"It's been a difficult weekend," I said.

"I know."

"Go easy" was something Abby said to me often. She knew I wasn't a person who glided through life in a relaxed manner. I wasn't easygoing; stress and worry had always been my steady companions. All my life, I'd had an active, examining mind—an asset when I had business decisions to make but self-destructive when problems caused my mind to spin wildly out of control, like over the weekend. As I climbed into the cab of my pickup truck, I was exhausted from lack of sleep and stressed out by the news about Matt's father. I wasn't in the best shape for the start of a new workweek.

* * *

The Mayfield home was the largest project I'd ever undertaken. Upon completion, it would have seven bedrooms, nine bathrooms, 5,700 square feet of living space, and a cost of $3.9 million. In early 2017, the home's exterior was complete, and it looked magnificent in its setting on a flat ridge beside a grove of Aspen trees. The interior was about 70% complete, which meant we'd finish in the spring. When I walked in the front door of the worksite, my project manager, Wyatt Dawson, was busy organizing materials in the great room for the day's work. He turned when he saw me enter the room.

"Hey bossman," he shouted across the mostly empty space, "we've got a lot of drywalling to get done today, so I hope Abby packed a sandwich for you."

"Roast beef and cheddar with a bag of chips," I said.

Wyatt hailed from Dallas, Texas, so if he didn't have a hard hat on his head, he wore a cowboy hat. He was clearly a product of his East Texas upbringing with blonde hair the color of straw, steel blue eyes that were often wide with wonder, and a knotted nose from a roping mishap in his youth. His work ethic matched the toughest ranch hands, and he had bullheaded determination whenever obstacles arose in our work. Wyatt was a genuine cowboy, not like the ones you saw two-stepping at cowboy bars on Saturday nights.

As I approached him, I pointed toward the window at the front of the house and said, "I just saw two whitetail deer as I came up the driveway. That's unusual this time of year."

"I don't like to see deer at any time of the year," Wyatt said. "I always feel sorry for them whenever I see one."

"Why?" I asked.

"They're cute and harmless creatures, and it never ends well for them. They get shot by hunters, hit by cars, or ripped apart by predators."

"Well, thanks for starting my week off on such a pleasant note."

"That's just the way of the world."

Wyatt wasn't always that gloomy, but he was very serious. His smiles were rare and heartfelt. He once asked me if I thought a recent spate of wildfires in our area was God's way of telling us to stop building homes in remote areas. Unlike many others I knew, Wyatt wasn't a guy who only believed in God when he was at church; he wore his faith comfortably like a good pair of blue jeans. Often, the task of lightening the moment fell to me. "If that was the case," I told him that day, "then God wouldn't have created insurance companies."

"How was your weekend?" Wyatt asked.

"Not great," I answered, not wanting to elaborate.

"Me either. Jessica filed for full custody of our girls last week."

"Oh crap. Why would she do that?"

"I don't know. I think it's probably got something to do with her new husband. Jack is the kind of guy who thinks he's entitled to whatever he wants."

"I'm sorry to hear that."

It was difficult timing for me because I was dealing with what I'd learned about Matt's biological father. In a weird way, I felt like I was in jeopardy of losing my son. I couldn't tell Wyatt about my situation because no one other than Abby, me, and a few family members knew the truth that I wasn't Matt's biological father. The worst part of Wyatt's news was the fact that I knew he was a great father. I'd seen him with his three young daughters on many occasions, and they had a wonderful relationship. They'd stayed at our house many times. One thing I knew for certain, I wished I was as close to my kids. I wished I was as good a father.

As soon as my other two workers arrived, we began hanging drywall in the great room, dining room, and basement. Even under the best conditions, when I'd slept more than I stressed the previous night, hanging drywall was demanding, dirty, exhausting work. That kind of hard work always made me sore the next day and reminded me that my age had a five handle. For more than six hours, we measured, cut, and maneuvered large slabs of drywall that were both heavy and awkward to handle. Having started the day in an already depleted state, my tank was empty in late afternoon as Wyatt and I rested in the great room while our team finished the basement.

Out of nowhere, Wyatt turned to me and said, "In her filing, Jessica accused me of molesting Amelia."

Amelia was their youngest child at four-years-old. Abby and I were her Godparents.

"Oh my God," I exclaimed, "how could she do that?"

"It must be Jack. Jessica wouldn't do that. He is Hell-bent on ruining my relationship with my family."

"That doesn't sound like Jessica."

* * *

Seven years earlier, I'd met Wyatt and Jessica when they stopped at my worksite on their way into Boulder. Three days earlier, they'd driven out of Dallas with little more than their unborn child, two suitcases, and Wyatt's tools in the bed of the pickup truck. While Wyatt told me about his skillset, Jessica waddled around the worksite like a mother duck and looked eleven months pregnant, but her face glowed with the anticipation of an ecstatic first-time mother. She had strawberry blonde hair, a smattering of light freckles on her cheeks, and a warm, beguiling smile consistent with her Georgia roots and southern hospitality.

"I am very pleased to make your acquaintance," she told me in her slow drawl.

"Is your husband as good as he says?" I asked.

"He is," Jessica replied, "and, more importantly, he is a good man. Wyatt is a man of his word."

"Well, that may be the best job reference I've ever heard. I think I can trust a pregnant woman."

"I've got a feeling we are going to be very good friends, Mr. Bryant," she told me as she rubbed her large belly in a circular motion. "In fact, you're our first Colorado friend."

"Call me Alex."

"Once we get situated, Alex, you and your wife will have to come to our home for dinner. I have a friend in Texas who swears my peach cobbler is proof that divine inspiration exists."

"I look forward to tasting it. My wife is an excellent cook too, so I'm sure she'll want to reciprocate."

Beneath his cowboy hat and studded shirt, Wyatt was as solid and strapping as anyone I knew, so I told him I'd give him a week to show me what he could do. Turned out he could do plenty, and he quickly became my best and most capable employee. I was fortunate he'd stumbled onto my worksite that day. Along with her endorsement, Jessica's prediction proved to be correct that day as well—Wyatt and Jessica became great friends to Abby and me.

* * *

With his revelation, Wyatt's eyes welled with tears. I hadn't said anything earlier, but I'd sensed something was wrong with him. More than the custody case. As we'd prepared and hung the drywall, he'd misplaced tools, measured incorrectly, and jumped every time someone's cell phone rang. Concerned for his safety, I'd kept a close eye on him. He was obviously distracted, and a worksite was a dangerous place for a distracted mind.

"Why didn't you tell me this morning?" I asked.

"I still can't accept that it's real. I'm afraid for my children and what they're about to be put through."

"Abby and I are here for you. Let us know if there is anything we can do."

Wyatt looked directly at me. "I didn't do it. I'd never hurt my daughters."

I didn't hesitate. "I know. I didn't have to ask."

"I felt like I had to say it."

I didn't think Wyatt had done anything inappropriate with his daughters. I'd seen the love between them, and I knew he was a great father. But the truth was we really don't know what goes on in another person's mind or what they're capable of in their worst moments. No one would ever have suspected my irrational actions on my hill. Everyone would've been quite shocked if my accident had occurred and I'd been killed. No one reveals everything to the world.

Chapter Three

My Uncle Bob, my father's older brother, was a well-regarded pediatrician in Boulder. He was a tall, lanky man with thick, curly auburn hair, bushy eyebrows, and a love for antiques and all things historical. True to his chosen profession, he was a warm and caring person who offered his hand and assistance to anyone in need. It was always a good day for me whenever Uncle Bob came to our home for a visit. He was my Godfather, and he always made me feel special and often brought gifts for me. My father and his brother were opposites, and, as I grew older and more aware, I sensed that my father resented his brother. Unlike my father, Uncle Bob connected with people.

One night, when I was six years old, my father poked his head into my bedroom and said, "Let's go. We have to go to the hospital."

"Why?" I asked.

He didn't answer. My father didn't show a lot of emotion, but I saw something in his eyes that night that was different. He was distraught.

"Get your coat and come with me."

"Why are we going to the hospital?" I asked again as he backed out of our driveway in an accelerated manner.

"Your mother and sister were in an accident."

"Are they okay?"

"Don't talk to me now. We have to hurry."

As he drove, my father clenched the steering wheel so tightly that his knuckles were white. He slowed for stop signs and red lights but never stopped at a single one. When we arrived at the emergency room entrance, Uncle Bob was waiting by the large automatic doors. Very uncharacteristic of him, he was wearing a white T-shirt which must have meant he'd rushed out the door the moment he got the call. He looked worried.

"What do you know, Ray?" he asked as we approached, my father four paces ahead of me.

"They were broadsided by a drunk driver who was speeding," my father said.

"Damn it," my uncle returned, shaking his head.

When I reached him, Uncle Bob took me by the hand, and we followed my father to the receptionist.

"Susan and Emma Bryant," my father said, and then my uncle led me to the chairs in the waiting room.

It was my first time in an emergency room, and I sensed anxiety and dread all around me. We were surrounded by strangers with sad eyes and worried expressions. A man passed me with a bandage on his hand that was red with blood. Seated across from me, a young woman with yellow hair had tear tracks on her cheeks. Instinctively, I didn't want to be there.

"Everything's going to be okay," Uncle Bob told me as I sat in a waiting room chair.

Once I was situated, my uncle returned to the reception desk beside my father. Side by side, no one would have thought they were brothers; they looked nothing alike. My father was three inches shorter with a stockier build, sparse brown hair that he combed straight back, and his eyes were framed by dark eyebrows and puffy bags from all his reading. If anything connected them, it was the slight hint of auburn in my father's hair.

My clearest memory from that night was the doctor in blue scrubs with a splotch of blood near his navel who emerged from a hallway and approached my father and uncle. Even at six years old, I could gauge the seriousness of the conversation from twenty feet away. The doctor didn't smile or shake hands with either brother, and he did all the talking. After a minute or so, my father slumped and raised his hand to his mouth. My uncle hugged him in a way that seemed to be holding him up. I'd never seen my father exhibit any weakness before or after that night, and it was the only time I ever saw him cry. In a strange way, it was almost as if he was a different man for one night.

Eventually, my uncle came over and knelt in front of me. He put his hand on my shoulder and told me that my mother and sister had died in the crash. He hugged me tightly as I cried.

"I am here for you, Alex," he whispered into my ear.

My uncle drove us home that night. My father and I didn't speak about the accident or the deaths until two hours before the funeral.

In my good Sunday suit, a blue one that I was starting to outgrow, I waited for my father in the front hallway of our home. We were about to leave to go to the funeral home. As I waited, I noticed my mother's purse on a chair by the door and I wondered how it got there. A smudge of motor oil on the leather flap made it clear that my mother hadn't placed it there. In his normal workday manner, my father came down the stairs and retrieved his coat and hat from the hallway closet. A holdout from another era, my father always wore a hat.

"Things are going to be different without your mom and sister," he told me, like he was talking to his staff at his law firm, "but we're going to be fine."

* * *

After my mother and sister died in the accident, our home, a brown and tan Tudor in central Boulder, became a quiet and still place. Where conversation and taunts and giggles and laughter once echoed through the rooms, silence took up residence. Even the natural light that once streamed through the ornate windows seemed dimmer and less frequent. In an attempt to restore some sense of normalcy to the household, my father hired a woman to serve as cook and housekeeper. For me, the presence of this stranger in our home only served as a constant reminder that my mother wasn't there.

Mrs. Morgan, a matronly woman with gray hair in a tight bun, eyes like a French bulldog, glasses that belonged in Palm Beach rather than Colorado, and a cookbook as thick as municipality codes, moved into a bedroom with its own bathroom on the first floor. During her first week on the job, she was talkative while she worked, but she quickly yielded to the melancholy that permeated our home. After her first week, we passed each other frequently during the day but hardly said a word.

Each night at 7 p.m., Mrs. Morgan served my father and me a dinner that consisted of multiple courses. At the start of the meal, my father always asked, "How was your day, son?" To which I replied, "Fine." And that was the extent of our dinner conversation. At his elbow, beside his plate, my father always had several yellow legal pads, which he read and made notes upon. He rotated utensils, his fork and pen, about every two minutes or so as he chewed or jotted throughout the meal. After several courses and about thirty minutes of elapsed time, I'd ask my father if I could be excused. "Certainly," he always responded, and I'd leave him at the table with his legal pads and glass of scotch.

Most of the time, my father and I barely interacted, but one evening, out of nowhere, he told me I could miss school the following day and accompany him to his office. He said he wanted me to see where he worked and what a lawyer's day was like. Though confused by the unusual invite, I was also thrilled by the prospect of spending time with my father and seeing his office. I'd never been there. Before I was born, my father founded the law firm of Bryant, Houston, and Wheeler, one of the most prestigious in Boulder. Before she died, my mother had always told me that "my father was a very important man." My father usually returned home from work after my bedtime, so I'd spent little time with him. When he told me to come with him to his office, it was about three months after the accident, and I thought this might be my father's way of showing me that he wanted to spend time with me. He wanted us to be closer. So, I was excited.

Early the next morning, I was seated at the kitchen table with a bowl of Cheerios before me when my father walked in. To my surprise, he was buttoning his overcoat and already had his hat on. His car keys jangled in his hand. Clearly, he was ready to leave.

"Come on, Alex," he said, motioning with his hand. "We've got to go, or I'll be late for my first meeting."

I stopped mid-spoonful. My jaw dropped, and I looked up in dismay. "I've got to pee," I told him as I abruptly placed my spoon on the table.

"You can pee at my office. We've got to go."

I retrieved my coat from the hall closet as we rushed out the front door. We drove towards his office but encountered unusually thick, stop-and-go traffic that added another twenty minutes to his normal thirty-minute commute.

"There must be an accident up ahead," he said at one point. "It's never this bad."

I squirmed in my seat. "I have to pee," I told him.

"Hold it until we get to my office. It won't be much longer."

We drove for another half-hour. When we arrived at his office building, my father saw the darkened area of my tan pants and realized I'd wet myself. He winced; he looked disgusted. I couldn't look at him and kept my eyes down on the floor mat.

"What have you done?" my father demanded.

"I couldn't hold it," I answered, never looking up, my cheeks red with embarrassment.

"I can't take you into my office like that. You'll have to wait here. I can probably get away in an hour and take you home."

My head was still down. "I told you I had to pee."

"Just stay here," he said as he closed the car door.

Ashamed of my mishap, I sat in the car alone as my father entered the lobby of the building. I saw him speak briefly with the receptionist and point toward the car. When he did, I ducked beneath the dashboard. I was uncomfortable and smelled of urine already. Worse still, I knew my father was ashamed of me. Three hours later, my father drove me home and dropped me off at the curb in front of our home. He didn't come in with me. By then, my pants were dry, but I still stank of urine. Unnerved, I ran inside and took a long shower. I never saw the inside of my father's law firm until a decade later when I was arrested for DUI at the age of twenty and needed a lawyer.

* * *

Late night was never a good time for me because the quiet stoked my mind like a strong wind gust across hot coals. I laid awake often, and into the wee hours, and thought about my mother and sister or worried about my world. My mind always revved up late at night, and I had difficulty sleeping. In the darkness and the silence, I felt small and alone. It was then that I missed my mother and sister the most. Eventually, around the age of eight or nine, I started reading at night to distract my mind and help me with my insomnia.

In his office in our home, my father kept a library of beautiful, leather-bound books on a bookcase that climbed twelve feet to the room's ceiling. On a weekly basis, I would sneak one out and keep it hidden under my bed. In the middle of the night, when the quiet arrived like a cat burglar, I'd retrieve the book from under the bed and seek solace from its pages. I often read until the morning light started to slink into my room. I later wondered if reading about the guerrilla fighters in *For Whom the Bell Tolls* or about the brutal killers of *In Cold Blood* was appropriate at that age. The truth was that I always read above my grade level and about subject matter that often confused or horrified me. But the books distracted me and helped me sleep, so I continued.

After the accident and throughout my adolescence, I had one memory of my mother that meant everything to me, but it was dream-like with a lot of missing details, so I wasn't sure if it was real or imagined. I also had photos of her, so her face was always fresh in my mind, but few actual memories. I kept the photos in a wooden box under my bed with my book stash. My mother was a petite woman with brown hair, emerald eyes, a kind smile, and a nose that crimpled when she laughed. On many nights, I opened the box and looked at the pictures; in most, she was smiling and laughing, so I believed she was kind. While I didn't have many memories of my mother, I clung to them like a life preserver.

In my most cherished memory, my mother and I sat in a grand building with a curved, white ceiling and tall arched windows divided by thin, black, iron muntins. She wore a red dress with a yellow sash and a white hat, and I was dressed in my best Sunday clothes. While I had no memory of a special occasion, our outfits made it seem that way. Together, we sat on a wooden bench and waited while people scurried all around us. As we waited, my mother held my hand tightly and only released it when I asked to walk over to a tall statue across from us. After I crossed the floor, I stared up at the bronze man as he towered over me until she grabbed my hand and led me back to the bench.

"Be a good boy, Alex," she said, "and wait patiently. We'll get an ice cream cone when we leave."

Then, she placed her hand on my head and mussed my hair while she smiled at me.

"You're my little man," she said, "and I love you to the moon and back."

A beautiful clock with a white face and Roman numerals was on the wall with the tall windows. She looked at it often and told me, "Just a little bit longer."

My memory of the occasion had no reason or finale. I didn't know why we went there, how long we stayed, or how it ended. I only remembered what I remembered, but I savored that memory and sustained myself with it. Through the years, I fought off my doubts that it never happened and constantly convinced myself it was real. It was all I had. It had to be real.

Sometimes late at night, I'd crawl out my window onto the tile roof so I could gaze up at the moon. In my young mind, I'd connected my memory of my mother to the moon, and I felt comforted when I looked up at it, most particularly on nights when it was full.

My mom loved me to the moon and back, I'd told myself, reclined on the roof beneath the bright moon.

Chapter Four

My Uncle Bob's home was a large, white Colonial-style house about a mile from our home, and I'd walk there often. Sometimes, I would spend the night and sleep on the leather sofa in his home office. They had a guest room, but I liked the supple feel of that sofa. After the accident, I fell asleep on that sofa often while my uncle worked at his desk into the evening. I'd found comfort and a sense of security there. Their home was always a lively place, so I would go there to escape the quiet and solitude of our home. I enjoyed the commotion and bustle, especially on the weekends when everyone was busy with hobbies and activities. My Aunt Maggie owned a restaurant in the downtown called Bonne Bouche, so their refrigerator was always full of leftovers. At least once a week, I had dinner with them. Uncle Bob and Aunt Maggie had two sons and a daughter: Tommy, who was two years older than me, Ethan, who was my age, and Sarah, who was two years younger than me. I didn't feel so alone when I thought of them as my siblings.

Somehow, after the accident, the tradition started that my birthday dinners were celebrated at their home. Each year in advance, my Aunt Maggie would ask me what I wanted for my "special birthday dinner," and my father and I would go to their home for the meal, which always included cake and ice cream afterward. And my aunt and uncle gave me great birthday gifts; on my tenth birthday, I remember they gave me a red Schwinn bicycle with a banana seat. They always treated me like I was their third son.

One evening, when I was about ten, Uncle Bob walked in his front door and found me sitting alone in the living room. He smiled when he saw me.

"Hey, it's Alexander the Great," he said.

"Hi, Uncle Bob."

"Where is everyone?"

"I don't know."

"Do you want to play catch before dinner?"

"Sure."

"Just give me ten minutes to change."

"Okay."

When I grew older, I realized Uncle Bob used the game of catch as a way to have conversations with his children and me. He knew that sitting a child down on a sofa for a talk was an ineffective way to communicate with them. With the focus on them, children tensed up. He also knew that the act of tossing a baseball back and forth distracted us so we'd speak freely and be less guarded. Uncle Bob understood kids; after all, he was a pediatrician. As such, he had a penchant for natural remedies.

Fifteen minutes later, we stood twenty feet apart in the backyard beside a large maple tree with our mitts on our hands, tossing the ball back and forth. Uncle Bob had a very old baseball mitt with a well-worn pocket that looked like Ty Cobb might have used it.

"Are you going to play little league this year?" Uncle Bob asked me.

"I haven't decided yet," I answered. I wasn't a very decisive kid.

"Well, you let me know if you want to. I'll sign you up."

"Okay."

A game of catch was a rhythmic activity where the action moved back and forth between the participants like a tennis match. Catch, throw, wait. Catch, throw, wait. During our catch, our conversation was constantly punctuated by the thud of the ball in the mitt

"You seemed sad after Sarah's ballet performance last week," Uncle Bob said.

Thud!

"I'm okay," I said.

Thud!

"Does Sarah remind you of your sister, Emma?"

Thud!

"Sometimes."

"I see a lot of Emma in Sarah," Uncle Bob remarked. "They're a lot alike, both physically and the way they act."

"I see it, too."

"Sometimes, when I see it, it makes me sad, but other times, I'm happy to see it."

"I know what you mean."

"I'd like to think that, as the years pass, we're going to get sweet reminders of Emma from Sarah, and that'll be a good thing."

"Yeah, maybe."

"We'll also get to see a little of the woman Emma would've become."

"I guess so."

Uncle Bob caught the ball and paused. He didn't throw it back. He lowered his mitt to his side.

"Have I ever told you," he said, smiling broadly, "that Emma once told me she had the best brother in the world?"

"You tell me that all the time."

"That's because I don't want you to ever forget."

"I won't."

"She loved you very much."

"Yeah, I know."

"And Sarah and I love you, too."

"I know."

He finally tossed the ball my way.

Thud!

"You know, Alex, as Sarah gets older, she is going to need all the big brothers she can get. I'm counting on you to be there for her also."

"I will, Uncle Bob."

"I know you will."

* * *

The great room in my childhood home was a splendid space clearly meant for entertaining. It had a beautiful granite fireplace where flames reached six feet high, two large crystal chandeliers that provided balanced lighting to the grand space, and a pool table and bar at the other end. The strange thing about the room was that I had no memory of any parties or large gatherings ever hosted there, and I was generally the only one in the room. As a young boy, I watched a lot of television alone in that enormous room.

One afternoon when I was eleven, the western television series Bonanza was interrupted for a "News Bulletin." A news anchorman wearing black-rimmed glasses appeared on the screen with a script in his hand, and he hastily began reading the report.

"We are sorry to interrupt our regularly scheduled program, but a Boeing 727 aircraft with ninety-three passengers and crew aboard crashed at Denver International Airport just minutes ago. The New West Airlines flight, which left Portland at 11:37 a.m. and was bound for Chicago, diverted to Denver when it experienced problems with its hydraulic system. Pilots reported difficulties controlling the plane but managed to make an approach to the runway."

As the anchorman spoke, the TV screen displayed film footage of the plane descending toward the runway. On arrival, one of its wings suddenly dipped and violently struck the ground, causing the plane to somersault down the runway. As it tumbled, a large fireball erupted, engulfing about a quarter of the aircraft's fuselage. Then, the plane slid for about 300 yards before coming to a stop in the field beside the runway. Thick, black smoke obstructed the view of the evacuation, but a few survivors could be seen emerging from the black cloud, coughing and wiping their eyes feverishly, and dropping to their knees in the field. It was a horrible scene to watch.

After showing the footage of the crash multiple times, a reporter began broadcasting live from Denver International Airport. Standing on a tarmac with fire trucks and ambulances rushing in all directions behind him, the reporter relayed a harrowing tale.

"Ninety-three were aboard the Boeing 727 aircraft when it crashed and burst into flames less than thirty minutes ago. The wreckage sits in a field about a quarter mile from my position. Debris is scattered everywhere, and toxic, black smoke is still billowing from the plane. I haven't been able to get an exact count, but it's my belief that ambulances have only transported seven survivors to nearby hospitals. Most of the injured have suffered serious burns. As authorities get a better handle on the situation, the death count is expected to be significant because escaping the tumbling fireball would've been difficult."

The plane crash happened in early afternoon while my father was at work and Mrs. Morgan was out of the home doing the grocery shopping and running errands. For two hours, I watched the continuous showings of the crash as well as live reports about the rescue efforts and casualties. Having lost my mother and sister in a car accident, the scene of the plane crash was, for me, a larger version of their fate. At the time, no one could have foreseen the long-term effects that afternoon would have on me, but I was clearly traumatized by what I'd watched.

When Mrs. Morgan returned home later that afternoon, she found me in a stupor, sitting three feet from the TV screen with a glazed and horrified look on my face.

"You shouldn't be watching that!" she exclaimed as she turned the TV off.

After I'd lost my mother and sister, I lived with the very adult notion that the world was a dangerous and scary place. The accident altered my childhood and changed my view of the world. Where I had previously explored with childlike curiosity, I backed away and cowered instead. On the afternoon of the plane crash, in the great room of our home, I lost whatever tidbits of innocence and security remained.

Chapter Five

Saturday mornings in our home had changed over the years. When our children were in elementary school, we called them to breakfast for pancakes, and they scrambled down the stairs to the table. While Abby worked her magic in the kitchen, I combed hair, tied laces, poured orange juice, and served as a multi-tasking problem solver. Her pancakes were claimed as quickly as she removed them from the griddle and put them on a plate. Together, we served breakfast to our children with the same efficiency as the cafeteria crew at Abby's school. Then, Abby and the kids would drive into Boulder to volunteer at whatever school function Abby was coordinating at the time. Often, it was a bake sale, rummage sale, school play, or an athletic event. Back then, Abby and I determined our family's agenda for the day, and we made it happen. A decade later, with a tween and two teens in our home, our authority was a distant memory, the era of enthusiastic cooperation was clearly over, and Saturday mornings were a chaotic free-for-all where we struggled to keep up with our children. Our kids dictated the agenda for the day, and our roles were limited to financier and chauffeur.

On a snowy morning in late January, Abby stood before the hot griddle with four large pancakes bubbling on its cooking surface. The picture window beside her looked out upon a white landscape where the trees and mountain peaks were frosted with freshly fallen snow. Turning toward the staircase, Abby called out, "Kids, come get breakfast."

Meanwhile, I sat at the kitchen island with a tall stack in front of me and a hot cup of coffee in my hand. On the counter, yesterday's newspaper was open before me, and its woeful reports made me feel like the larger world was as troubled as my smaller one. I tried to savor my pancakes, coffee, and the placid scene out the window, but my mind felt as chaotic as the rest of the globe. Anxiously, I thought about the difficult countdown ahead for Donny Reed and its connection to my oldest child. I wondered if Matt got his husky build from him. After five minutes elapsed and no children appeared, Abby asked me to find a deserving child for the fresh stack in front of her.

"I'll see what I can do," I told her.

Two minutes later, I returned with Nate by my side.

"Nate's ready for his stack," I said. "Christi told me she's having granola and yogurt, but she'd be right down. Matt wants a very tall stack."

"Well done," Abby said.

A short while later, we were all gathered around the table while everyone finished their breakfast. A single pancake remained on a plate in the center of the table, and the kids' napkins remained untouched. I guess the manners we'd taught our children had also been lost with the passage of time. Outside the window, the snow was tapering off.

"Who can help me out at rehearsal for the third-grade play?" Abby asked.

"Not me," Christi said. "I'm going to Brooklyn's house to prepare our debate points for this week."

"Am I dropping you at Brooklyn's house?" Abby asked.

"Yes, please."

"Okay. What's the debate topic this week?" Abby asked.

"Does social media make people less social?" Christi said.

"What do you think?" I asked.

"It doesn't make me any less socially active," Christi insisted.

"Nothing could make you less socially active," Abby said, smiling at her daughter as she did.

"Ha ha, Mom," Christi said.

"I can't go either," Nate said as he reached for the syrup. "I've got a video game tournament at noon."

Abby smiled at Nate. "I think you just provided your sister with some data for her debate."

"Nate's just a nerd," Christi said. "You can't blame social media for that."

"Well, you're just a social butterfly with a knack for spinning facts," Nate said, razzing his sister.

Christi stuck her tongue out. "You're so lame."

Nate giggled.

Occasionally, when my family gathered in the same room, I experienced a strange sensation. I felt like I was eleven years old again in the great room of my childhood home, and I was put off by their intrusion on my space. The commotion and clamor of their voices unsettled me. I yearned for the aloneness again.

"I can come," Matt said. "I don't have anything to do today."

"Way to go, Matt," I said. "You're a good son. It's nice of you to volunteer to help your mother."

Abby grinned at me. "Really?" she said, questioning the complimentary nature of my response.

"Matt's going to help you," I said.

"Okay," Abby said, glancing my way and winking, a gesture that said, "I'm on to you."

Fifteen minutes later, only Abby and I remained downstairs. The kids had retreated to their bedrooms to get ready for their days. The change in the energy level of the room was palpable. With my mug in hand, I savored the calm.

"I take it from the way you gushed over Matt, you've been thinking about Donny." Abby said.

"Only every minute of the day."

"Have you come to any conclusions?"

"Good riddance."

"Seriously, what are you thinking?"

"I am serious. The State of Texas is going to solve this problem for us."

"Texas isn't going to get us off the hook. We've got to decide whether to tell Matt about Donny before they execute him so he can contact him if he wants. He may resent us for it one day if we don't."

"I'd rather not tell him about Donny ever."

"We can do that, but it may come back to haunt us."

"I'll take that chance."

"I lied to you about Donny, so I'll support whatever you decide. Just tell me you'll think about it."

"Oh, I'll be thinking about it, all right."

* * *

Matt's favorable station from his volunteer work with his mother didn't even last a week. On the following Friday night, he went to a house party in downtown Boulder hosted by one of his former football teammates. In those days, his curfew was 1 a.m. Abby and I were asleep in our bed when we got a call just after midnight.

"Hello," I said, with trepidation in my voice due to the late hour.

"Is this Alex Bryant, the father of Matthew Bryant?"

"I am."

"This is Officer Lorenzo Grant at the Boulder Police Department."

"Is Matt okay?" I asked.

"Who is it?" Abby asked, concerned.

"The police department."

"Your son is fine, Mr. Bryant," the officer informed me, "but he's in our custody after a fight that our officers broke up earlier this evening."

According to the police report, officers responded to a home on a residential street at approximately 11 p.m. in response to a 911 call about a fistfight. When the police arrived, they found a party in progress, loud music blaring, alcohol present, the smell of marijuana in the air, and approximately fifty people in the residence. In the main living area of the home, three young men were exchanging punches and all three were bruised and bloodied. Additionally, several holes were punched in a wall, and an interior door was torn from its hinges. All three assailants were arrested and taken into custody.

"Are there charges?" I asked.

"Charges," Abby exclaimed. "What's going on?"

I placed my phone on speaker so Abby could hear the conversation. In the dark, we huddled over the light from the screen like scouts around a campfire. She had her hand on my shoulder, and I felt her trembling.

"He is being held on assault and disturbing the peace charges," the officer said.

"Oh my God," Abby blurted.

"That's his mother, Abby," I told the officer. "I've got you on speaker."

"I'm sorry to call with bad news at such a late hour, Abby, this is Lorenzo Grant, you taught my daughter two years ago."

"Heather Grant, of course, I remember."

The officer's voice softened. "She loved having you as her teacher."

"That's so nice of you to say."

We all paused for a moment as if we'd collectively decided to ignore the actual problem at hand. Then, Abby brought us back to reality by asking, "What's his condition, Lorenzo?"

"Well, he's got a couple bruises and scrapes, but he's okay."

"Is he drunk?" Abby followed up.

"He's pretty inebriated and he smells of pot."

"That's not good," I said, glancing over at my wife.

"No, it's not," she said.

"Seventeen is a tough age for parents," Officer Grant said.

"It sure is," I added.

"Should we come get him tonight?" Abby asked.

"That's up to you," the officer said. "We'll keep him overnight if you want."

"That might do him some good," Abby said. "He has been on the wrong path lately."

Her words caught me by surprise. Despite the late hour, I was sure we were going to drive into town to get him. I never would've thought she'd leave our son in jail overnight. She'd stopped trembling and seemed steady again.

"Well then, come to the station tomorrow. He'll be waiting."

"Thanks, Lorenzo," Abby said.

"Get some sleep," the officer said and then he hung up.

"Are you sure you want to leave him there tonight?" I asked Abby.

"He needs to know his actions have consequences. He's practically an adult now."

* * *

At the police station the next day, we waited beside a large steel door that made a loud buzzing sound every time it swung open. Like a nervous kitten, Abby jumped whenever it sounded. Opposite us, the sign on the wall read, "Holding Cell Processing." During our time there, a handful of uniformed police officers and what appeared to be wrongdoers in their custody walked by; sometimes cuffs were involved, other times, not. As we waited, Abby fidgeted in her seat and checked her cell phone frequently, and I wondered about her apparent unease but didn't ask. Nothing remained a secret with Abby for very long.

"I haven't been in a police station since my days with Donny," she told me.

"Does it bring back bad memories?"

"It sure does. I bailed him out of jail more than a few times."

"Why'd you stay with him?"

She shrugged. "I don't know. I guess I was young and stupid at the time."

"I think we're dealing with a case of that right now."

Abby smiled. Her lip quivered as she did. "God, I hope he doesn't turn out like Donny."

"He won't. He has a great mother."

"I'm not talking about death row type offenses. I just mean petty crimes and stupid stuff."

"I know what you mean."

"Matt seems to keep things bottled up inside these days until he snaps," Abby said. "I know he's a teenager, but that's not healthy."

"High school kids get into fights," I said, trying to minimize the charges and reassure her.

"I sure hope this isn't the start of anything bad."

"It's not. Fortunately, I can console myself with the fact that he doesn't get it from me."

She smiled her nervous smile again. "Not funny."

After a half-hour wait, the buzzer blared, Abby practically leapt out of her skin, and Matt walked out of the steel door. He had a large scrape on his forehead, a swollen lip, and a significant tear in his shirt. His hair was mussed, and he looked like he hadn't slept at all. When I first saw him, he didn't even look like the kid who rambled about our home.

"I can't believe you left me in there," he said, glaring at his mother.

"You get arrested, you're going to spend time in jail," Abby returned, unruffled. "That's how it works."

"It wasn't my fault," he said. "A couple of asshole jocks were picking on Wesley."

Wesley Stone, a friend of Matt's since elementary school, had a pituitary gland issue that stunted his growth. Wesley was four feet eight inches tall on his tippy toes and considerably overweight for his size. That combination made him the subject of an inordinate amount of bullying in the hallways at school.

"I hate bullies," Abby said, disdain in her eyes.

"I had to do something," Matt said.

"I'm not as concerned about the fight," Abby told him, "as I am the drinking and the pot."

I nodded in agreement.

"I wasn't drunk or high," Matt said. "I'd only had a couple of beers and shared a joint."

I usually remained silent whenever Abby talked with Matt about drug use. After all, I was pretty sure I'd done more drugs at his age than he'd done. Hell, I was best friends with a pot dealer and even sold product for him. While I wanted my children to stay away from drugs, I was conflicted about lecturing them. I couldn't get past the hypocrisy. As Abby scolded Matt about pot, I kept quiet and nodded in support.

"Don't lie to me, Matt," Abby demanded.

"I'm not."

"We'll talk about this at home," Abby said, "as well as how long you're going to be grounded. Let's go to the car."

Chapter Six

A bby was a really good cook. She always said that cooking was her favorite distraction whenever she had a lot on her mind, so I guess I should have expected an exceptional meal that evening. After all, she'd spent the better part of the afternoon at the police station bailing her oldest son out of the slammer. A difficult duty for any mother. Reveling in her favorite distraction, Abby prepared a wonderful meal consisting of a hearty beef stew with yellow potatoes and fresh vegetables, biscuits made from scratch, and a luscious chocolate layer cake for dessert. Whether her delicious meal was the reason or not, I didn't know, but our family had a lengthy and lively dinner conversation that evening. Abby and I often lingered after the meal, but the kids were usually quick to leave the table for their rooms. Whatever the reason—good food, good company, good conversation, or nothing else to do—for once, no one was in a hurry to leave the table.

"What was that music you played on the piano this afternoon?" Abby asked Nate as we all took our seats at the table.

"Beethoven's Moonlight Sonata," Nate said. "I heard it on a snow-boarding video, so I bought the score."

"It's quite beautiful," Abby said.

"I haven't nailed it yet, but I'm getting close."

"You played it wonderfully."

"How is the Mayfield house coming along?" Christi asked me.

"The interior is starting to take shape," I said. "We're probably about eighty percent complete on the whole project."

"Can I come see it again?" Christi followed up.

"Sure, the next time I go there on a weekend, I'll take you with me."

"Can I do some work again?"

"I'm sure I can find something for you to do."

"Great."

Of my children, Christi was the one who wanted to get dirty and work alongside me at my sites. She was a decent carpenter for her age and proficient with power tools, but she stressed me out because she was fearless. From my experience, power tools and motorcycles were two things that commanded respect; in an instant, both could cause irreparable harm. A couple projects back, Christi and I spent a beautiful spring afternoon building a deck on the back of a house. She did some good work that day but was way too casual with the power tools for me. I was so relieved when the deck was done and we were going home instead of the emergency room.

"Mom," Christi said, turning her attention to the other end of table, "now that we have a criminal in the house, I need a lock on my door."

"Innocent until proven guilty," Matt said. "The charges are totally bogus."

"Christi is right," Nate said. "Most serial killers are quiet, social outcasts like Matt. Ted Bundy was a rare exception. We shouldn't ignore these warning signs."

"That's enough, you two," Abby warned them. "Be kind to your brother. You're going to miss him while he's away in prison."

"Thanks a lot," Matt said, sneering at his mother. "I can always count on you to come to my defense."

"With your fat lip and scraped forehead," I said, "you do look like a bit of a thug."

"Can I just eat my dinner in peace?" Matt asked.

"Sure, let's move along," I suggested. "I think we've made fun of Matt's crime spree long enough."

Half smiling and nodding, Matt didn't seem upset or angry about the ribbing. He seemed to take it in stride, and I was thankful for that small morsel of maturity after his antics the previous night. It occurred to me that I mostly interacted with Matt when he'd done something wrong, and I didn't like that thought because it reminded me of my relationship with my father.

"I read that ten percent of serial killers pose their victims," Nate said.

Christi turned to her mother and pleaded, "That's not appropriate dinner conversation."

"Who wants cake?" Abby asked, deftly changing the subject, and everyone answered, "Me," in unison.

"I guess that was a dumb question," she added.

Over slices of rich, gooey chocolate cake, Christi told us all that she planned to try out for the softball team next month. Since the age of ten, she had played on several softball teams. For a solid fifteen minutes, we all heard about her chances of making the squad and why second base was her best option. Christi always analyzed everything in great detail, and she probably got that from me.

"Do you really have time for another extracurricular activity?" Abby asked with a whiff of concern in her voice.

"No, I don't," Christi said. "If I make the team, I'll probably have to drop something."

Abby and I lingered at the table with our coffee after the kids had departed. After such an unusually pleasant meal with our family, I couldn't help but notice her pensive, almost troubled look. She was sitting with me, but her mind seemed a million miles away.

"Something on your mind?" I asked.

"It's Nate," she answered.

"What about Nate?"

"We have to make sure he has a childhood," she said.

"What do you mean?"

"With most kids, you worry about them learning and keeping up, but Nate is the opposite. Tonight, he talked about classical music and serial killers. He is interested in everything, and he absorbs information like a sponge. We have to make sure he has fun."

"I hear you. Nate is one unique twelve-year-old."

"When the warm weather comes, let's make sure we do some fun stuff with him."

"That's a good idea."

"That was a really nice meal, wasn't it?"

"Everything was delicious."

"I meant our family. We've got three pretty good kids there, don't we?"

"You're forgetting that we just picked one up from jail today."

"Oh yeah. There was that."

* * *

A month had passed since I searched for Donny Reed's story on the internet, and I'd come to regret that action. Unfortunately, the article included a mug shot of Donny from his arrest and his face was making its way into my daily thoughts and even crossing my mind as I lay in bed at night. In his mug shot, he looked callous and unsavory to me; in my mind, his appearance fit his crime. Donny had eyes like lumps of coal, a thin scar on his forehead, a blue tattoo of a cross on the side of his neck, and black hair spiked like a thug who'd never outgrown his rebellious teen phase. Because of that picture, Donny was no longer an omitted figure from our past; he was flesh and blood and real to me. That night, I dreamed I was behind the counter at the Quick Stop Market & Gas on the night that Donny came to rob it. As he entered the store, a bell jangled above the door, and I looked down at his gun and then up at his face.

My memories of my dreams were always hazy and disoriented, but the gist of the conversation follows...

"You're the sucker raising my son, Matt," Donny said, a cocky smile on his face as he did.

"He's a good kid, but no thanks to you."

"He's my son, asshole, and you'll never be anything more than his stepfather."

"I'm the one who's there for him every day. I'm the one watching him grow up."

"Face it, no kid loves their stepfather. They want the real thing."

"Matt doesn't know I'm not his biological father."

"See, you know I'm right. You're a coward."

"He'd love me just as much if I told him."

"No way! Not even close!"

"You're about to be executed, Donny. Any day now, they're going to stick a needle in your arm and end your miserable life."

"I fucked your wife, and now you're cleaning up my mess. Who's got the miserable life?"

"Hey, don't talk about my wife that way!"

"I'm the one with the gun. I'll say any shit I want."

With that said, Donny raised the gun, pointed it directly at my face, and pulled the trigger. I heard a blast, sprang upwards in my bed, and screamed, "No," as loudly as I could, waking Abby.

"Are you okay?" she asked, now upright beside me. "You must've had a horrible nightmare. You're drenched in sweat."

"Oh my God, Abby. You'll never believe it."

Chapter Seven

As punishment for his arrest, Matt was grounded for two weeks. In our home, that meant he could drive his SUV—a 2011 Land Rover that had been his mother's—to school and back home but nowhere else. He couldn't participate in any extracurricular activities, and he had to forfeit the use of his phone. Basically, he could be in the classroom or his bedroom. This punishment was much more effective on a kid like Christi than Matt because Matt didn't participate in any extracurricular activities, and he didn't interact with his small circle of friends on the phone often. He wasn't one to text or gab like his sister did. The only real punishment for him was his lack of freedom and choice, and he did seem to resent the mandated confinement to his room.

"Where's Matt?" I asked Abby late on a Saturday afternoon, having noticed his empty room.

"He left around 4," she said. "His grounding ended today."

"Did he say where he was going?"

"You know Matt," she said, "he mumbled something about getting pizza with some guy named Ron. I barely heard him."

"Do we know Ron?"

"I don't think so."

About an hour later, Abby hastily descended the stairs and came over to where I was seated on the sofa in the living room. She had a panicked look and two little orange pills in her right hand.

"Look what fell out of Matt's jeans," she said, the pills in her trembling palm.

"Oh crap," I said.

A minute earlier, when she'd picked up a pair of Matt's jeans off his floor to include in her load of wash, the little orange pills fell to the floor in front of her. Having lived with a meth addict in her younger years only heightened her concern about her children using drugs, especially Matt. Her time with Donny had clearly scarred her.

"Do you know what they are?" she asked, her head tilted as she prepared for my response.

"My guess would be ecstasy."

"Oh no."

"Sit down next to me and calm down. We'll talk to Matt when he comes home tonight."

Late that night, Matt walked in the front door and wobbled as he crossed the living room in front of me. When Abby heard the front door close, she came out of the kitchen to meet her son as he tried his darnedest to conceal the fact that he'd been drinking. With his eyes focused on the staircase ahead, he tried to avoid his mother entirely by calling out, "Good night, I'm tired, and I'm going straight to bed." But Abby wasn't having any of that nonsense, and she made a beeline for the staircase to block his escape. She positioned herself in his path with her arms firmly crossed in front of her, the universal sign for disappointed parents.

"Have you been drinking?" she asked as he approached. "I can smell beer on your breath."

"We shared a six-pack with our pizza," Matt replied, slurring the word "six" as he said it. "What's the big deal?"

"The big deal is you designate a driver or take an Uber when you drink," she said. "You know the rule."

"I only had a couple," he said, again slurring his words.

"You're drunk, Matt."

"I am not."

"What are these?" Abby asked, holding the pills in the palm of her hand.

"So, you're searching my room now?"

"What are they?" Abby's exasperated tone made it clear that she wasn't in the mood for a discussion about privacy or personal space. She wanted an answer right now.

"Molly," Matt said reluctantly.

As he spoke, I'd finished walking across the room to join them beside the stairs. Abby looked my way.

"It's ecstasy," I said.

"Have you taken these before?" Abby asked.

"I've taken Molly plenty of times, Mom. Kids take it all the time at parties."

"God damn it, Matt," she blurted. "What is wrong with you lately?"

"It just makes you feel happy. It's not a big deal."

"That's the problem," Abby said. "Nothing is a big deal to you anymore."

"Well, everything is a big deal to you."

Her arm flinched. For a second, I thought Abby was going to hit him. I guess she caught herself and stopped the impulse, but I'd never seen such rage in her eyes before. She took a deep breath, seemed to gather herself, and then she spoke through gritted teeth.

"Get out of my sight. You are grounded indefinitely this time."

After Matt turned at the top of the stairs and proceeded towards his room, Abby and I walked to the sofa and sat down. She was trembling.

"Take a deep breath," I told her.

"I think that went well," she said sarcastically, as tears began rolling down her face.

"You did a great job."

"I'm just so scared for him. I watched as meth took Donny over and slowly robbed him of everything else in his life. It was horrible."

"We won't let that happen."

"Sometimes, I could see in Donny's eyes that all he could think about was his next fix. I don't want that to happen to Matt."

"We won't let that happen," I repeated. It was all I could think of to say.

* * *

When I returned home the next night, Abby whisked me off to our bedroom. Along the way, she pulled me by my right elbow and did all she could to quicken my pace. In an unsteady tone, she told me, "I've got something to show you," and I sensed this wasn't good news. Earlier in our marriage, she'd once hustled me off to our bedroom to show me a new teddy she'd bought. This wasn't going to be one of those nights. Once inside, I noticed a few baggies, two pints of liquor, and a cough drop box on the comforter of the bed that looked like they'd been retrieved from a trash basket. Standing at the foot of the bed, Abby seemed unnerved and unhinged by the items.

"What are we going to do?" she asked, shifting back and forth anxiously. Her glazed eyes locked on mine.

Without telling anyone, Abby had taken the day off. With no one else around, she methodically searched every drawer, cabinet, closet, nook, and cranny in Matt's room. Her search lasted almost three hours, and she left no signs that she'd been there. Taped to the bottom of a dresser drawer, Abby found two baggies containing loose marijuana and four rolled joints. In a desk drawer, she found a box of Mr. Smith's Cough Drops that contained three real cough drops and eleven ecstasy tablets. In the pocket of a robe in the closet, she found two pints of vodka, one open with half of its contents gone, the other still sealed.

"When we finish dinner," I told her calmly, hoping to calm her, "we'll ask Matt to stay so we can talk to him."

"Good," she blurted, gathering the contraband from atop the bed. "I've got a lot to say to him."

The mood at the dinner table that night could best be described as unusual. Abby, in particular, was quiet and unengaged, only nodding and feigning interest in her children's tales and remarks. Even Christi, who always brought a handful of stories to the table each night, seemed to sense her mother's distraction, and her storytelling slowly petered out. For the first time in memory, Christi seemed to lose interest in recounting her day. Within twenty minutes of us sitting down, Matt, Christi, and Nate all rose from their seats to leave.

47

"Could you stay at the table, Matt?" I said. "Your mother and I would like to talk with you."

"Damn," Matt mumbled beneath his breath.

"What did you do now?" Christi asked.

"Did you rob a convenience store?" Nate followed up.

Nate's innocent teasing caused me to lose my train of thought. My mind flashed to Donny Reed and the murder lurking in the shadows of our family history. Because of Donny, convenience stores were no longer innocuous places where I grabbed sodas and snacks while out and about. These days, I couldn't drive past one during errands without thinking of him, without his dark persona overshadowing my thoughts. Abby noticed my faraway look and spoke up.

"Off you go," she instructed Christi and Nate, waving her hand as she did.

"What now?" Matt asked as he retook his seat.

From the pocket of her sweats, Abby began removing items and placing them on the table. First, she placed the bag of pot and rolled joints on the table. Matt's eyes widened. Then, she emptied the box of cough drops onto the table and the legitimate lozenges stood out like diamonds amongst gravel. Finally, from both her side pockets, with exaggerated movements of her arms, she unloaded the two pints of vodka, one after the other. Matt scooted back in his chair like he was under attack.

"You searched my room?" he said, his voice rising.

"I did," Abby replied without a hint of remorse.

"We're concerned about you, Matt," I interjected.

"No need," he said. "I'm fine."

"Have you taken any drugs other than these?" Abby asked.

"No."

"Matt?" Abby blasted back, her eyes narrowed and her brow ridged.

"I dropped acid a couple of times."

I expected Abby to explode with that revelation, but she didn't react. I could see she had steeled herself for this conversation. She was a mother on a mission.

"Matt," she told her son, "I have watched as friends destroyed their lives with drugs. You may think you are in control, but addicts never realize until it's too late that the drugs have control of them."

"I'm fine, Mom. I'm not a drug addict."

"Your mother is right, Matt," I said. "I've seen it, too. You're not a drug addict now, but we don't want you to become one. Drugs will grab you and not let go."

"I do a little innocent experimentation, and you guys act like I'm an addict. Give me a break."

"Matt," Abby said, "make no mistake about it, I am your mother, and I will not stand by or enable you while you throw your life away. You can drink beer and smoke pot occasionally, but you're not to do any other drugs. Do you hear me?"

"I'm seventeen years old. I'm old enough to decide."

Her eyes narrowed. "Do you hear me?"

"Yes."

"Well, hear this, too. I've never said anything like this to you before, but I mean it. Do not fuck with me! I love you more than anything in this world, and I will do whatever it takes to keep you safe, even if that means protecting you from yourself. I didn't raise a wonderful young man to bury a wonderful young man. Got it?"

"Geez, Mom, back off. This is ridiculous."

"Got it?"

The only retreat available, Matt slumped in his chair. "Yes. Okay. I got it."

Abby surprised me with her stern warning. She was the most determined I'd ever seen her, an unyielding force of nature. Living in the mountains, I'd seen mama bears protect their cubs as they wandered along through the trees, keeping any and all threats at bay. Add a thick coat of fur, and this would have been comparable. We were all quiet for a moment as we let her words sink slowly from the air. Finally, I spoke.

"You're seventeen," I said, "and you're going to graduate in a few months. What are your plans?"

"I'll get a job," he said, "and then I plan to move out. Don't worry about me."

His words were uncomfortably familiar. Many times, I'd made similar statements to my father. My heart sank in my chest because I'd always hoped I'd do better with my children. Looking at Matt, I felt like I'd continued the dysfunction in my family.

"We don't want you to move out," Abby said. "Have you considered the community college?"

"I'm a C-student at best. I'm not exactly college material."

"Just think about it, okay?" Abby suggested. "If nothing else, it might help you figure out what you want to do."

"Can I go?" Matt asked. "Are we done?"

"You can go," Abby told him, "but you are grounded until I tell you otherwise."

Chapter Eight

B lue skies were the norm in Boulder. Elevated and surrounded by mountains, I often felt like the city was somehow situated in the big blue sky, like it was more a part of the heavens than earth. It's the only place I'd ever lived, but I'd never thought about leaving. On a beautiful spring-like Sunday morning in late March, Christi and I drove to the Mayfield job to drop off some materials and give her a chance to view the progress. A whole season had come and gone since she'd last been there. We passed several fields where wildflowers were bursting into bloom and painting the landscape with blues and reds and yellows. In my business, signs of spring were always a welcome sight.

When we arrived at the worksite, Wyatt's truck was parked in front of the home, which wouldn't have been unusual except for the fact that he'd told me his daughters were staying with him that weekend. He had them every other weekend and usually planned special activities for them. Through the large front window, we could see his three daughters, the oldest only seven, wearing pretty, pastel dresses like they'd just come from Sunday services. As soon as I put the truck in park, Christi jumped out of the cab and ran inside to join Wyatt's kids in the living room. After a little wandering, I found Wyatt in the basement. He looked worn and frayed, in stark contrast to his children's shiny appearance in the other room.

"What are you doing here?" I asked.

"I need a place to think," he said. "I need a plan."

"A plan for what?"

"I don't know. I'm just feeling very confused. I don't know what to do."

"About what?" I asked, basically repeating the same question again.

Wyatt had a lost look in his eyes, and I was starting to feel the same way. All I could deduce so far was that he needed help. He didn't respond to my question, so I made it more basic.

"Tell me what's going on."

"My lawyer advised me to talk to a counselor who specializes in parenting, so I've been going there once a week."

"That's good. That will help with the custody case."

"This week, my counselor told me that Child Welfare will probably start conducting interviews with my kids in the next few weeks."

"That's good, too. The sooner they get started, the sooner it will be over."

"I can't put my kids through that, Alex. It's going to scar them for life."

"Kids are more resilient than you think. They'll be okay. Just be there for them."

"What if I lose custody? I can't lose my children. I just can't."

"You won't."

"I can't take that chance."

When Wyatt said that, I realized what he meant earlier when he said he needed a plan. Wyatt had come to our worksite to concoct a plan to take his kids and run. He was afraid he was going to lose them.

"Are you thinking about running?" I asked him.

"I can't lose them."

"You can't run. You'll ruin their lives."

"I can't lose them."

"Did you hurt Amelia?"

"No. Of course not."

"Then you won't lose them."

"How can I be sure?"

"You can't. You can only fight for them."

"I'm supposed to drop them off in an hour. I don't know if I can do that."

Like a man facing an incalculable loss, Wyatt looked confused. Clearly, he wasn't thinking straight; he wasn't in his right mind. Apparently, he couldn't imagine his life without his daughters, and, frankly, neither could I. His girls were everything to him. Nothing else mattered. Wyatt's plan to run was totally absurd, but it illustrated his conundrum: Any risk was better than the alternative. Losing his daughters was simply incomprehensible to him.

"You're their father," I said. "You've got to do what is best for them. You've got to put your own interests aside. Running will make a mess of their lives."

I was talking to Wyatt, but my words ricocheted right back at me. A father must do what is best for his child and put his own self-interests aside. I'd said it myself. Clearly, Matt deserved to know the truth about his father and contact him if he wanted. It was wrong of me to hide the truth from him. As a general rule, the truth should always be the default setting in life. My only reasons for not telling Matt about Donny Reed were my own self-interest and fears. How had I avoided such a simple and obvious truth for as long as I had?

"I'll just take them and run," Wyatt blurted, like it was that simple.

"That's no life for them," I said. "You'll probably get caught and things will be even worse. Think of those beautiful, little girls. As their father, you've got to do what's best for them. You've got to fight for them."

"You're right. I know you're right."

Wyatt's head and shoulders were hung low, like he was carrying a heavy load on an exhausted frame. From the look of him, I was sure he hadn't slept the previous night. I patted him on the back.

"By the way," I said, "a worksite isn't the best place to bring little girls. There are plenty of ways for them to get hurt around here."

"Oh God, you're right again. I'm not thinking clearly today. Let's go find them."

"It's okay. They're with Christi."

"Good."

"You should take your daughters to their mother."

"Yeah, thanks. I almost did something really stupid."

"We've all been there, my friend."

* * *

That night, with Matt and Wyatt and his children so occupying my thoughts, Donny made another appearance in one of my dreams. This time, Donny stood behind the Quick Stop Market & Gas counter as I walked in the front door with a gun in my hand. Looking pretty ridiculous, my hair was black and spiked in the same style that he wore his hair back then. Suddenly, Donny was the innocent victim in his own robbery and murder scenario.

My memory of my dream was hazy, but it unfolded something like this...

"Can I help you, sir?" Donny inquired, with a cocky look on his face, his head tilted slightly, his lip arched.

"You don't work here, Donny. What the hell is going on?"

"Would you like some gas or a Clark bar? Maybe some condoms?"

"Knock it off! You know who I am."

"I do. You're the coward who won't tell my son who his real father is."

"Well, you're wrong. I think I'm going to tell Matt the truth."

"You think?"

"It's complicated."

"No, it isn't. You either tell him or you don't."

"I'm going to tell him."

"No, you're not."

"Why do you say that?"

"Because that's why you're here. You're looking for an excuse not to tell him."

"You don't know me."

"I know you're afraid you'll lose him."

"He is my son."

"No, actually, he's my son. And you can't face that."

"If I tell him, he'll love me just the same."

"Let's see, will he still love his fake father, or will he love his new celebrity dad?"

"Celebrity? You're a fucking murderer."

"Tell that to the women who write me in here and pledge their love to me."

"He'll see you for the murderer you are."

"You so underestimate me. Many bitches would love for me to fuck them the same way I fucked your wife."

"What did I tell you about talking about my wife that way?"

"You got the gun, asshole."

With that said, I raised the gun, pointed it directly at Donny's face, and pulled the trigger. A thin stream of water squirted from the barrel and landed on his shirt pocket. He looked down at the wet spot and smiled. Then, Donny reached beneath the counter and retrieved a real gun. He raised it to shoulder height and pointed it at my face. I heard a blast, sprang upwards in my bed, and screamed, "No," as loudly as I could, waking Abby.

"Is it Donny again?" Abby asked, now upright beside me.

"He shot me again," I said. "The fucker did it again."

Donny's first appearance in my dreams was bad enough, but I found his encore even more problematic. I'd already spent too many waking hours fretting over him and whether to tell Matt about him, so the fact that he was now invading my sleep was very bothersome. Once and for all, I had to decide what to do about him. I couldn't allow this torment to continue. Perhaps I could start a letter-writing campaign to move up his execution date?

Chapter Nine

From my observations, good friendships were the product of mutual respect, common interests, and shared history between people that had been cultivated over many months or even years. Friendships were a lot like good wine—mellowing and improving with the passage of time. The first time we invited Wyatt and Jessica to our home for dinner in the summer of 2010, Abby and Jessica bonded faster than any two people I'd ever known. In fact, they'd become best friends before we'd even finished our salads and started the main course. As it turned out, they had a lot in common.

Abby and Jessica shared a birthday. Their fathers died when they were thirteen. Both had one sibling, a younger sister. Both worked at an elementary school. To them, cooking and baking were sacred institutions. Both incorporated yoga and meditation into their weekly routines. They believed dogs were the best life form on the planet. Both were proficient with a pottery wheel and owned a kiln. They loved quilting. Abby and Jessica were so enthralled with one another that, during the course of our meal, Wyatt and I barely got a word in.

"I'm going to tell my sister we have a new sister," Jessica told Abby.

"I'll do the same," Abby replied.

They both laughed. They even shared a similar kooky sense of humor.

During dinner, Jessica described her hometown of Savannah, Georgia, as a mystical place with narrow, red cobblestone streets lined with Colonial homes and oak trees draped with Spanish moss. After her father died, Jessica and her sister walked those quiet streets after dark beneath gas lampposts to visit their father's gravesite at the cemetery, about ten blocks from their home. In their small hands, they each carried a black, steel-cased flashlight for use when they reached the unlit cemetery grounds. Surrounded by headstones that dated back to the Revolutionary War, Jessica and her sister wholeheartedly believed their father was present at his gravesite each night, along with many other spirits who lived on in mystical Savannah. The sisters sat on each side of their father's headstone—Henry Otis Fuller inscribed between them—and watched the full moon dance with the wispy clouds in the sky above them.

"It was eerie," Jessica told us, "sitting amongst the old oaks and gray stones, but we were never afraid. We knew our father wouldn't let anything bad happen to us."

"I can't imagine two little girls sitting in a cemetery after midnight," Abby said. "What did your mother say?"

"My mother was devastated by the death of my father," Jessica said. "She kind of lost track of us for a while."

Abby nodded. "I remember how empty my mother's eyes were after my father died."

"I know that look," Jessica said.

For dessert, we were treated to Jessica's renowned peach cobbler, and it was every bit as good as she'd told me. Once again, Wyatt and I were largely excluded from the conversation as Abby raved about the delicious peach cobbler, and Jessica raved about the crispy yet moist fried chicken. If there had been any outsiders at the dinner table that night, they would have thought Abby and Jessica had grown up together and known each other their entire lives.

Despite Abby and Jessica's immediate connection, one remarkable shared experience would seal their bond of friendship that night. Within hours of sitting down at the dinner table with them, Abby and I became an integral part of their family history.

"Oh Gawd," Jessica said as we finished our cobblers, "I think I just wet my rags."

"Say what?" I asked.

"My water just broke."

Wyatt and I sprang upwards from our chairs. Unfortunately, I had no plan in mind for once I was upright. Across from me, Wyatt appeared equally unprepared. We both stood there with confounded looks on our faces.

"Have you been having contractions?" Abby asked.

"I think so," Jessica said. "I wasn't sure, so I didn't want to ruin dinner."

"For land's sake, Jessie," Wyatt exclaimed.

"How long since the last one?" Abby asked.

"Several minutes."

Still, Wyatt and I stood motionless, apparently waiting for directions or an idea to come to mind. Wyatt's face was pale, and his eyes were wide. I imagine I looked the same.

Abby turned my way. "Call for an ambulance and tell them to meet us as we drive south on Route 3."

I patted my pants. "I don't know where my phone is," I said, a quiver in my voice.

"It's on the counter," Abby said.

At that moment, Jessica cried out with a long, agonizing wail. It echoed in our great room. Finished, a couple of tears fell from her green eyes and slid over her faint freckles. "They're contractions, all right," she said calmly.

Abby checked her watch.

Wyatt wobbled a bit and looked like he was about to faint. He grabbed his wife's hand, but I couldn't tell whether it was to support her or himself. She comforted her husband.

"It's going to be fine, Wyatt. We're going to meet our daughter soon."

Fifteen minutes later, we'd loaded into my SUV, Wyatt and I in the front, Abby and Jessica in the back, and we were rushing down the mountain road toward the city of Boulder.

"Slow down," Abby barked as we rounded a sharp curve. "This is no time for an accident."

"We've got to reach the ambulance," I called out.

"Drive, Alex, drive," Wyatt said.

The scene inside the vehicle was chaotic and panicked. Jessica was stretched out across the backseat with her legs propped up on the side window, breathing loudly and rhythmically as Wyatt hovered over his seat and tried to coach her, just as they'd practiced in their classes.

"Breathe, Jessie, breathe," he said.

"Just shut up," Jessica said. "Can't you hear me breathing? I'm two feet from you."

All the vehicle's interior lights were illuminated as we scurried through the darkness like an enormous steel firefly. Abby sat on the floor beside Jessica and monitored the baby's progress. She spotted the crown of the baby's head as we drove, so we all knew we were dealing with an impatient baby. As part of her job at the elementary school, Abby had taken first aid and CPR classes, but she'd never delivered a baby. Still, she was an oasis of cool in an otherwise frantic vehicle.

"Get ready to push," Abby instructed Jessica.

"Push!" Wyatt objected. "No pushing!"

"I need all the men in this vehicle to just shut the hell up," Jessica demanded.

"Alex," Abby said, "pull into the Valley Overlook when we reach it. This little girl is going to be born there."

"Oh my God," I responded. My grip on the wheel tightened until my knuckles turned white. I felt sweat appear on my brow.

"Where is that damn ambulance?" Wyatt shouted.

"We'll hear the siren as it approaches," I told him.

When we reached the overlook, I brought the SUV to such a screeching halt that all its occupants lurched forward, so much so that Jessica almost fell on top of Abby.

"Good driving," Abby said as she pushed Jessica back onto the seat. "Go flag down the ambulance when it arrives."

As she spoke, the sound of a siren was audible in the distance.

"There it is," Wyatt declared. "I hear the ambulance."

"I hear it, too," I said.

"Go," Wyatt said, shoving my right shoulder toward the door. "Go meet it."

Again, Jessica wailed with agony as another contraction moved within her.

"It's time," Jessica screamed. "I've got to get this baby out of me."

"Get ready to push," Abby said to her as I climbed out of the vehicle.

I hustled from the overlook to the roadside—a distance of about fifty yards—so I could flag down the ambulance when it arrived. Over the course of three minutes, the siren gradually got closer and closer until I could finally see the flashing red and blue lights coming up the road. When it reached me, I pointed to our SUV in the overlook, and the ambulance drove right past me. By the time I reached the scene, I had heard the first cries of a newborn echo through the Colorado night. At 10:57 p.m. that night, Hailey Abigail Dawson was born at the Valley Overlook on Route 3, high above the city of Boulder. The birth was anything but uneventful.

Chapter Ten

I n the warm weather months, Abby loved to venture out to the Longmont Market in downtown Boulder, a farmers' market where the streets were lined with colorful tents and booths, and vendors sold everything from fresh produce to meats, cheeses, and ice cream. Personally, I enjoyed the fresh, hot corn on the cob from a tattooed woman with her corgi sidekick and a roaster on a trailer. Once a month or so, I'd tag along. On this particular outing, Abby was as radiant as ever in a red and gold cardigan and jeans that had faded to the same shade of blue as her eyes and the Boulder sky. Totally present in the moment, she was in high spirits and seemed to be taking in every person, tent, booth, and offering around her. In contrast, I was lost in memories and unaware of much else.

"Do you remember when Matt doubled over at the playground, and we had to rush him to the hospital?" I asked as we strolled.

"Of course," Abby said. "He had to undergo an emergency appendectomy."

"It was about six months after we married, and you were pregnant with Christi."

"That sounds right."

"I was thinking about us in that waiting room because that was the day I realized I was truly Matt's dad."

"What do you mean?"

"While Matt was in surgery, we sat in the waiting room, and I felt like I was going through it. My son was hurting, so I was physically hurting too. It was very real for me."

"How come you never told me this before?"

"I don't know. I'm not very good at that."

"Lord, don't I know it?"

"I think it was the first time I ever prayed. I was that scared for him."

"You never prayed as a child?"

"We went to church before my mother died. I'm sure I probably said some silly, juvenile prayers, but that was the first time I really prayed."

"You stopped going after your mother died?"

"We stopped doing a lot of things."

"That's sad."

"In the waiting room, I remember looking at your pregnant belly and worrying about having a second child. I thought that it might actually kill me if the two of them were ever hurting at the same time. It would be more than I could bear."

"I've had plenty of those moments. I still do."

"Clearer than ever before, I knew how much I loved Matt, and I knew I'd do anything for him."

"That's a father, alright."

Her timing was perfect. It was almost as if her words had set the stage. Abby and I paused and watched a father and his four-year-old son as they crossed the street in front of us, hand in hand. Both had an ice cream cone in their other hand. The boy licked his ice cream scoop, and it toppled from its cone to the street. His eyes welled, and his face reddened. Ahead of the tears, the father leaned over, lowered his cone, and gave his son a lick, and then the two walked on, alternating licks. Abby and I smiled at one another. We also walked on silently until I continued my reminiscing.

"In the waiting room that day," I said, "was also the first time I had considered how much pain my father must've experienced losing my mother and my sister."

"He must've been devastated," she said.

"I know. I'd never thought about it from his perspective."

"You were so young when it happened."

"I was just a kid at the time, and I was devastated, but I never thought about how much it must've hurt him."

"He never showed it, did he?"

"No, not at all."

"You strong, silent types are a pain in the ass."

"I can't argue with that."

Again, we paused in the middle of the street. To our right, a busker, a barefoot girl in a yellow beret, was belting out a decent version of "Me and Bobby McGee," and we listened for a few minutes. Always quick to participate, Abby swayed with the rhythm of the guitar, bumped her hip gently against mine, and then joined in with the singer on the final chorus. In a hushed voice she sang, "Freedom's just another word for nothin' left to lose. Nothin', and that's all that Bobby left me. Well feelin' good was easy, Lord, when he sang the blues. Hey feelin' good was good enough for me, good enough for me and my Bobby McGee."

With the final strum of the guitar, Abby pulled a couple of bucks from her pocket and tossed them in the singer's open guitar case.

"That was great," she told her.

We'd covered about half the market and Abby hadn't purchased anything yet. That was unusual.

"We've been talking so much," I said, "you haven't been able to shop."

"That's okay," she replied. "I'm really enjoying our conversation."

I nodded. "Me too." Then, I continued.

"The thing is, I think my love for Matt finally caused me to understand how much the death of my mom and sister must've affected my father. Until that day in the emergency room, I had no sense of the pain he must've endured."

"I'm sure it changed him."

"That's just it. I was so young at the time that I don't remember him before the accident. He may have been an entirely different man."

"Did the issue of Matt's birth father bring on this soul-searching?"

"Of course."

"Well then, maybe something good is coming of it."

"I want to tell Matt about his father."

"I know."

"What do you mean, you know?"

"I knew you'd decide to do it. You're a good man, Alex, and it's the right thing to do."

"How do you think he'll take the news?"

"These days, your guess is as good as mine. Two years ago, I thought I knew my son. Now, I guess the kindest thing we can say is he's at a difficult age."

"I want to tell him, but I'm very concerned about his reaction."

"He may react badly in the moment, but he'll come around in time."

"I've got to brace myself for a bad reaction."

"When should we tell him?"

"Let's try to find a good moment."

"We can't wait too long; the State of Texas isn't going to wait."

At the time, I could've jotted everything I knew about being a father on the back of a postage stamp and still had room to sign my name. Amazingly enough, I'd been at it for over fifteen years without ever really contemplating the task at hand. As was true of so much of my life, I never applied myself to anything until my subpar results demanded it. My decision to tell Matt about his birth father might have been my first well-thought-out, fatherly act.

Chapter Eleven

A s his parents, Abby and I had discussed how much Matt's room concerned us on several occasions. Items scattered about the room reflected his past interests, but nothing suggested any current interests. It had been that way for two years. From his elementary school days, meticulously assembled and painted model trains were parked on a shelf near the window. For about five years, Matt loved trains and everything railroad related. During junior high school, he became interested in the Harry Potter book series, and his complete collection was displayed on his bookcase, along with statuettes of a few characters and some collectibles. Matt also played three seasons of little league baseball, and his baseball mitt, cap, and a trophy sat atop his dresser. In a heap in a corner of his room, his football helmet, jersey, cleats, and letter jacket remained as souvenirs of his one season, but since his last outing on the gridiron, Matt hadn't shown interest in anything else. At such a key stage of his development, it seemed to us as his parents, a bad time to lose interest in everything. Whenever we passed his bedroom's open door and looked in at what was clearly ancient history, Abby and I were reminded of our concern.

Early one evening, Matt looked up and saw Abby and me standing in his doorway, so he reluctantly removed his headphones. "What did I do now?" he asked.

"Nothing," Abby said. "We want to talk to you."

"That's never good," Matt said.

We entered his room, and I closed the door behind us. Though I'd hoped for a relaxed conversation, it felt awkward right away because there wasn't any place for us to sit. Abby and I were adrift in the center of the room while Matt remained on his bed. He may have noticed our seriousness because he reached up and hung his earphones on a hook over the bed. His face was gradually filling with concern.

"We have something to tell you," I said, moving from spot to spot, still trying to figure out my location for this conversation. "You're old enough now to understand."

"What is it?" Matt asked.

My "old enough" reference only added to the rising tension in the room. Alerted, Matt sat up on the edge of his bed in anticipation. Suddenly, I wished we had some great news for him. Anything but what we had.

"Matt," Abby said, "I lived with a man in Texas before I met your dad. We had a child together, and that was you. You were two years old when Alex became your father."

Matt straightened his back and shook his head. "What the hell?" he blurted.

"We feel it's time for you to know," I said, "but this doesn't change anything. I'm still your father."

My words felt awkward. I'd rehearsed them in my mind, but they sounded flat and wrong when I said them. Dismayed, I watched Matt for a reaction. He'd lowered his head.

"Do you know where my father is?" Matt asked, looking up at his mother.

I felt dropped from the conversation. Just like that, I was nonessential; I was excluded. This conversation was now limited to blood relations.

"He is in prison in Texas."

"What did he do?"

"He murdered a grandmother during a convenience store robbery," I said, squeezing my way back into the conversation. I knew I'd phrased it harshly, and I was a little ashamed of my choice of words.

"That's cold," Matt said, expressionless.

I hoped he was referring to the actual murder and not my words.

We stood in silence for several minutes while Matt stared at the floor. In the still, I noticed Abby's right hand nervously tugging on the bottom of her blouse. When Matt finally looked up, his face had reddened, and his eyes were welled with tears.

"What's his name?" Matt asked.

"Donny Reed," Abby said.

"His execution is scheduled for August 23rd," I added. Again, I felt like I was slanting the message, but I couldn't stop myself. It felt instinctive.

"Is that why you're telling me this now?"

"It's part of it," Abby said. "We also think it's time for you to know."

Matt looked overwhelmed. Tears slowly trickled from his eyes. His tone was biting when he next spoke. "You're telling me my whole life has been a lie."

"No, Matt," Abby pleaded. "Please don't think that way."

I shook my head. "Nothing has changed," I said. "I'm still your father."

I so wanted him to acknowledge it, but we'd barely made eye contact. Though I knew telling him was the right thing to do, it didn't stop my heart from filling with regret.

"You're not my father," Matt said, scowling at me. "You're just a dude who sleeps with my mother. We're not even related."

"Don't say things you're going to regret later," Abby warned him. "This is a difficult moment, but we'll get through it."

Matt glared at both of us. "You've lied to me every day of my life. Why should I listen to you?"

"We're your parents," Abby said. "We only want what's best for you."

"You're my mother," Matt shot back, "but my father is some dude locked up in a Texas prison."

"I'm still your father," I said.

My words felt desperate, like I was trying to convince myself. Now aware of Donny Reed, the man who'd actually begotten him, Matt barely acknowledged my presence. He looked down and away but never at me. Years ago, while in rooms with my father, he had always looked right past me, like I wasn't there or I was invisible. In his presence, I felt nonexistent. With Matt now, I felt that way again—ignored, unseen, disheartened—but it was worse coming from my son.

"I want to be alone," Matt said as he rose from the bed. With his arms wide open, Matt herded Abby and me toward the door. We shuffled our feet awkwardly.

"We need to talk about this," Abby protested as we both backpedaled across the room.

"We've talked enough," Matt said. "I need space."

Matt opened the door and guided us out of his room. He nudged my shoulder to make sure that I'd cleared the doorframe. Dumbfounded, Abby and I were left standing in the hallway as the door slammed. We looked at one another, heartbroken. On the other side of the door, Matt sobbed. My spirit sank even lower.

"He needs time," Abby said.

I nodded, but I wasn't sure I agreed. All the time in the world couldn't erase the horrible things he'd learned about his father and his past, or my role as substitute.

*　*　*

The next morning, a Saturday, everyone was up and planning activities by 9 a.m. While Christi and Nate gathered their breakfast in the kitchen, I sat at the island with my cup of coffee and a half-eaten bagel in front of me. Last night had been difficult, and I didn't sleep well, so my plans for that morning wouldn't take me any further than the sofa in our living room. I'd planned a long nap once the kids cleared out, and then later, I'd meet Wyatt at the site to complete some work. Thinking about Wyatt, I wondered how he was doing.

In a hurried manner, Matt descended the stairs and joined Christi and Nate in the kitchen to grab breakfast for the road.

"Good morning," he said, his focus directed at Nate and Christi only. Then, he turned and said, "Good morning, Alex," with a scowl upon his face.

"Good morning, Matt," I replied.

His scowl was the same look I saw last night, and I figured I'd simply have to get used to it for a while. The fact that we were suddenly on a first-name basis was news to me. It reminded me of my relationship with my own father, and I'd always hoped for better for us. Once again, our dysfunction was continuing in my family.

In less than three minutes in the kitchen, Matt grabbed a bagel, banana, two donuts, and a juice and headed for the front door.

"I'll be gone all day," he said, once again scowling at me. "Have a good day, Alex."

He slammed the front door behind him and was gone.

"Since when does Matt call you Alex?" Christi asked.

"We'll talk about that when your mom comes down," I said.

"We've got a lot to do today," Abby announced as she descended the stairs. "Eat your breakfast, kids."

Abby grabbed a cup of coffee and a donut and sat beside me at the island. Her eyes were only partially open as our conversation with Matt had hampered her sleep as well. Squinting from the morning light, she stirred her coffee.

"Where's Matt?" she asked me.

"He's gone," I said. "He left ten minutes ago."

"He's still grounded."

"After last night, I thought we'd cut him some slack."

"He's grounded," she repeated in a no-nonsense tone.

"I'm sorry."

"I've got to drop Christi at her softball practice and then take Nate to the mall for clothes shopping."

"I think we'd better have a conversation with them about last night first."

"Oh damn, you're right."

While Christi and Nate ate their breakfast, Abby and I repeated what we'd told Matt the previous night. Almost in unison, when we told them about the execution, they moved their plates to the side, like they'd either lost their appetites or couldn't focus on their food any longer. Seemingly immobilized by the news, Christi sat frozen in place, with a blank stare on her face and her mouth slightly agape. Unusual for her, she said nothing. In retrospect, I underestimated the impact this news would have on our children's senses of well-being and security. At their young ages, learning that things were different than they believed was unsettling for them. In my assessment, they seemed less confident and more unsure about their world.

"Matt is still your brother," Abby said, concluding our conversation. "Nothing has changed."

"You mean half-brother," Nate corrected her glumly. "Technically, Matt is our half-brother."

"Nothing has changed, Nate," Abby said, with the same tired impatience she directed at me earlier.

Weighted by the news about their brother, Christi and Nate trudged off to their rooms to get ready to go into Boulder. Abby and I remained at the island. Alone, we just looked at one another, a look all parents know, the "what are we going to do now look." We knew our family was in tatters, and we had work to do. We also knew it would take time. Less than an hour into the new day, Abby's normal glow was conspicuously absent.

"Can you please buy Nate something other than blue shirts?" I asked.

"I doubt it," Abby replied. "Ever since he read that biography about Steve Jobs, he has worn nothing but indigo shirts and khakis. He says it's his signature outfit."

"Our twelve-year-old has a signature outfit?"

"Yup."

"That's it," I said, "that's the final straw. How do I quit being a parent?"

"If you find a way, let me know."

* * *

Matt didn't come home on Saturday night. Or the next night. Or the four that followed. Fortunately for us, a friend of ours called Abby on Saturday to tell us that Matt was staying at their home, so we needn't be concerned about his safety. We were, however, very concerned about his mental state. Abby briefed our friend on what was going on with Matt, and together, they decided it would be good for Matt to spend a few days there. Give him a little space.

"Don't worry, Abby," our friend said, "we'll keep a close eye on Matt."

It was a long week for Abby and me. We knew our child was hurting, but we had no interactions with him. Our only consolation was the fact that we knew our friends would take good care of him. They were good people. Abby and I were waiting in the living room when Matt finally returned home on Friday evening, almost a week later.

"Come sit beside me on the sofa," Abby called out as Matt walked in the front door with his backpack over his shoulder.

Slowly, Matt walked into the living room and sat beside his mother, without making eye contact with either of us. Apprehensively, he looked up at Abby and asked, "What's the matter?"

"We just want to talk," Abby assured him. "How are you doing?"

"I'm okay."

"Really, Matt," she pressed him. "How are you?"

"I feel like I'm not the person I thought I was," he said, "like I've been living a lie."

Abby nodded. "It's going to take time. You have a lot to process and come to terms with. I just want you to know we are here for you."

"Okay."

Matt was clearly hurting and couldn't even look me in the eyes. We were five feet apart, but it felt like miles. Sitting across from him, seeing my son in so much pain, two things were clear to me: first, I needed to give him space and time to adjust to his new reality, and second, I needed to be a better father.

"When you're ready to talk," Abby said, "let us know. And, if you want to talk to someone else, like a counselor or therapist, we'll arrange that."

"Okay."

"We're going to get through this together. We're a family, and that's what families do."

"I know."

"Do you have any questions for us?"

"Was Donny a good man when you were with him."

Abby sighed. "He was at first. He was a really nice man, but then he got into meth, and the man I knew went away. The drugs took over."

"Do I remind you of him?"

"Not really," she answered. "You're much more like me than him."

"Good." He seemed relieved.

Then, Matt looked pensive. His brow creased, his eyes narrowed. "Do you think I should contact him?" he asked.

"I think you have to make that decision," Abby said.

"Well, what do you think?"

"I don't know which Donny will respond, the nice guy or the drug addict."

Matt nodded. "I get it."

"What else?"

"That's all."

"All right then," Abby said, extending her hand out before him. "Give me the car keys and your cell phone."

"What?" he exclaimed.

"You're still grounded."

"Aw, Mom."

Matt retrieved his keys and phone from his pockets and placed them in his mother's palm. His jerky movements made his displeasure obvious, and his now familiar scowl returned to his face.

"I love you," Abby said as Matt walked away.

He mumbled something unintelligible.

Chapter Twelve

I had one memory that I always relied upon during hard times to lift my spirits and restore my hope. When times were darkest, I went back in my mind to the day I met Abby, the one remarkable day in my otherwise unremarkable life. The date was July 17, 2001, a bright, beautiful summer day without a single cloud in the sky, at a time when I was building an A-frame home for a client who lived in Napa. Twenty minutes or so before noon, Abby was gassing up her Mini Cooper with a Union Jack on its roof when I pulled up on the other side of her pump to fill my tank. Thirty-five years old and still single, you can bet I noticed her even before I'd gotten out of my truck. Once I placed the hose in my gas tank, she glanced my way between the pumps. As she did, her curly, blonde locks fluttered in the breeze.

"I feel like I know you from somewhere," Abby said.

"If we had met, I'm sure I'd remember," I said, hoping to flatter her.

"Will you remember me now?"

I smiled. "I'm sure I will."

"I think we crossed paths somewhere."

"Did you go to Boulder High?"

"No," she said. "I went to high school in Texas. I just moved here a month ago.

"What brings you to Boulder?"

"I'm counting on the mountain air for a fresh start."

"You picked the right place. Boulder air has magical powers when it comes to cleansing and reinvigorating the soul."

"I believe you."

As a child, Abby's family lived one mile from the Pacific Ocean in Del Mar, California, until her father died from a brain tumor prior to her starting high school. Devastated by the loss and needing family nearby, her mother moved with Abby and her younger sister to Austin, Texas. For more than a decade, Abby felt like a fish out of water in Texas, but it wasn't until a year after the birth of her son while living in Abilene that she decided to move somewhere that inspired her once again. She'd felt so much happier and alive in Del Mar than she ever did in Texas. It simply wasn't the right place for her. Confident she could teach anywhere, Abby decided she wanted a new start in a new town. As a young, single mother, she knew she couldn't afford Southern California so, after a lot of research, she picked Boulder, Colorado. She sensed it had the natural beauty and close-knit community that were typical of beach towns. Just no beach. Her application with the Boulder school system was quickly accepted.

"Maybe our eyes met one day in this mini-mart," Abby said, "when we both reached for a blueberry muffin."

"Again, I'd remember that."

"How can you be sure?"

"Because you have such beautiful blue eyes."

"You're very sweet."

"My name is Alex."

"I'm Abby."

That day at the gas station, Abby was wearing cut-off blue jean shorts and a white V-neck T-shirt, and, at times during our conversation, she clutched the frayed threads at the bottom of her shorts. She winked at me at one point in our conversation and it felt like she'd thrown a switch within my heart. Too quickly, her pump made a loud, clanking sound and shut off, and I suddenly felt pressured to keep her from simply saying goodbye and motoring away.

"I wish I could ask you to lunch right now, but I'm building a home near Cathedral Peak, and I'm not going to have time for lunch today. Can I call you, and we'll have dinner one night?"

"Sure. I'll give you my number."

Two hours later, while perched on the roof of my A-frame project, I spotted Abby walking up the dirt path that would eventually be the home's driveway with a bucket of fried chicken in one hand and a six-pack of beer in the other. For a moment, I thought I'd been in the hot sun too long, and my mind was playing a trick on me—it looked like a scene from a beer commercial. After I removed my work gloves, I wiped my eyes and took a second look. She was still there, strolling my way. Then, Abby removed all doubt when she called out, "Hello again, Alex. I brought lunch for you."

In the clean, crisp mountain air, we sat in the shade of a large cottonwood tree, drank beer, nibbled on fried chicken, and shared the journeys that had brought us to that moment. She told me she loved teaching elementary-aged children because they made her smile and laugh every day. They were so sweet and innocent. I told her I loved building homes because I felt like I'd found my purpose in life. I was proud of the finished homes. I even showed her some pictures of a few projects that I had with me. She said she had a two-year-old son named Matt, whose father had never been in his life. And just like that, it was her turn to show me pictures of Matt from her wallet. He was a chubby child with a constant gleam in his eyes. I said I'd never married or had children, but I wanted both someday. Abby and I talked and laughed and had a great time together, but I couldn't get past the notion that she was out of my league. She was smart and funny and beautiful, so I pictured her with a doctor or lawyer or college professor, but never someone like me. I so enjoyed her company, but I cautioned myself not to get my hopes up. It wasn't until she quoted Hemingway, when she joked about "what if" we'd already crossed paths previously, that I thought I had a chance.

"I didn't say you looked familiar just to talk to you," Abby said. "We've crossed paths somewhere."

"It's not a big town," I said. "Maybe we did."

"What's your favorite lunch place in town?"

"I eat at the Mountain View Pub a lot. Maybe it was there?"

"Nope. That's not it. I've never been there."

"Well, you've only been in town a month, so we haven't lost a lot of time if our paths crossed earlier."

"Oh, Alex," Abby said, taking on a theatrical tone, "we could have had such a damned good time together."

"Yes," I said. "Isn't it pretty to think so?"

Our exchange was the last lines of *The Sun Also Rises*.

"Oh my God," she said, her face aglow. "You've read Hemingway."

"I read *The Sun Also Rises* when I was twelve."

"You were ahead of your time."

"Maybe, but time has certainly caught up."

We both laughed.

For another hour, we talked about our favorite books, most of which we had in common, classics as well as modern works from great writers like Fitzgerald, Lee, Salinger, Irving, King, Tartt, and Oates. I told her about the leather-bound books in my father's office and how I regularly snuck one out and kept it under my bed. She told me her book collection was the only material thing she truly valued. Like she was sharing something with me that she treasured, Abby quoted a passage from *The Great Gatsby* that almost brought a tear to my eye. At the time, I didn't know if it was the beauty of Fitzgerald's words or the sadness in her tone that moved me so.

"I felt a haunting loneliness sometimes, and felt it in others—young clerks in the dusk, wasting the most poignant moments of night and life."

It was only then, while basking in our mutual love of great literature, that I thought we both felt a connection, and I had hope.

* * *

Another date forever locked in my memory was September 25, 2016. On that day, Abby spoke the thirteen cruelest, most soul-crushing words I'd ever heard.

"I had a brief affair with someone I met through school. I'm sorry."

When Abby said those words to me, my insides collapsed. It felt like my heart sank deep within my body until it came to rest atop other organs, much lower than normal. A hollowness resulted that caused me to slump over in my chair and focus on my breathing. What happened naturally before required concentration and effort now. Where my body had structure before, there was rubble now. All normality was gone; I was broken. In my shattered condition, the only thing happening normally was the tears sliding down my cheeks. That part of me was working. It was all she'd left of me.

"I don't love him," she said. "I love you."

Those seven words only made me angrier. All the more, I questioned how she could betray our vows, the commitment we'd made, and the love we felt for one another. In my sunken heart, I knew I could never betray her with another, never bring that sacrilege into the sanctity of our marriage. I could never hurt her that way. Beyond the emotional betrayal, the thought of Abby in the arms of another man, kissing and caressing him, making love to him instead of me, infuriated me. It made me want to punch something really hard; it made me want to scream out as loudly as I could. By my side, I clenched my fists as a way to manage my anger, a way to vent the rage within me. My fists were squeezed so tightly I thought a finger might snap. In that moment, something had to give.

Unable to think clearly or convert my thoughts into words, I felt incapacitated. Silent, I kept my head down, unwilling to look her in the eyes. Her eyes had always been my salvation, and now I didn't know what I'd see in them. I was afraid to look.

In a timid manner, Abby crept over to the sofa and sat beside me. She placed her hand on my knee, but I didn't look up at her. Instead, I only raised my gaze as high as a photograph of Abby in an ornate, gold frame on the coffee table in front of me. It was taken a few years back at an awards dinner where I'd received the "Boulder Builder of the Year" honor. In the photo, Abby was attired in a beautiful, red, sequined evening gown, and the camera had caught her by surprise as she turned. Her face was aglow, but her eyes were wide from the start like she'd been caught in a mischievous moment. It was my favorite photo of Abby because it captured her playful, uninhibited nature. Despite her objections, I'd framed it and placed it there. Looking at the photo, her confession fresh in my mind, I suddenly hated her playful, uninhibited nature.

In my life, one that had included much pain and isolation, Abby was the physical embodiment of my hope. She was my sunshine during dark days, my comfort when I felt bruised and defeated, and a beacon of light in a safe harbor when storms threatened. Most scary to me was the thought that my collapse might lead to my disappearance because she was so much of me now that I wasn't sure how much of the old me still existed. Couples jokingly referred to their "better halves" when they talked about their spouses, but the truth was that Abby was my better seventy or eighty percent. She was my whole world. I couldn't imagine my life without her.

Finally, I looked up at Abby. Her face mirrored mine, with tear tracks visible on her cheeks and creases beside her eyes. I saw a mixture of pain, remorse, and embarrassment in her eyes. Face to face, she had trouble maintaining eye contact with me. She diverted her eyes. Abby was always hard on herself when she made mistakes or let people down, and this was obviously one of her worst failings. She appeared weighted by heartache and regret. Her body shook as she wept.

"How could you?" I demanded.

Abby lowered her head. "I don't know what I was thinking," she answered. "I wish I could undo it."

"You betrayed our vows," I said.

She looked up at me once again. Her lip quivered. "I love you so much, Alex, but I need more of you."

I shook my head. "This isn't about me, Abby."

"I know."

"How brief of an affair?"

Abby hesitated. She bit her lip. "We met three times. It was meaningless. I'm sorry."

"It means a hell of lot to me," I said.

"I didn't mean it that way," she said, reticent.

Side by side on the sofa, I felt indignant, an unusual emotion for me. In sixteen years of marriage, we'd argued as couples do, but I'd never felt like I couldn't look at her, like I didn't want to be near her. At that moment, her presence annoyed me, and I wanted to be away from her. I wanted to be someplace else. Anyplace else. Suddenly, every day we'd spent together and everything we'd shared felt like a lie.

"I can't be in the same room as you," I said. "I'm going out."

I rose from the sofa and headed straight for the front door, snatching my keys from the entry table as I walked past it. I didn't pause. I didn't look back.

"I'm sorry I hurt you, Alex," she called out to me, desperation in her voice. "Please forgive me."

Her confession came one month to the day after the death of Uncle Bob, and something became unhinged inside of me. It was all too much. The next day, I accelerated and changed lanes as I approached my hill for the very first time.

Chapter Thirteen

B ack in my twenties, I spent many long nights at poker tables with coarse, unshaven individuals who lied as often as they spoke, and I became proficient at the game. From my first hand, I was drawn to poker because it was a wonderful distraction from whatever issues and problems occupied my mind. Poker required focus and analysis, and I found I could immerse myself into the game to the exclusion of everything else. With cards in front of me, my entire world consisted of the dealer, the cards, the chips, and the eight other players at the table. In my thirties and forties, with both business and family obligations competing for my time, I continued to play poker but much less frequently.

At a poker table, I studied the other players to learn their playing styles. Good players play the other players as much as their own cards. It's easy to win with the best cards, but good players win even when they don't have the best cards by making lesser players believe they do. Years ago, I won my first hand at a poker table with a pair of threes. Though new to the game, I sensed my opponent was trying to bet me out of the hand, so I raised him, and he quickly folded. Back then, I realized that my mind, relentless and analytical by nature, was well-suited (no pun intended) to the game of poker.

After the death of my uncle and Abby's affair, I once again sought distraction at the poker table. Lying is common to both poker and affairs, so the irony wasn't lost on me that I sought refuge from my wife's big lie with a table full of liars. But this time around, two things were different: my mind wouldn't let go of my troubles, and small stakes tables weren't sufficient. I decided to play at the no-limit table, where wins and losses were significantly larger.

When I arrived at the table, I recognized several regulars from previous outings, including a loudmouth named Larry, who was my least favorite player to have at my table. A mechanic by trade, Larry was about my age, with blonde hair, a nearly transparent mustache and soul patch, dark stubble, and fingernails rimmed with grime. He always wore wrinkled Henley shirts with a pack of Lucky Strike cigarettes in the breast pocket. Larry coughed frequently, talked incessantly, and made obnoxious comments like, "Why don't ya'll just pass your money to me? That way, we'll give the dealer a break, and the result will be the same." Some players had table personas, but Larry was just plain obnoxious.

"Haven't seen you in a while, Alex," Larry said as I placed my chips on the table.

"I've been busy," I said.

"Nothing gets in the way of my poker," Larry declared. "I've got priorities."

"I've got a wife, kids, and a business."

"So do I, but I make sure they don't get in the way of my poker. Like I said, I've got priorities."

Larry laughed boisterously at his own remark, and then he followed it with a long bout of hacking coughs.

"If you keep *coffin* like that," I said, "you're gonna end up in one."

"Hey, that's good."

During my first hour of play, I lost $3,000. Players referred to the suckers at the table—the ones who would inevitably lose their money—as "fish." I was playing so badly that the other players must have seen scales and gills when they looked my way. Making matters worse, I couldn't get my mind to focus on the game, so I hadn't learned anything about the playing styles of my opponents. Who chased straights and flushes? I had no idea. Who bluffed by raising and tried to buy pots? Again, I didn't know. When I arrived at the casino, I felt depressed and disheartened, and now, after making four horrible calls that had cost me three grand, I could add frustrated to the list.

Even worse than Loudmouth Larry was the player at seat 5. Everything about him annoyed me. He was trim and fit, with chiseled cheekbones and long brown hair that he pushed backward in a careless manner, and he was wearing a pink-striped Oxford shirt and brown corduroy pants like an Ivy League Professor wannabe. Aside from his betting, he never said a word, but he annoyed me nonetheless because, in my mind, seat 5 had become a proxy for the dude that had stepped out with Abby when she betrayed her vows. I'd never met her paramour, but I knew he was a principal at a Boulder school, and that guy looked like how I pictured him. In my mind, I'd labeled him "the Principal."

Around midnight, one of my favorite players joined our table and sat beside me. Rufus Snow, a dapper gentleman with a matching bow tie and pocket square, was an attorney who'd worked at my father's law firm in the early seventies after he passed the bar exam. About a year after my father died, Rufus and I met at a poker table, and he told me many stories about my father as we played in the subsequent months. My father, it turned out, was somewhat legendary amongst the Boulder legal community, and young lawyers studied and emulated his courtroom tactics. When Rufus spoke of my father, his words were always laced with reverence.

"How have you been?" Rufus asked as he arranged his chips before him.

"I'm on a really bad run," I said.

"Are we talking about cards or life?"

"Both."

When the dealer tossed my second card my way, I picked them up from the felt, cupped them to not reveal them, and spied the ace and jack of diamonds in my open hands. In the game of Texas Holdem, an ace and a "face" were decent hole cards and worthy of a bet.

"$100," I said.

In Texas Holdem, players are dealt two cards face down, five community cards are dealt face up in the center of the table, and each player makes the best hand possible with five of the seven cards. In the end, the players reveal their hole cards, and the best hand claims the pot.

All the other players folded except one.

"$200," the Principal said.

"Let's make it $400," I said, looking directly at him.

"Call," he said, unruffled.

With the first round of betting complete, the dealer placed three cards, also known as the "flop," face up in the middle of the table: the jack of clubs, ace of hearts, and ten of spades.

Opponent		Dealer		My Cards	
J	A	10		A	J
♣	♥	♠		♦	♦

"$300," I said without hesitation. I had two pairs, a strong hand, but he could have had a straight or three of a kind.

"Call," he said.

In my estimation, the Principal was a cowardly player because he never looked my way. In my mind, the only thing worse than a poker player who wouldn't make eye contact was one who wore sunglasses at the table. Staring opponents down and reading their faces was an integral part of poker, and players who couldn't handle that interaction should've stuck to Old Maid. This guy was exactly how I imagined Abby's lover. I didn't even know his name, but I hated him.

On what is known as the "turn," the dealer placed the five of spades beside the ten.

Opponent		Dealer			My Cards	
J	A	10	5		A	J
♣	♥	♠	♠		♦	♦

Still believing my two pairs were probably best, I bet again.

"$300," I declared.

"Call," he said. Once again, his eyes remained down and focused on the table in front of him. He never looked my way.

Revealing the final card of the hand, or what is known as the "river," the dealer placed the ten of diamonds at the end of the row of cards.

Opponent			Dealer				My Cards	
		J	A	10	5	10	A	J
		♣	♥	♣	♠	♦	♦	♦

"$300," I said.

"$600," the Principal said. He raised me.

I paused. I looked his way, but he didn't return my gaze. His raise meant one of three things: his hand was already better than I thought, the ten improved his hand, or he was trying to buy the pot. I lost in two of my three scenarios, but I couldn't fold to this guy. I couldn't back down. I hated him.

"I call," I said. I placed another $300 in the pot.

With that said, the Principal turned over the ace and ten of clubs, so the river gave him a full house, tens over aces, which beat my two pairs.

Opponent		Dealer					My Cards	
A	10	J	A	10	5	10	A	J
♣	♣	♣	♥	♣	♠	♦	♦	♦

"You got burned on the river," Larry said, stating the obvious. "You had him until then."

"Tough loss," Rufus said to me.

I nodded. "It sure was."

"By the way," Rufus added, like his previous comment had reminded him, "I heard about your uncle and I'm really sorry. He was a good man."

"Now that was a tough loss," I said.

"I'll bet."

The dealer dealt the cards for the next hand. Rufus and I checked our cards and promptly tossed them into the middle of the table, folding. The hand continued without us.

"How have you been, Rufus?" I asked.

"Not so good either."

"How come?"

"My nephew was arrested for robbing and stabbing an elderly woman, but he didn't do it. My brother wants me to represent him."

"Are you gonna do it?"

"I've got to, but there's nothing a lawyer hates more than an innocent client. The stakes are so high."

On the morning in question, at around 11:10 a.m., Louise Greer, a sixty-eight-year-old retired nurse, was standing at a bus stop on the corner of Fifth and Dalrymple when a young black male approached her with a knife in his hand and demanded her purse. Still feisty for her age, Ms. Greer refused to hand it over. The robber grabbed the purse by the strap and a struggle ensued. After a protracted tug-of-war, her assailant slashed her upper arm with the blade. Startled by the sight of blood, Ms. Greer released the purse, and the young man fled through a nearby alleyway.

"Are you sure he didn't do it?" I asked.

"I'm sure," Rufus said. "I've known him all his life."

"Do you think you can get him off?"

"Hell no. My nephew's alibi witness is a sixteen-year-old black kid with a record."

"What did he do?"

"Possession."

"Crap."

"And the victim picked my nephew out of a lineup."

"Well, that's not good either."

Rufus nodded. "Victim identifications are known to be unreliable, but that's hard to overcome in a trial."

"Were there any other witnesses?"

"Only the victim."

"You've got a tough case there."

"My nephew didn't do the crime, but he may do the time."

Rufus's words made me think. When it came to infidelity, which spouse did the time, the cheater or the betrayed? It sure felt like I was the one doing the hard time for Abby's crime. Clearly, nothing about love was fair or logical.

Chapter Fourteen

W ithin three weeks of Abby's confession, I'd made the poker room my home away from home, playing until well after midnight on plenty of nights. At home, Abby and I barely spoke to one another, unless you counted my frequent "I'm going to play poker" announcements and her relieved "Okay, good luck" responses. I wasn't having fun or playing well, but I needed time away from my marriage, and I'm sure Abby welcomed the respite from my sad face. As a couple, we were in a place we'd never been before, a dark and lonely place where we guarded our emotions and left words unsaid. Our normally light and breezy interactions were now weighted and tense, with little eye contact. Night after night, we had a hard time being in the same room together, but neither of us wanted to end our marriage. We comforted one another by saying that things would get better with the passage of time. I hoped that was true.

As I approached the poker table, I saw all the usual suspects already in place: Larry in seat 8, the Principal in seat 7, and Rufus in seat 2, with an empty seat beside him. With $5,000 in chips in one hand and a tumbler of scotch and rocks in my other, I sat beside Rufus in seat 3. Rufus was having a prosperous night as his stack towered over all the others and easily totaled more than $20,000. He smiled when he saw me.

"I hope you came to play poker tonight," Rufus said in a ribbing kind of way. "Frankly, I'm not sure what you've been doing at this table lately."

"Yeah," I replied. "I hope so, too. I've been a little distracted lately."

"Well, get your head in the game. I'm tired of watching you lose."

"I'm gonna turn it around tonight."

"That's the attitude."

Before I'd even finished stacking my chips, the dealer dealt the cards for the next hand. In succession, Rufus and I glanced at our cards and promptly tossed them into the middle of the table. The hand continued without us.

"How is your nephew's case going?" I asked.

"Not so good," Rufus said. "I met with my nephew and his friend, Darnell, and they told me that they bought pot around 10:30 a.m. on the morning of the attack and then went to Darnell's house to smoke it and shoot hoops in his driveway."

"None of that sounds good."

"I know." Rufus grimaced. "And, to make matters worse, Darnell's house is about ten blocks from the scene of the attack."

"So, their alibi also puts them in the vicinity."

"Yeah." He shook his head.

"Is there any other evidence?"

"On the day of the lineup, the police took photos of bruises on my nephew's right arm."

"Well, that's not good. How did he get them?"

"Playing hoops."

"Makes sense, but it doesn't look good."

"I don't know what I'm going to do. I can't let them take him off to prison. He's my nephew, and I know he didn't do it."

"You're a lawyer. Trust in the system."

Rufus glared at me. "Are you kidding me?"

"I'm sorry, Rufus," I added quickly. "I didn't know what else to say."

At a little before midnight, after I'd begun telling myself that I needed to call it a night, I found myself looking at the two red aces, the aces of hearts and diamonds. I was on the "button," which meant I'd be the last to bet in each round of betting, a distinct advantage for me. Confident in my cards, I waited patiently while the action moved around the table.

"$100," the Principal announced.

"$300," Larry said.

"Call," Rufus said.

"Call," I said, tossing my wager forward.

Raised, the Principal tossed the additional $200 into the pot.

With the first round of betting complete, the dealer placed the flop face up in the middle of the table: the ten of diamonds, jack of diamonds, and queen of spades.

Opponent		Dealer	My Cards	
10 ♦	J ♦	Q ♠	A ♥	A ♦

"$100," the Principal said.

"$300," Larry said as he rechecked his cards.

"Call," Rufus said.

I called too, and the Principal promptly folded, leaving three of us in the hand.

On the turn, the dealer placed the three of diamonds beside the queen of spades.

Opponent		Dealer		My Cards	
10 ♦	J ♦	Q ♠	3 ♦	A ♥	A ♦

The board contained three diamonds, so a flush was a possibility. The board also contained three consecutive cards, so a straight was a possibility. It was a difficult board for pocket aces and one where I had to worry about them being "cracked," table lingo for when pocket aces got beat.

"$500," Larry declared.

"Call," Rufus said.

I called too.

As the final card of the hand, the dealer placed the nine of diamonds at the end of the row of cards.

Four diamonds on the board with three consecutive diamonds meant that the winning hand would most likely be either a flush or a straight flush. I had the ace of diamonds, so I had the highest flush possible, so only a straight flush could beat me. Sure of my ace, I watched as Rufus and Larry both checked their cards.

"$1,000," I declared.

With a disgruntled look on his face, Larry tossed his cards into the middle of the table and folded.

"Call," Rufus said, moving a grand forward.

Suspecting I'd won the hand, I flipped my cards and displayed my ace high flush.

"Straight flush to the king," Rufus said as he flipped over the king and queen of diamonds.

The dealer pushed the chips his way.

"Thanks for not going all in," I said in a hushed tone. "I would've called."

Rufus nodded as he gathered the chips. "You're my friend, Alex."

"A long time ago," I said, "you told me there were no friends at poker tables."

"What can I tell you?" he said, shrugging his shoulders. "I'm a poker player. I lied."

At that particularly trying time in my life, Rufus's words about our friendship meant a lot to me.

Chapter Fifteen

"At this rate," Larry said to me as he raked in another large pot full of my chips, "you're going to put my kid through college."

It was a Friday night in late December, and I was having yet another miserable night at the poker table, down over $7,000 and totally incapable of distinguishing a bluff from a winning hand. Without exception, I'd bet every time I should've folded and folded every time I should've bet. My poker instincts were as busted as my wallet. The only thing worse than losing that much money was losing most of it to Larry, who bombastically gloated over every chip he won. Larry was a bad loser and an even worse winner.

"Keep it up, Alex," Larry blared, "and Larry Jr. will have a single dorm room and the best meal plan next fall."

I was steaming mad. My head actually felt warm. I'd only been at the table about an hour, and I'd already lost several large pots to Larry and one to the Principal. Both men had large stacks of chips in front of them —many of them once mine—that stood as monuments to my stupidity and poor judgment. Looking for distraction from my bitterness, I addressed Rufus, who was seated across the table from me.

"Any news on your nephew's case?" I asked.

Rufus's face lit up. He smiled the elated smile of a lottery winner or someone who'd just pulled off a heist. Pausing momentarily, he glanced at the two cards in front of him and folded them just as quickly. Obviously, he had a story to tell.

"You're never going to believe it," he began.

Shortly before the robbery and stabbing occurred, Rufus's nephew and his friend were playing basketball in the driveway of his friend's home. It was a simple game of one-on-one, but with bragging rights at stake, it was always a fierce contest. With the score tied at ten and a next-basket-wins scenario in place, Rufus's nephew launched a shot from twenty feet away that swished through the net while barely ruffling it. Celebrating his victory, Rufus's nephew danced and strutted up the street while waving his arms and emphatically exclaiming, "Game, sucker!"

Fortunately for Rufus and his nephew, one of the homes on the street had a security camera. While the driveway and basketball court weren't within its range, the security camera recorded Rufus's nephew as he danced up the street celebrating his victory. For fifteen seconds at 11:11 a.m. that morning, one minute after the assault occurred, the camera recorded his nephew's antics after the game-winning shot and provided an ironclad alibi for the time of the incident.

"I knew the camera wouldn't show their game," Rufus said, "but I hoped I might see a neighbor driving by who could give him an alibi. Sure enough, as I'm watching the video of the empty street, here comes my dang fool nephew strutting up the street at exactly the right time."

"So, what happened?" I asked.

"I showed the video to the district attorney, and she dropped the charges."

"That's unbelievable," I said.

"It's practically a miracle," Rufus added.

As Rufus concluded his story, I picked up my hole cards and saw two lovely ladies staring back at me, the queens of spades and diamonds. After my miserable start to the night, I needed Lady Luck by my side, and I hoped these ladies' arrival was a sign my luck was about to change.

"I bet $500," I said when the betting reached me.

"Call," the Principal said as he tossed five chips onto the table. True to his cowardly playing style, he never looked my way.

All the other players folded, so it was just the Principal and me remaining in the hand as the dealer placed the ten of spades, queen of clubs, and seven of diamonds in the center of the table.

The flop had given me three queens, which was a very strong hand. I was the first to bet. I gathered my chips, and then I announced my wager.

"$500 more," I said.

"Call," the Principal said.

On the turn, the dealer added the six of hearts to the row of cards before him.

The addition of the six meant that a straight was now possible if the Principal had a nine and an eight. However, I didn't think that was likely because he was a conservative player who tended to play hands when he had aces and face cards. It was more likely that he had either an ace/queen or king/queen. Since I had three queens, I figured I had control of the hand.

"$1,000," I declared.

"Call," the Principal said.

With the round of betting done, the dealer placed the two of diamonds on the table.

Clearly, the two was inconsequential to the hand and hadn't changed either of our positions. I believed I had him.

"$1,000," I said.

"$3,000," the Principal announced.

Crap, I thought. *He's got the straight. The Principal never raises unless he is sure he has the best hand.*

I looked his way, but he kept his eyes on his chips before him. He never looked up at me. Looking at the board, my three queens were a powerful hand and the winner unless he had the straight. I picked up $2,000 in chips and held them in the palm of my hand. I hated the Principal and didn't want to make the wrong decision. A full minute passed while I considered the wager.

If this is the guy who had sex with my wife, I thought, *I'm not giving him my money as well.*

"I fold," I said, tossing my queens face down onto the felt in front of me.

Though I'd folded, and he didn't have to reveal his cards, the Principal flipped over the ace and queen of hearts. Disgusted, I watched as the dealer slid the pot across the table to the Principal. He had a pair of queens with an ace. He didn't have the straight.

I had the winning hand, I thought, furious at myself. *I folded the winner.*

In poker, players who'd suffered bad losses, lost their equilibrium, and weren't acting prudently were said to be "on tilt." Clearly, I was on tilt. Even worse, my tilt extended beyond the lights and noise of the casino; my entire life was on tilt. My uncle's death and my wife's indiscretion had obliterated my equilibrium and left me unable to act prudently. My mind was awash in a searing pain that made good decisions unlikely. It was suddenly clear to me that Abby and my uncle were the foundation my life was built upon and the bracing that kept me upright. Without their support, my foundation cracked and became unstable, and I teetered.

As I walked out the mechanized doors of the casino into the cold night air, I acknowledged my predicament, and I decided to give up poker for a while. I had to stop. I was throwing money away. Since Abby confessed her affair to me, I'd lost close to $50,000. I told myself I wouldn't play again until I regained my equilibrium and wasn't teetering any longer. I'd take a break from my losing streak until I'd figured out how to mend my cracked foundation. But more importantly, I also decided to stop my weekly antics at my hill. That craziness had gone on for too long. I'd been racing up that hill in the wrong lane once a week for three months, and I was fortunate that I hadn't been killed already. I didn't understand why I did it, but I knew I had to stop doing it. That night, I made a commitment to myself: I would drop these two out-of-control behaviors from my life.

As I arrived at my SUV, I acknowledged the timely moral in Rufus's story about his nephew: No matter how bad things may seem, there is always a way forward.

I need to look forward to the New Year, I thought. *A fresh start is exactly what I need. With some stability reclaimed, I sure hope 2017 will be better.*

Chapter Sixteen

T he building was as utilitarian as anything I'd ever seen. It was square, nondescript, and the color of sand, with narrow, rectangular windows at equal intervals across its three floors. Looking at its bland facade, I could only surmise that all design elements were removed during the drafting stage because the budget only allowed for functionality. The building was just plain ugly. On the inside, I envisioned long lines of people desperate to be done with the forms and the bureaucracy: think the Department of Motor Vehicles. In the final analysis, the building served its purpose—a place for local government work to be conducted—but it didn't add a hint of a pleasing aesthetic to the neighborhood or provide a modicum of enrichment for its visitors.

As a homebuilder, I appreciated beautiful, well-crafted things, not for their monetary value but for the way they made me feel, pleasing to my eyes and enriching of my spirit and soul. I'd found purpose in my chosen profession because my product elevated and improved the lives of my clients. Nothing was more satisfying to me than building a spectacular home on a spot where only dirt and rocks existed before. When my homes integrated perfectly with their natural surroundings, I felt I'd done it right; I'd merged people's lives with the beauty of the natural world. My homes were places for the human spirit to soar. Looking at the drab, soulless building before me, I felt empty.

I'd come to this architectural monstrosity because I had an interview with a caseworker as part of Wyatt and Jessica's custody case. Abby and I were Amelia's Godparents, and we knew the family well, so I wasn't surprised when the caseworker called. Scheduling the appointment, I felt uneasy about getting involved in another family's rift, but I hoped I could help Wyatt. Certainly, I could say good things about his character and work ethic.

Anxious, I waited in a cream reception area with splashes of beige until a twenty-something woman with a large turquoise necklace and matching earrings called my name. She had a file in her hand, and I could see the name "Dawson" on the tab.

"I'm right here," I answered nervously, my voice cracking as I did, and then I followed her to a small conference room.

Why am I so nervous? I thought as I sat in the only other chair in the room.

"My name is Hannah Peters," she said like she had formalities to get out of the way. "I am the caseworker assigned to the Dawson case. At Child Welfare, our responsibility is to ensure that the child's best interests are served. We always do what is best for the child without regard for the feelings or interests of the adults involved."

I'm nervous because the stakes are so high, I thought, answering my own question. *Now I know how Rufus felt about representing his nephew.*

"I'm here to help in any way I can," I said.

"How long have you known Jessica and Wyatt?" she asked, readying her pen for my answer.

"Seven years," I said. "We've been friends with them through the births of all three of their children."

"How would you describe their relationship during the years you've known them?"

"They were very happy for most of it, but then their marriage seemed to unravel."

"Do you know the cause of that unraveling?"

"Well, I know Jessica had an affair and left Wyatt for another man."

"Do you blame Jessica for the breakup?"

"I don't blame either of them. I think that's their business, not mine. I don't think you can judge someone else's marriage."

With my marriage at a low point, I knew from where I spoke. Would I blame Abby if we couldn't mend our marriage? I knew it wasn't that simple.

"Are you aware that Jessica and her new husband, Jack, have accused Wyatt of molesting Amelia?"

"I am aware of the charge, but I don't believe Wyatt is capable of that."

"Why do you say that?"

I shuffled nervously in my chair. "Because I've watched Wyatt with his children for seven years, and I think he is the best father I know. There is no doubt in my mind that he loves his daughters and would never hurt them."

"Do you have a daughter?"

"I do. I have a fifteen-year-old named Christi."

"If Christi was four years old, would you trust Wyatt to care for her in your absence?"

The question really caught me off guard. I hesitated. *Say something,* I thought, *say something.* I remained silent as a very uncomfortable few moments elapsed. With these accusations pending, would I leave a four-year-old Christi in his care? I didn't know.

"Of course I would," I said unconvincingly. "I wouldn't hesitate."

What am I saying? I thought. *I just told the Child Welfare case-worker that I'd leave my young daughter in the care of an accused child molester. They're going to knock on my door next.*

"Well, thank you for coming in, Mr. Bryant. You've been a big help."

Oh my God, I thought. *What have I done? I'm both a horrible father and a horrible friend.*

My phone rang before I even reached my vehicle. When I looked at the screen and saw Wyatt's name, I got a lump in my throat. He was counting on me to turn the tide for him, and I couldn't tell him I felt like I did. Heck, I might've made it worse.

"Hey, buddy," Wyatt said when I put him on speaker. "How did it go?"

"I think it went well," I said right away, trying to avoid any hesitation that might convey my doubts.

"Did Hannah seem to like you? That's important, you know?"

"We got along fine."

"Did you tell her I was a good dad?"

"Of course I did. I told her you were a great dad."

"I know. Thank you for doing the interview. I'm just so nervous."

"It's going to be okay."

"I hope so."

"Just hang in there."

"Jessica just left me a message to call her. She seemed upset."

"Well then, you'd better call her."

"I will. I wanted to talk to you first."

Once we'd finished our call, I looked back over my shoulder, and the architectural monstrosity appeared oppressive and foreboding to me now. My visit complete, its bureaucratic nature had taken on an Orwellian Big Brother quality. Inside those walls, decisions were made about who was a good parent and who wasn't. Families were reduced to files. I knew children needed protection, but I also understood—more so now than at any other time of my life—how difficult it was to be a parent. The fact that those government workers had the power to take Wyatt's children from him caused a pit to form in my stomach. I felt ill. At that moment, a twenty-something with turquoise jewelry seemed like the perfect front for a soulless and diabolical bureaucracy.

Chapter Seventeen

With my son barely speaking to me or even acknowledging my presence when we were in the same room together, another dream about Donny seemed unavoidable. Once again, I stood behind the counter at the Quick Stop Market & Gas when Donny came in to rob it, but, this time, Matt was by his side. They both had a gun in hand and big smiles on their faces. My son and a convicted killer side-by-side like Butch and Sundance or Jesse and Frank about to rob a convenience store. It was the realization of my worst fears about telling Matt about his father. They'd teamed up and were ruthless criminal and naïve sidekick now.

"I can't thank you enough for telling my son about me," Donny said. "I always wanted a partner in crime."

Desperate, I pleaded, "Matt, what are you doing?"

"I'm joining the family business," Matt said. "Donny is going to teach me everything. He's a great guy."

I couldn't believe what I'd heard. I was appalled. "He shot a grandmother in the face," I said.

"I know," Matt said. His face lit up. "He's going teach me how to shoot people in the face too."

"Like father, like son," Donny said.

"Matt, please," I said, "don't get involved with this guy."

"He's my dad."

My heart broke. Not only was Matt calling me, Alex, but now he was calling Donny, Dad. I was crushed.

"I've just got to break him of a few bad habits you taught him," Donny said, "and we'll be right as rain."

"Bad habits?" I asked.

"Yeah," Donny replied, "like all that please and thank you shit for starters."

I clenched my fist. "He is my son!" I blasted. "You stay away from him."

"Now that's not true," Donny returned calmly, "we both know my seed found its way to Matt's egg, not yours. You weren't even around yet."

"He's right, Alex," Matt said, "you're not my father. You're just the dude who sleeps with my mother."

"No, Matt, no," I pleaded.

"Oh, for Pete's sake," Donny said, "let's get down to business." He nodded at Matt.

"Give us your money," Matt said, almost gleefully, while pointing his gun at me.

"Well done," Donny said. "You're a fast learner."

Donny raised his gun and pointed it at me also. I raised my hands and took a step backwards. Limited by the cashier's station, I was flush against the cigarette display.

"Don't do this," I pleaded, directed at Matt.

"Fuck it," Donny said. "Let's skip ahead to the fun part."

"Time to shoot him in the face?" Matt asked.

"Yeah," Donny answered, smiling at me.

I heard two blasts, sprang upwards in my bed, and screamed, "No," as loudly as I could, waking Abby.

"Again?" she asked, now upright beside me. "This is getting old."

"Matt was with him," I said, breathing heavily. "They both shot me."

As far as I was concerned, August 23rd couldn't get here fast enough. The sooner Donny Reed was out of my life (and my dreams), the better.

Until then, I sure hoped Matt wouldn't develop an interest in his birth father and want to meet him.

* * *

One evening in May, Matt lingered at the dinner table after the meal while Abby and I drank coffee. I noticed immediately because Matt was usually the first to depart after dinner. It often seemed like his objective was to spend as little time in our company as possible. Slyly, I glanced over at Abby. She subtly raised her eyebrows, signaling to me that she was suspicious too. Neither of us spoke. We tended to our cups. Once Christie and Nate ascended the stairs and were out of view and earshot, Matt let us know what was on his mind.

"I got a letter from Donny today," he said.

Once again, I glanced at Abby to gauge her response. I could tell she was as surprised and caught off-guard as me, but she knew not to overreact. I took a silent breath and waited on her to speak first.

"You wrote him?" Abby said.

"I did," Matt replied.

"Can we read Donny's letter?" Abby asked timidly.

Matt retrieved a folded sheet of paper from his pants pocket and handed it across the table to Abby. We took turns reading the short note.

Hi Matt,

I'm locked up on death row, so you know I've done stupid stuff. I've hurt a lot of people. The truth is I fucked up my life. I wasted it. One of my worst mistakes was leaving your mother before you were born. I was a meth addict, and I made really bad choices. I won't ask you to forgive me. I don't deserve it. I'd like to meet you if you want. If not, I understand. Donny Reed

Part of me hoped there'd be something in the letter that made Matt <u>not</u> want to meet his father, some indication that he was still a drug-addicted criminal, but he didn't come across that way at all. Instead, Donny seemed sincere, clean, and contrite, a trifecta of trouble for me. When I finished reading, I felt like my adversary had just made a smart move and put me in a weakened position. I didn't want to feel that way, but I did.

"What do you think about the letter?" Abby asked Matt.

"He doesn't make any excuses," Matt said. "He admits his mistakes."

Abby nodded. "He does."

"He doesn't sound like an addict anymore," Matt said.

"He doesn't specifically say it," Abby said, "but he sounds clean."

"He said he wants to meet me."

"Do you want to meet him?" I asked. I did my best to say those six words without revealing my preference that he didn't.

"I think I should."

"I think you should, too," Abby said. "If you don't, you'll always wonder what if?"

"I think so, too," I said. I felt like a politician, saying what my constituents wanted to hear. While I knew I should support Matt, I was conflicted.

"Can I go to Huntsville?"

"Of course," Abby told him.

"Mom and I will work out the details," I said.

"Thanks," he said as he rose from the table.

Abby and I sat quietly while Matt left the room. She waited until she heard the door of his room close, and then she finally spoke.

"He needs to meet his father before he dies."

I nodded reluctantly. "I know," I said. It wasn't what I wanted, but I knew Abby was right.

"I'll take Matt, and we'll fly to Huntsville."

"No way, Abby," I objected. "I've got to go too."

"We both know you're not going to fly."

"We'll drive. It'll only take a couple days."

I didn't want this meeting to happen, but if it did, I wanted to be part of it. I wouldn't cede my role to a man whose entire contribution to Matt's life was a spoonful of ejaculate. In some manner, I needed to loom over their meeting. I needed to be there.

"I'm not driving all the way to Huntsville," Abby said. "We'll have to cross the whole state of Texas in the summer heat."

"It'll be fun. We'll take Christi and Nate and make a family road trip out of it."

She smirked and shook her head. "You're out of your mind."

"You said you wanted us to do some fun stuff with Nate. This is our chance."

"There is nothing fun about this trip. We're going to meet a man who is about to be executed."

"We can have fun on the way. We'll stop in Dallas. We'll have a good time."

"Well, you should be there with Matt too."

"Then it's settled. We'll all go."

"Oh geez. I know I'm going to regret this, but okay."

"You won't regret this."

Chapter Eighteen

T alk about famous last words...

"By dinner time tomorrow," I said enthusiastically, as we all loaded into the SUV, "we'll be in a beautiful hotel in Dallas, getting ready for a great meal to celebrate Matt's eighteenth birthday."

"Where are we staying?" Christi asked.

"Nate's going to work on that while we drive," I said. "And once Nate finds our hotel, Matt will figure out where he wants to have dinner."

"What about me?" Christi asked.

"Why don't you find us some options for things we can do the next day in Dallas. Something fun."

"Okay."

"What about me?" Abby asked.

"You just sit there and look beautiful," I told her.

"I can do that," she replied with a wink.

Six hours into the journey, somewhere south of the Oklahoma/Texas border, something went wrong. While on cruise control at seventy miles per hour, the SUV suddenly lost power, decelerated, and started to coast. I pressed the accelerator to the floor several times, but it wouldn't respond. We continued to lose speed. Certain we had a mechanical problem, I steered our vehicle to the side of the road, and we stopped beside a highway sign that read, "Abilene 287 Miles." As soon as I put the shifter in park, everyone offered their opinions and suggestions.

"We'd better call for help," Abby said.

"It's going to take a long time for a tow truck to reach us," Matt said.

"It's hotter than hell out there," Nate said. "We'd better come up with a plan quick."

"I won't last in that heat," Christi said.

"I think it's best if we leave the vehicle here and just go to the next town," I said. "Let me see if I can flag someone down."

"No serial killers, Dad," Nate said.

"I'll see what I can do," I replied with a smirk.

"Killing an entire family would be quite a feat for a serial killer," Matt said.

Nate nodded and grinned. "His masterpiece."

"Mom," Christi cried out, "make them stop."

I put the flashers on and exited the vehicle. In the hot Texas sun, I stood beside the rear taillight and waited for the next vehicle to come along. Fortunately, I didn't have to wait long as a salesman in a Chevrolet Impala pulled up behind our vehicle after about five minutes. He put on his flashers and joined me on the roadside.

"There is a small town with a couple service stations about thirty miles up the road," he told me. "If you want, I can drop your family there, and you can get your SUV towed into town."

The salesman was a kind man who knew the route well and even told me which of the service stations he recommended. After a crowded ride in his car, with his sales materials and samples on our laps, the salesman dropped us in front of the Lone Star Motel at the edge of town. Standing in the midday sun, looking at the motel's weathered signage, dilapidated lobby, and cracked concrete near the outlying rooms, I wondered if that one-star designation was its name or guide-book rating. In silence, we all stood for a moment and took in our surroundings—a motley collection of roadside establishments that passed as a town, though it clearly wasn't a town. There weren't any homes, churches, or schools, and the closest post office, police station, or pharmacy was in the next town, another ninety miles down the highway. Set on desolate land, this pseudo town was a clump of structures surrounded by nothingness that made a person thirsty just to look at it, with its searing glare, unrelenting sand, and prickly vegetation.

"We're fucked," Matt said.

"Matt, please," I objected.

"I agree with him," Abby said.

"Oh, I'm not disagreeing," I said, "I was just hoping we could be more civil."

"We're not staying here, are we?" Christi asked.

"We have to, honey," I told her.

"For how long?" she said.

"Hopefully, just tonight."

"If we survive this road trip," Christi said, "I'm not going on another with you for as long as I live."

"That's fair."

The proprietors of the businesses that operated along this stretch of highway had obviously decided that this location offered a unique opportunity. The highway provided a steady flow of travelers who needed the town's basic services, namely restaurants, motels, convenience stores, and gas stations, with two providing towing and repair services. And, with the essentials covered but nothing for the morale of the passersby, The Blue Lizard Lounge somehow emerged onto the terrain and filled that need. Nothing in the town was clean or well-maintained, but their offerings would suffice in an emergency. If the town had a marketing slogan (which it didn't), I imagined it would've been "Stop for a while and make do with us."

"Let's get a couple of rooms," I said, "and then I'll see about getting our vehicle towed."

Twenty minutes later, I retrieved the yellow pages from the end table and dialed the phone.

"Walt's Auto Repair and Towing," the voice on the other end of the line blared. "This is Walt."

I briefed Walt on our breakdown and asked him to tow our SUV to his station. He told me he could go in an hour as he was busy replacing a radiator on a Mustang for a retired couple from Phoenix. Immediately, I sensed two things about Walt's service station: There wasn't a team of mechanics standing by, and all work was accomplished on an unhurried basis.

"Do you think we'll be able to get back on the road tomorrow?" I asked.

"I doubt it."

"Why not?"

"Well, Mr. Bryant, for starters, I don't know what's wrong with your vehicle yet, and, when I do, I don't stock any Land Rover parts. It will take at least a day to get the parts from Dallas."

Oh no, I thought, *we're going to spend Matt's eighteenth birthday in the town my family has affectionately dubbed, We're Fucked, Texas.*

"Call me when you know more, Walt."

"I've got your number on a sticky."

One thing I'd learned in life was to never tell myself that things couldn't get any worse because, if I did, they inevitably would. I'd learned not to jinx myself in that manner, but that never stopped things from getting worse. It often happened anyway. Somehow, I knew this was one of those times.

Long before it got dark, I spotted a red neon sign a little up the road that flashed the words, "World Famous Texas BBQ In AC Comfort," to lure patrons from the highway into its large dining hall. The structure had a mess hall quality about it.

"Texas is famous for BBQ," Nate said, "but I seriously doubt that's it."

"Hopefully, the air conditioning is better than our rooms," Christi said.

"It's got to be," Matt said.

"It's walking distance," Abby offered.

"It's still ninety degrees outside," Nate said, "so maybe we should eat there. It's close."

Gradually, we talked ourselves into BBQ for dinner and set off into the still-simmering West Texas evening to partake in a meal together. The sun had descended to a spot where it had almost reached the horizon, but the glare was still unyielding. The walk from the Lone Star

Motel to Uncle Rusty's BBQ was about a quarter mile. On the emotional spectrum, our collective mood was a long way from jovial and much closer to irritated.

"It's like being inside an oven," Christi grumbled as we walked.

"We're mountain folk," Nate said. "We're not made for this climate."

Uncle Rusty's was an enormous space that looked like a meeting hall with picnic tables and benches and red checkered tablecloths. It was cool and comfortable, as promised. When our orders were ready, each was served on its own tray with about a pound of ribs—or chicken in Christi's case—French fries, coleslaw, baked beans, and biscuits. It was a lot of food. Everyone's spirits seemed lifted by the prospect of a good meal, so I tried to forget the calamity-filled day.

"This is good," Nate said. "How's the chicken?"

"Good," Christi replied, looking up from a bite with BBQ sauce all over her face.

We all laughed.

"Matt," Abby asked, "when are we scheduled to meet with Donny?"

"We can only see him on the weekend," Matt replied. "All visits happen on Saturday and Sunday."

"That's good," I said, "because I don't think we'll have the Rover back tomorrow."

"Say what?" Matt asked. "Are you telling me I've got to spend my eighteenth birthday here?"

"It looks that way," I said. "The parts will have to come from Dallas."

"That's great," Matt exclaimed, pushing his tray away from him. "I'm going back to the motel."

He rose from the table and walked away.

"Wait, Matt," I called out. "Don't go."

My plea didn't slow him any, and he marched right out of the door.

"Let him go," Abby said. "We have to come up with something we can do to make his birthday special tomorrow."

"I think Dad has taken care of that," Nate said.

"Yeah," Christi added, "we're all going to remember this trip."

Christi and Nate laughed while I looked at Abby for consolation.

Abby shook her head. It had been a long, hard day, and, at that moment, I didn't know this miserable day wasn't done with us yet.

At the motel, we had three rooms in a row. Abby and I were in the center room, Matt and Nate were on one side, and Christi was on the other. Sometime after midnight, I awoke feeling warm and nauseous and coated by a thin layer of sweat. Immediately, I threw off the covers and made a beeline for the bathroom. As soon as I dropped to my knees in front of the toilet, I vomited violently and continued for several minutes. Whenever I paused, I could hear Abby throwing up in the other room. We'd formed a late-night chorus of violent puking. When I finished and opened the bathroom door, Abby was waiting with a motel trash bin in her hand.

"Damn that Uncle Rusty," she said, her face moist with sweat, and then she slipped past me on her way to the toilet.

Done for the moment, I sat on the edge of the bed while Abby vomited in the bathroom. Through the thin motel walls, I heard similar retching sounds coming from Matt and Nate's room, as well as the sounds of frequent flushing. Still nauseated, I sensed more vomiting in my future. My nightmare wasn't over yet. As I sat there, I also noticed that Christi's room was conspicuously quiet.

I should've ordered chicken, I thought to myself.

Only Christi stirred early the next day. The rest of us slept in until almost noon. When we'd all gathered in early afternoon, Nate summed up everyone's displeasure with me when he said, "You almost killed us three times yesterday."

"What are you talking about?" I asked.

"First," he said, "you stranded us on a Texas highway in 90-degree heat. Then, you hitched a ride for us with a potential serial killer. And, finally, we all got food poisoning."

"No one died," I said, my only defense.

* * *

Our time in We're Fucked, Texas, passed in an excruciatingly slow manner. I found myself gazing periodically at the telephone on the nightstand like I was trying to will it to ring. Desperately, I wanted to hear that the Land Rover was ready. Though we were all leery about what we ate, each afternoon, while the thermometer recorded its high for the day, we sent a volunteer out into the heat and glare to bring back lunch for everyone. One day, with his double cheeseburger in hand, Matt remarked, "I hope we don't get Uncle Rusty'ed again," which caused everyone to pause and examine their food more closely. Late on our second day, Walt called to advise me that the problem with our Land Rover was a busted fuel pump. He said he'd ordered the replacement. It felt like a call from the governor though I'd never use that analogy around Matt.

* * *

"We need to start drinking," Abby said to me on the third night around 10 p.m. She looked exhausted and overwhelmed. Her hair was uncombed, her blouse wrinkled. Looking at her reminded me of our younger days when these types of predicaments were more common.

"I can't argue with that," I replied. "Do you want to walk to the bar?"

"Hell, yes."

It had cooled down nicely, so it was a pleasant fifteen-minute walk beneath a black night sky dotted with twinkling stars to The Blue Lizard Lounge. We chose a little booth near the back and ordered the first of several rounds, maybe many. As I slowly unwound, I noticed a common look in the eyes of all who came into the bar, a look of hopelessness and despair, like they were unsure of their ability to survive in this harsh environment. We shared a common knowledge that we were all on our own out here in the middle of nowhere, with no line tethering us to the civilized world. As I sipped a tumbler of whiskey, I fully understood the need for The Blue Lizard in this town of otherwise essential services.

When our third round arrived, Abby seemed more relaxed. At a minimum, her look was less desperate. The alcohol was having the desired effect.

"When we reach Dallas," she said, "I think I should take Christi and Nate and fly back to Boulder."

"Really."

"Yeah, we're all exhausted."

"Okay."

"I also think it might be a good idea for you and Matt to go to Huntsville without us."

"I agree. I need to do this with him."

Me, Matt, and a convicted murderer just sitting around chewing the fat, I thought. *Won't that be fun?*

"Let's enjoy a couple of relaxing days in Dallas," Abby said, "and then go our separate ways."

"Sounds good."

The call finally came around 4 p.m. on the fourth day. The Land Rover was ready.

Chapter Nineteen

The State of Texas executed a lot of people, more than any other state, more than all other states combined. Ron White, the popular comedian, once said that while other states put moratoriums in place against the death penalty, Texas put in an express lane. The state penitentiary in Huntsville, Texas, was that express lane and on an overcast morning in late May, Matt and I were driving towards it. We, however, were only concerned with one execution, the execution of Donny Reed on August 23rd. During my academic career —a polished term for my lackluster time in school—I seldom studied for my exams. On our way to Huntsville, I spent a lot of time on the internet learning what I could about penitentiary life, death row, executions, and the facility in general. Matt was about to face the most difficult challenge of his young life, and I wanted to support him by educating myself. He barely talked to me, but I was determined to help him through this visit.

The execution site, a 225-cell facility known as the Walls Unit because of the red brick walls that encircled it, was a medium security penitentiary that didn't look like a prison. Built in the middle of the nineteenth century, the structure was architecturally appealing and similar to many commercial buildings of the era, with a red brick facade, large, square multi-pane windows, and a clock near its peak. It was not where death row was located or Donny was housed; death row inmates were moved to the facility the night before their execution.

On the morning of our first scheduled visit with Donny, we stopped in front of the Walls Unit because it was on our way to the maximum-security penitentiary where Donny was housed, about a half-hour away.

"It doesn't look like a penitentiary," Matt said. "I expected something more intimidating."

"The entrance looks like a restaurant," I remarked. "Not what I expected either."

"I'm sure Donny thinks about this place a lot."

"I'll bet he does. Maybe we shouldn't mention that we were here today?"

"That's a good idea."

"Do you have some questions you want to ask him?"

"I've got a few."

"You know, Matt, this will be an emotional day for you. If at any time you feel like it's too much, you let me know, and we'll call it a day."

"I'll be all right, Alex."

"Okay, let's head for the real prison."

After a short drive, we arrived at the Polunsky Unit, a supermax penitentiary in West Livingston where death row inmates were held until their execution.

"Now that's a penitentiary," Matt said as we parked in the massive lot.

Unlike the Walls Unit, this penitentiary was built with containment as the sole consideration. It appeared both impenetrable and indestructible, made of solid concrete with unscalable walls and thin slats for windows. From the outside, it looked more like a medieval fortress than a correctional facility. Guard towers where armed correction officers watched over the grounds rose from the structure like fire lookouts in national parks. The perimeter of the complex was lined with many layers of fences and each fence was topped with glistening razor wire. The complex itself was enormous and seemed to go on endlessly, and I couldn't fully gauge its size from our vantage point. It was built to hold up to three thousand of the most hardened criminals and appeared to be up to the task.

"I'm a little afraid to go in," I said.

"I know what you mean," Matt replied, nervously wiping his brow. "Are you ready?"

"Let's sit for a minute."

This is starting to get real for him, I thought.

Judging by the apprehensive look in Matt's eyes, he hadn't considered the site where he'd meet Donny when he decided to meet him. Sitting in the SUV, staring at the ominous gray walls in front of us, we both knew it was an ugly, scary, violent world inside. We'd never been this far out of our element in our entire lives. Sensing his reluctance, I felt like I needed to give him a little push.

"We can only bring our IDs and quarters for the vending machines," I said.

"I know," he snapped. "I can google too."

"Shall we go?"

"Give me a minute, will you?"

This was it; this was my chance. He was having second thoughts. If I said the right words, maybe he'd cancel the meeting. We could end this fool's errand right now. But I couldn't bring myself to do it. Instead, I sat quietly and waited while he bolstered his resolve.

"Okay," he finally said. "Let's go. I'm ready to do this."

Getting into a maximum-security prison made a TSA checkpoint at an airport seem like a day at a country club. We walked through a metal detector, we were patted down aggressively, we were buzzed through six metal doors, we presented our IDs to a woman in a fortified booth, and we were escorted by an armed guard the entire time. It took us more than thirty minutes to reach the visitation center, a simple cinderblock building with only seven booths, a couple of round tables and chairs, and vending machines inside. For over an hour, we waited in the room until I finally heard inmates being escorted into booths on the other side, chains rattling as they walked. Another ten minutes slowly ticked away and then a female officer standing beside the last booth called out, "Reed."

Hearing his father's name, Matt suddenly looked like he was the one about to be executed, his eyes wide, his hands trembling. He looked over at the guard and swallowed hard. I put my hand on his shoulder.

"You can do this," I told him in my most reassuring tone.

"Okay," he said in his most unsure tone.

We slowly walked to the booth.

* * *

Chronologically, Donny Reed wasn't an old man, but as I stepped into the visitation booth, I saw a frail man with gaunt features, thinning hair streaked by gray strands, creases in his forehead and beside his eyes, and purple veins on both his cuffed hands. Looking at him through the glass, I knew the calendar was only partly responsible for his sapped state; waiting for his execution had also inflicted a toll. On his forearm, in faint blue ink, was a tattoo in fancy script that read "Fearless," and I suspected it predated his incarceration. I also suspected that the cockiness of the young man who chose that word had faded as well. Immediately, all my preconceptions about him evaporated like summer rain on a Texas highway. In front of me, I saw a man weighted by guilt and remorse over what he'd done, like he'd carried a corpse on his back every day for the last seventeen years. Suddenly, my adversary was sympathetic; once again, Donny Reed had outmaneuvered me. That didn't sit well with me.

Matt slipped into one of the two plastic chairs in front of the glass, where a black phone with its metallic cord dangled beside him. Rather than sit beside him, I stood behind him because I didn't want to be intrusive. I wanted to fade into the background. This was clearly their moment.

For what seemed like an eternity, father and son stared at one another through the glass with inquisitive eyes, squinting ever so slightly at times to better focus on the person before them. Neither smiled or reached for the phone, and neither even mouthed, "Hello," or any other greeting. To me, it felt like strangers linked by DNA results searching for signs of commonality to confirm their genetic connection. As I looked at Donny, his connection to Matt was evident to me in their eyes, noses, and brows; they were clearly father and son. Finally, Donny reached for the phone, and Matt followed his lead by turning the speaker on. Positioned for conversation, Donny seemed to be at a loss for words. He tapped the phone against his skull like he was trying to loosen his thoughts.

"How old are you?" Donny asked.

"Eighteen," Matt replied.

Another long silence ensued.

"You look a lot like me when I was your age."

"I do?"

"Yeah, you do."

"Okay."

"I thought I knew everything back then. Obviously, I didn't."

Once again, they stared at one another. The silences weren't uncomfortable as both men seemed content to simply survey the other.

"How is your mother?"

"Good."

"Do you have any brothers or sisters?"

"I have a sister named Christi and a brother named Nate."

"That's good. Abby wanted a family."

For more than an hour, the conversation proceeded at a sluggish pace and with little depth or emotion until Donny finally addressed the abandonment. Apparently ashamed, he hung his head and looked down at the counter in front of him as he spoke. His tone was hushed.

"I'm sorry I wasn't there for you, Matt. I walked out on you and your mother. Hell, what am I saying? I ran off. The truth is I wasn't a good man back then."

"It's okay, Donny. I have a good family."

"I sure wish I'd seen you grow up."

"You didn't miss much," Matt said as if trying to lighten the moment.

Donny looked up. "Yes, I did."

Matt was silent. Donny lowered his gaze again. He told Matt that leaving his mother was the biggest mistake of his life. He regretted it every day. From my vantage point, standing over Matt, I saw a few tears fall on the counter in front of Donny, but I didn't think Matt saw them. A female corrections officer called out, "Five minutes," and Donny slowly raised his head.

"Thank you for coming," he said.

"I'm glad we got to meet," Matt said.

"Me too."

Well, it's over, I thought. *I don't know what the impact will be on our relationship, but at least it's over.*

During the long trek out of the facility, Matt didn't speak. He didn't even look my way. Once again, we were buzzed through door after door until we finally reached the parking lot and our SUV. Back in the driver's seat, I looked over at Matt, who was mostly still, silent, and expressionless. Typical of the last few years, I had no idea what my son was thinking, only this time, I really wanted to know. This time, I needed to know.

"Are you okay?" I asked.

He nodded.

"Is there anything you want to talk about?"

He shook his head.

"Are you hungry?"

He nodded again.

"What do you want for dinner?"

"How about Mexican?"

"Sounds good."

I started the Land Rover, and we set off for the drive back to Huntsville. I suspected that I'd not seen or heard the last of Donny Reed. Though locked in a maximum-security prison, I believed he'd follow us in ways I didn't want to think about. I focused on the road.

Chapter Twenty

A cross the street from our hotel was a little shop with the words "Garcia Girls Coffee" painted across the front window in white. During our stay, several times a day, Matt offered to get coffee, and I always appreciated his willingness to make the coffee run. After three days, I couldn't help but notice that our hotel room was littered with many cups with their "GG" logo on it. Our thirst for their coffee was well-documented. Far and away, the Garcia Girls made the best iced coffee I'd ever tasted, and I struggled with every cup to figure out their secret.

"What makes this so good?" I asked Matt as I sipped.

"I think it's the vanilla," he answered.

"It's the vanilla all right, but it's something else also."

"Don't analyze it, Alex. Just enjoy it."

On our final day, we checked out of our room at the front desk and then walked out the lobby door onto the still street. The sky looked like a gray, velvet drape that enclosed the town.

"It's friggin' hot already," Matt said.

"Let's grab an iced coffee for the road," I said.

"Sounds good to me."

We walked across the street to the little coffee shop where we were greeted by two beautiful women with shiny black hair who called out from behind the counter in unison, "Hello, Matt." The Garcia Girls were Rosalita Garcia and her daughter, Angelica, and it didn't take me long to figure out that my son was smitten with Angie. Before I had my cup in hand, Angie handed Matt his cup, and the two of them made their way to a table in the corner. While I waited, they talked quietly and giggled intermittently like two teenagers in their own world. Eventually, Rosalita handed my cup across the counter to me and smiled and said, "They've been acting like that for three days."

I grinned. "Now I know why we had so many of your cups in our room."

"You're my best customers."

* * *

Leaving Huntsville around 10 a.m., Matt took the first shift driving while I napped in the back seat. When I awoke in early afternoon, our SUV wasn't moving, and I spotted a sign through the front windshield that read, Quick Stop Market & Gas. Alerted, I scanned my surroundings and realized we were parked at the gas pumps at the Abilene convenience store where Donny Reed committed his crime. Even worse: Matt wasn't around. He wasn't in the driver's seat, and he wasn't pumping gas. No one was around.

He must be in the store, I thought. *I'd better get in there.*

As I walked in the front door, Matt stepped up to the counter with an armful of snacks and drinks. He unloaded the items onto the counter and nodded at the woman behind the cash register, a redhead in her thirties wearing a Quick Stop gas station style shirt with Ruby on the nameplate. I waited near the door.

"That gonna do it?" she asked.

"That's it," Matt said. "I paid for the gas at the pump."

She picked up items one by one and scanned them into the register. The register made a loud beep as she moved each past the reader.

"Does Mary Jo Donovan's family still own this business?" Matt asked.

No, Matt, I thought. *Don't talk about that.*

119

"She was my grandmother," the woman answered. "Why do you ask?"

Matt hesitated and then spoke. "My father is Donny Reed."

Oh no, I thought.

In an instant, Ruby's expression went from welcoming to offended. Even from a distance, I sensed indignation stirring within her, and I knew it emanated from the day Donny Reed walked into their family's market all those years ago. On her forearm, she had a tattoo that read "Nana" in crimson letters that told me she'd carried her grandmother's murder with her every day, on her arm and in her heart. She was young when it happened, probably in her teens, but that didn't blunt its impact on her life; in fact, it might have accentuated it.

When Matt spoke the name, her arm stopped its waving motion with a bag of potato chips in her hand. She froze momentarily, and then she placed the chips on the counter. With her hands on the counter to support her weight, she leaned forward. Matt leaned backward. I braced myself.

"You've got a lot of nerve coming in here," she said, her tone biting.

"I just want to say I'm sorry my father did that."

"Did what? Shot my grandmother in the face? Do you think your apology makes a difference?"

"I guess not. It's just something I have to live with also, so I wanted to say it."

"I don't want to hear anything you have to say."

"I'm sorry."

"Just get out of our store. You're not welcome here."

"What about my purchase?"

The woman pressed the cancel button and the total on the register cleared with a loud ding. She waved her hand. "Take your business elsewhere," she snarled.

"Come on, Matt," I said, stepping towards the counter. "We should leave."

Once we were back in the SUV, me in the driver's seat and Matt in the back, I turned around to face him.

"Why did you say that?" I asked.

"I don't know. It just came out."

"Do you understand why she doesn't want to hear what you have to say?"

"I do. I get it. But, when she said she was her granddaughter, I just felt the need to say something, to say I'm sorry."

"What if someone shot your mother in the face? Do you think we'd ever get over it?"

"I know it was horrible. I think about it all the time."

Our voices were raised. Our anger was also rising. The fact that Donny's blood—and not mine—coursed through Matt's veins enraged me. It made me want to scream. And worse still, going forward, we'd have to live with the reality that Donny was his birth father; after Huntsville, we couldn't ignore that now. It was like having a mother-in-law who'd inserted herself into the marriage and was ruining everything. We had one too many people in our father/son relationship. Donny was ruining it. Infuriated, I was raging against him. At his young age, this was all too much for Matt to fully understand. He was raging against life.

"You didn't rob that store," I shouted. "You didn't shoot that woman."

"Damn it," Matt shouted back, "I'm his son. I'm connected to the murder. It's part of my history."

"You didn't do it, Matt. He did."

"You don't understand."

I turned around in my seat and looked straight forward. I didn't know what more to say. I had no words. Matt's words had stopped me in my tracks. I inserted the key, started the engine, and drove away from the Quick Stop. I'd had enough of Donny Reed and his legacy for one weekend. At that moment, I just wanted to go home, and I knew it would be a long, quiet ride to Boulder.

* * *

When we were about an hour from our home, Abby's affair began to dominate my thoughts. The idea of her in the arms of another man was like a poison seeping into my soul, decimating my spirit. She was the love of my life and my life partner, but without trust and commitment, those were only words. I had believed in Abby and me more than I'd ever believed in anything. I'd believed we'd always be there for one another, always be true to one another, unwavering, no matter what. We were in this thing together, forever. Nothing could've ever caused me to betray her. Nothing. Obviously, her level of commitment wasn't as resolute as mine. Could I move past her transgression?

Chapter Twenty-One

When I drove up to the Mayfield job, only three pickup trucks were parked out front, which alerted me to the fact that a lot had been accomplished in my absence and work was winding down. At the height of the work, ten or more trucks were parked on the grassy area in front of the home. After hearing my truck approach, Wyatt emerged from within with a big smile on his face, excited to show me the progress. While I was away on the Huntsville trip, the kitchen and three bathrooms were tiled and finished, the media room was wired and setup, and the entire interior was painted. Once he gave me an update, we walked the house together, and he pointed out what was completed and what remained. After more than sixteen months on the job, we were two weeks from completion.

"This is fantastic," I said. "I can't believe you guys got so much done."

"We can accomplish a lot without you looking over our shoulders," Wyatt said, chuckling.

"I should go away more often."

"The house looks really good, Alex, but believe it or not, I've got even bigger news."

Wyatt looked like he was about to burst at the seams. His eyes were wide, his smile bright. As elated as he looked, he looked even more relieved. Before he said anything, I knew something huge had happened while I was in Texas.

As it turned out, the ongoing turmoil in Wyatt's life had taken a drastic turn for the better. Two days earlier, Jessica called him and apologized for accusing him of molesting their daughter. In an emotionally charged and tear-filled phone call, she said she'd realized that her husband, Jack, was manipulating her and Amelia and basically trying to push Wyatt out of their lives. In her heart, she knew Wyatt would never hurt their daughters, and she felt terrible that she'd let Jack convince her otherwise. In the past few months, Jessica told Wyatt, she'd seen a whole different side of her husband, and she didn't like the man she'd married.

"Jack is controlling and abusive," Jessica said, "and I never should've married him. He's not good for the kids or me."

Jessica also told Wyatt that she planned to find an apartment in the next few days and tell Jack she wanted a divorce over the weekend. They'd only been married a year, but she was done.

"That's great news," I said. "I'm happy for you."

"Jessica also said she'd called the case worker, Hannah, and told her she no longer believed the accusation. I should get word that the investigation is over any day."

"I knew this would resolve itself somehow."

"It did."

"I feel very relieved."

"Me too."

"Will you and Jessica will get back together?"

"Maybe. I don't know."

Was it possible that both our parental nightmares were over? Had Jack and Donny darkened our lives for the last time? I didn't know if that was true or not, but I was thrilled by the possibility.

* * *

Five days later, in the entryway of the Mayfield job, Wyatt and I prepared to leave for the day after spending the better part of the morning installing flooring in two hallways and the basement. Just as we locked the front door, Wyatt's phone rang, and he clumsily retrieved it from his pocket, almost dropping it on the slate.

"It's Hannah," he said with a confused look on his face. "Why would she call me on a Saturday?"

His question concerned me, so I lingered while he answered the call.

"Hello, Hannah," he said, holding the phone in front of his mouth on speaker. "I'm with Alex Bryant at our work site."

"That's good," she said. "Put me on speaker."

"You're on speaker," Wyatt advised her.

"I have bad news, Wyatt. You should sit down before I tell you."

Wyatt stepped backward. "What is it?" he said.

"An hour ago, Jack shot Jessica at their home. When the police arrived, Jessica was dead."

"No," Wyatt screamed. "No, it can't be!"

Though a strong man, Wyatt was also an emotional man. I'd seen him cry on several occasions before, generally brought on by difficulties in his marriage, but I'd never seen him cry like this before. Tears streamed down his face as he slowly sat down on the top step, and he sobbed uncontrollably. He kept repeating, "No, no, no," in a desperate tone. Then suddenly, his sobbing stopped, and he spoke into the phone again.

"What about the kids, Hannah? Are they okay?"

"They're with Patricia Watson, and they're fine. They weren't in the home at the time of the shooting."

"Oh, thank God," Wyatt blurted.

Wyatt placed the phone on the step beside him, rested his elbows on his knees, and placed his face in his hands. Once again, he sobbed loudly. Both Hannah and I remained silent. In my case, I was in shock and had no words of comfort for my friend. I sat beside Wyatt and wrapped my left arm around his back and shoulder. I felt tremors roll through his body as he wept beside me. Eventually, I remembered Hannah on the phone and called out to her.

"What should we do, Hannah?" I asked.

"Meet me at the Watson house," Hannah responded. "I'll be there with the kids. We won't tell them anything until you arrive."

"No, no, no, no, no," Wyatt continued saying in a quieter tone now.

"I'm so sorry, Wyatt," I said, finally finding some words.

He looked up at me. His tears continued to stream down his cheeks and drop from his chin. His eyes were empty; his spirit had vacated them.

He shook his head. "She can't be dead," he said.

I felt like Wyatt wanted me to tell him it wasn't true. It was all a big mistake. I couldn't. I wished that was true, but I knew it wasn't. Once again, there was nothing I could say. I put my free hand over my eyes and hung my head. I couldn't bear looking at the pain and sorrow and emptiness in Wyatt's eyes. I thought about Jessica and how much my family loved her too. Though I had plenty to deal with beside me, I was already dreading the thought of telling Abby and my children about what happened. They would be devastated. For Abby, it would be like the loss of a sister. Seated on the front steps beside Wyatt, I braced myself for my family's inevitable agony.

Chapter Twenty-Two

I n a state of complete shock, I sat with Abby on the sofa in our living room. Over the last two days, we'd spent close to twenty hours with Wyatt and his children, at our home and Wyatt's home in Boulder. Watching young children grapple with the idea that they will never see their mother again was a gut-wrenching experience. Only their oldest, Hailey, seemed fully able to understand the tragedy. It was particularly difficult for me because I'd experienced a similar loss when I was young. Firsthand, I knew their pain and anguish. Firsthand, I understood the confusion and feelings of uncertainty that accompanied their predicament. Though my loss happened more than forty years ago, I vividly remembered what it felt like to be in their tiny, little shoes.

Suddenly, from his bedroom upstairs, Matt wailed, "Oh no, not again!"

It was an ear-piercing wail, laden with anguish, that seemed to echo throughout the house.

Abby and I rushed toward the staircase and scaled its seven steps in leaps and bounds. When we arrived at his door, we found Matt in a heap in the corner, pointing at the laptop on his desk. A newspaper article was on the screen, and together, Abby and I leaned over the desk and began reading...

Local Dentist Held in Wife's Death

Jack Barnett, a prominent Boulder dentist, has been arrested and charged with the murder of his wife, Jessica Fuller Barnett. At 12:03 p.m. on Saturday, on the 300 block of Maplewood Road, neighbors called 911 and reported hearing a gunshot from the Barnett residence. When police arrived, they found Jessica Barnett dead from a gunshot wound to the face, and the accused shooter, Jack Barnett, seated on the living room sofa with a 38-caliber handgun in front of him on a coffee table. Neighbors told investigators that they heard shouting coming from the residence in the hour before the shot was fired. The Barnetts had married a year ago and had three children living with them, but none were in the residence at the time of the shooting. According to their neighbor and friend, Patricia Watson, Jessica Barnett left the children in her care earlier that morning. At his arraignment, Barnett pleaded not guilty to all charges and is being held without bail until his next court appearance. In 2015, Jack Barnett was honored in a reader's poll by Colorado Living Magazine as one of the "Ten Best Dentists in Colorado."

Before I even finished, Matt wailed again.

"He shot her in the face. He shot her in the face."

Matt's tone turned hysterical as he rocked back and forth on the floor, holding his head between his hands. As soon as Abby finished reading, she rushed to his side and cradled him.

"He shot her in the face," Matt cried out again.

"That's horrible," Abby said. "I'm here."

Apparently, Abby hadn't made the connection, but Matt and I made it immediately. Because of the location of the gunshot wound, Matt had linked Jessica's murder with Mary Jo Donovan's murder. Though seventeen years apart and in a different state, Matt had connected the two horrific crimes. Even worse, he'd made himself the connection.

"Don't go there, Matt," I said. "This has nothing to do with you or Donny Reed."

"God wants me to know Ruby Donovan's pain," Matt cried out. "This isn't a coincidence."

"Oh no," Abby said, finally making the connection. "It is a coincidence. Nothing more."

"God is punishing me," Matt said while wiping tears from his cheeks. "God wants me to understand Ruby's pain. He wants me to feel her heartache. I do now."

"No," Abby said. "It's got nothing to do with you."

"It's got everything to do with me. He's my father."

"Jack killed Jessica," Abby said. "He was upset because she was leaving him. That's all there is to it."

Matt raised his head and seemed to cry out to the heavens. "I get it now. I get it. I never should've spoken to Ruby."

When Matt finished, I could see Abby hug him even tighter. It must've been something instinctual that made her tighten her hold. In the trauma of the moment, she was doing whatever she could, whatever came naturally, to comfort Matt. Desperate, she looked up at me, pleading with her eyes, apparently hoping I had words of consolation. I didn't. Worse still, I felt like I never had the right words for anyone in my life. I had no words for Wyatt during his time of need, and now I had no words for my son. Words were like oxygen, floating all around us, and still, in that moment, it was like I couldn't breathe. I couldn't find the right words. I felt like I needed to do better for the people in my life.

"What's going on?" Christi asked as she and Nate arrived at the door.

"Matt's having a hard time with Jessica's death," I said.

"We all are," Christi said.

"I could do some research," Nate offered, "and find a therapist, Matt. It might help to talk to someone."

To an outsider, a twelve-year-old suggesting a therapist might've seemed unusual, but, in our family, we all knew Nate was smarter and more mature than his age. He was twelve going on thirty.

"No, Nate," Matt responded in an agitated tone, "I don't want to talk to a therapist."

"I might need a therapist," Christi said, her face forlorn.

"Go back to your rooms, kids," I said, waving my hands, causing Christi and Nate to backpedal away from Matt's door.

As Christi and Nate retreated to their rooms, Abby and Matt continued to rock back and forth on the floor, and they remained that way for twenty minutes. For that eternity, I stood beside them without so much as a word of consolation.

I need to do better, I scolded myself.

Chapter Twenty-Three

L ying in my bed each night, staring out the window at the conifers beside our home, shrouded in darkness while dimly lit by the moon, I thought about how tragic events robbed me of so much. I thought about my mother and sister and all the things we never got to say to one another. All the smiles I missed, all the laughter I never heard. We could have filled a lifetime with those words and moments, but we didn't get the chance. A drunk driver ended their lives. I felt that same loss with Jessica because Wyatt and Jessica were our best friends. Abby and Jessica were as close as Wyatt and me, and we'd had many happy moments in their company. Much like my mother and sister, I thought about the loss of all the words and moments still to come, the memories that would never form in my mind. In Jessica's case, a jealous and unstable man had ended her life, but the common thread between the two tragedies was that the losses forever diminished our lives.

My family faced the cruelest juxtaposition of events imaginable in the coming days. On Saturday at noon, Jessica's funeral was scheduled at Mountain View Memorial Park on the north side of Boulder. On Sunday at noon, Matt's graduation was scheduled at Boulder High School, just three miles from the funeral site. As I lay in bed each night,

I wondered if twenty-four hours and three miles were enough of a buffer between those two very different ceremonies. How could we possibly bury our friend and then celebrate a graduation? More importantly, I wondered how my family would make it through the weekend.

When we arrived at the funeral, Wyatt stood at the head of the casket flanked by his three young daughters dressed in spring-like dresses with flowery prints and pastel colors. Later, Wyatt told me that he simply refused to introduce funeral colors into his daughters' lives at such a young age. Surrounding the casket were about thirty mourners dressed in dark suits and black dresses, and the little girls shone in that ring of gloomy garments like the glow of the Promised Land. Their innocence stood out in stark contrast to the somberness that surrounded them. We sat in five seats that had been reserved for us directly in front of the casket.

My family was dealing with the tragedy in unique and complicated ways. Nate and Christi had never known a tragic loss of this magnitude, and they were, unfortunately, coming to the fast realization that the world could be a cruel and dangerous place. Whatever childhood innocence they'd managed to hold onto so far in their lives would surely not survive the afternoon. They were disillusioned. Matt had merged Jessica's murder with the murder at the convenience store and found himself struggling with guilt, sorrow, and remorse. At that point, the year of 2017 had produced more confusion and tragedy for Matt than any eighteen-year-old ought to know. He was reeling. As for Abby, she'd lost one of her best friends, so she embraced the little girls with their mother's strawberry hair like a tight hold would somehow protect them from the truth. The thought of them without their mother was simply more than Abby could bear. She was heartbroken.

The first time Wyatt and Jessica came to our home for dinner, Jessica surprised me when she told us that she was a Buddhist. She said she first encountered Buddhist teachings when she visited a monastery in the Catskill Mountains, and she was drawn to their humility and thoughtful examination of life. In my mind, I'd had a notion of her based on her southern roots, but, as I got to know her, she proved to be someone who defied cataloging. Listening to Jessica talk about Buddhist philosophies in her slow, southern drawl made me realize she was a complex person, far more complex than Wyatt (but then, women often are), who was content whenever he had a tool or a beer in his hand. As I watched a somber (and rather chubby) monk in a red robe make his way to the casket, I thought about how I'd miss her unpredictable nature.

"When children lose a parent," the monk began, "their view of the world is changed."

He paused like he was reflecting and developing his eulogy as he spoke.

"For these children," he said as he continued, "the sky is no longer a beautiful shade of blue, the sun no longer warms their precious faces, their paths are no longer clear and safe, and people seem less kind."

He paused again, squinted his eyes against the bright glare of the midday sun, and then gazed at the crowd of mourners. After a full minute of silence, he began again.

"We don't know why such upheaval occurs in the lives of innocent children, but the one thing we know with certainty is that we, the people who love this family, are now called upon to provide color, warmth, security, and love."

He smiled. He nodded. "We, as a community, must embrace this family and help restore their view of the world so they can move forward in a healthy way. We can't replace Jessica, but we must do all we can to help them recover from their loss."

All my life, I'd hidden my brokenness like a master magician on a stage, making his audience notice only what he wanted them to see. Looking at Wyatt beside the coffin, unsteady and on the verge of collapse, I knew my friend would never be able to hide his brokenness. Like an unwanted tattoo, he'd try to conceal his pain but with little success. It would always be there. At that moment, my only consolation was that I knew my family would be there for Wyatt and his girls, and we would make sure they had support.

When the service concluded, Abby stepped forward to hug Wyatt as we approached him.

"I love you, Wyatt," she said as she wiped away tears from his cheeks with her bare hand. When Wyatt needed her, Abby had the right words.

* * *

If it were possible to fill a home with so much sorrow that the windows shattered from the pressure, it would have happened at our home the next morning. In mid-morning, we all gathered at the table with untouched boxes of cereal, cartons of milk and juice, and English muffins occupying the space between us. Collectively, we looked like we'd used our last ounces of energy to make it to the table, and it was hard for me to imagine us leaving to go anywhere. Abby, in particular, seemed to wear the funeral pall like a pair of flannel pajamas. She'd taken her friend's death to bed with her and lain with it all night. And still, there was family business we couldn't ignore—it was Matt's Graduation Day.

"I'm not going," Matt said. "I can't even think about the graduation ceremony today."

"You have to go," I said. "It's your graduation."

He shrugged. "I don't care. I'm not going."

For several minutes, we sat quietly with Matt's proclamation. Other than me, no one objected or even commented. Seated around the table were five sad faces that seemed to be putting forth all their efforts to hold back their tears. Personally, I was so worn out from the funeral that I couldn't even think about driving into Boulder again. Several days earlier, we'd canceled the party we were hosting at our home to celebrate Matt's graduation. As I thought about it, I wondered if, under the circumstances, we should skip the graduation ceremony also.

"Do you think we should go?" I asked, looking at Christi.

"I don't know if we should go or not," she said, her eyes red and barely open, "but I'm going to cry a lot during the ceremony."

"How about you?" I said, glancing Nate's way.

"It's Matt's graduation," he said, "so if he doesn't want to go, we shouldn't."

"Abby?"

"I hate the thought of not seeing Matt graduate," she said, "but I don't know if the pomp and circumstance of a graduation ceremony is the right place for our family right now."

"Are you sure that's what you want, Matt?" I asked him.

"I'm sure."

"All right then, it's decided," I said.

The graduating class of 2017 at Boulder High School was short one graduate that day.

Chapter Twenty-Four

My father always drove Cadillacs. A holdover from a bygone era, to him, Cadillacs were a symbol of a man's success and a vestige of the illustrious America in which he grew up. In the mid-1980s, after the gas shortage of the 1970s, Cadillac produced Eldorados and Coupe de Villes that were small, boxy, and uninspired; gone was the golden era of standout Cadillac automobiles with sweeping tail fins, flashy grilles, regal hood ornaments, and wide whitewall tires. The Cadillacs of the 1980s were a mere glimmer of their once brilliant heritage, but that didn't stop my father from buying them. I'd always hated my father's Cadillacs, but never more than when it pulled up to the curb in front of the Boulder Police Department to pick me up after my arrest for DUI. I was twenty years old at the time.

The previous night, I'd gone to a party for Cinqo de Mayo near the university, where I had my first margarita and learned that "mamada" was the Spanish word for blowjob. In the interest of full disclosure, I had my first six or seven margaritas that night, and I don't believe I got one, despite my effort to persuade a CU sophomore to give me one. When I left the party at about 2 a.m., the streets of the university district were a blurry obstacle course that I didn't navigate very well. Neither the red traffic light nor my excessive speed caused me to consider slowing down as I approached the turn at Broadway. In an ironic twist of fate, I clipped the telephone pole on the corner, crossed the center line, and plowed into the side of a Cadillac Eldorado parked in front of a Mexican restaurant. In the police report, the officer wrote that he found me seated on the curb in front of the restaurant with a sombrero (from the party) on my head. As he placed the cuffs on my wrists, the report also stated that I'd asked him, "Have you ever had a margarita?" When he didn't respond, I added, "They're really good."

"What the hell were you thinking?" my father asked as I climbed into the passenger seat of his burgundy Cadillac, my head throbbing and eyes bleeding.

"I guess I wasn't," I replied.

"No, you weren't."

I wasn't in any shape to listen to a verbal pummeling from my father, but I knew I had to sit there and take it. I was beholden to him. Thanks to my rampage, I'd need a good lawyer and a replacement for my totaled Toyota. My father and I were never close, but he always provided for me.

"Do you know how I earn a living?"

It hurt to nod, but I did it anyway.

"I practice law in the courtrooms of this town," he said. "I know every judge in Boulder, and some are close friends."

I nodded again.

"Do you have any idea what an embarrassment it will be for me when my son goes before one of those judges charged with driving under the influence?"

"I'm sorry."

Not only did I hate my father's Cadillacs, but I hated the way he drove them. We proceeded home at a leisurely rate, and he slowed to a crawl at every corner like he was steering an ocean liner around the bend. Every ride in his Cadillacs took twice as long as usual.

Stopped at a light, he looked over at me. He shook his head in disgust. "I'll arrange for one of the junior attorneys at my law firm to represent you, but you'll have to use your mother's maiden name when you come for the consultation. Your attorney will know you're my son, but no one else needs to know."

"Thanks."

"You could have been killed."

"I know."

Two weeks later, I stood in the lobby of my father's law firm and was greeted by the receptionist.

"Can I help you?" she asked.

"Alex Walsh to see Peter Thompson."

It was the first time I'd ever stepped inside my father's law firm. I was there under an alias, but I was there, nonetheless. At least I didn't piss my pants on the way over this time.

While the receptionist alerted Mr. Thompson that I'd arrived, I marveled at the exquisite furniture and art that filled the space. A statue of Lady Justice, blindfolded and holding a scale, stood in a corner of the lobby, and made up for its cliché nature with the beauty of its stone. On the wall behind the receptionist, I saw our name in large gold letters and wished I could reclaim it.

Sometime in the future, I thought, *when I inevitably return to this law firm for another embarrassing offense, I hope I can use my real name.*

In a matter of minutes, a tall, thin man with shaggy blonde hair appeared in the doorway and addressed me.

"Come with me, Mr. Walsh," he said.

As he shook my hand, the lawyer winked at me.

* * *

Three years after my DUI, I was back in my father's law firm for only the second time in my life. This time, though, I hadn't broken any laws, been arrested, or even crashed my car into an Eldorado after a night of partying. This time around, I walked into the lobby as someone who'd been invited to attend a meeting in one of the firm's conference rooms. It took my father's death for that invitation to be extended, but I was invited, nonetheless, for the reading of his will. As I walked the hallway towards the conference room, I passed the lawyer with the shaggy blonde hair who'd represented me three years earlier.

"Nice to see you again, Mr. Walsh," he said, again with that same wink.

In the conference room, about fifteen people had gathered for the reading of the will. All were dressed in business attire while I wore a rugby shirt and blue jeans. When I dressed that morning, I expected only three people to attend, me and my aunt and uncle.

"Am I dressed okay?" I asked my Uncle Bob as I took a seat beside him.

"You look fine," he told me.

"Is Aunt Maggie coming?"

"No, she's at the restaurant."

After a short wait, a heavyset man with a ruddy complexion and red, tartan vest that attested to his Edinburgh heritage entered the room and sat in a lone chair in the front. A small side table accompanied his chair. The man had my father's will in one hand and a mug with the law firm's logo in the other. A week earlier, at my father's funeral, I'd learned that the proud Scot was my father's original partner in the law firm, Wallace T. Wheeler. I'd never met him until that day.

"First, let me say that Ray's death has affected our law firm and me greatly," Mr. Wheeler said in a raspy voice. "He was a brilliant legal mind and one of my best friends. To Bob and Alex, his immediate family, seated in the front row before me, I want to express my sincere condolences once again."

"Thank you, Wally," my Uncle Bob said.

I wasn't ready for the attention, so I fixed my eyes on the logo on his coffee cup.

After a few legal formalities, Mr. Wheeler began reading my father's will.

"I, Raymond Ulysses Bryant, being of competent and sound mind, do hereby declare this to be my last will and testament and do hereby revoke any and all wills and codicils heretofore made jointly or severally by me."

I sure hope this document is written in English, I thought, *and not legalese so I can understand it.*

Eventually, the lawyer arrived at the most pertinent section, the distribution of assets.

"I leave my son, Alexander Robert Bryant," Mr. Wheeler said, glancing my way, "the proceeds from the sale of my home and the entirety of my brokerage account held at Western Financial Services

Company of Boulder, Colorado. The home must be sold within one year of my death, and the proceeds deposited into my brokerage account at WFSC. All funds will remain in the brokerage account until Alexander's fiftieth birthday, when he may access them and use them at his discretion."

"There it is," I blurted, rising from my chair, "the final slight. I can't access my inheritance until I'm fifty years old. That's crazy."

"Calm down, Alex," Uncle Bob said, grasping my shirt sleeve.

"No," I said, pulling my arm from his grip, "I won't calm down. He was ashamed of me my whole life, and this is his final slap in my face."

I stormed out of the conference room and strode up the hallway to find a quiet place to be alone. In one corner of the building, I noticed a dark office with Raymond Bryant on a silver placard on the door. In all the years he'd worked in that office, I'd never set foot in it. I paused for a moment like I wasn't sure I belonged. Then, feeling defiant, I strolled through the door and sat behind his massive oak desk in his leather chair.

Good God, this is nice, I thought to myself.

For a couple of minutes, I simply savored the splendor of the office —the floor to ceiling bookcases, leather and marble seating area, original artwork, and fully stocked wet bar—and then I addressed my father in my mind.

You were never a father to me, Ray. You never took any interest in my life. And now, you've slighted me again. I'm not surprised. What surprises me is that I feel sorry for both of us today. You're gone, so we can never have a good relationship. We're left with what we had.

"Can I come in?" my Uncle Bob asked from the doorway, breaking my train of thought.

"Sure."

"I knew my brother a lot longer than you," he said once he sat in a chair in front of the desk, "and I can honestly tell you that I never understood him either. He was an unusual man."

"He was an ass."

"At times, he was an ass."

"Most times."

"Maybe, but I can assure you, he loved us both."

"He had a strange way of showing it."

"It's probably more correct to say he didn't show it."

"Why was he like that?"

"I don't know. He had a brilliant mind, but once he latched onto the practice of law, it was at the exclusion of everything else."

"That's true."

"After the death of your mother and sister, he held onto it even tighter."

"That was a hard time."

"He was articulate in a courtroom but inarticulate in his relationships."

"Is it wrong that I don't miss him?"

"Feel whatever you feel, Alex, and don't question it. Family is complicated."

"In the end, he screwed me again."

Uncle Bob nodded. "I know he did, and I don't like it. I don't understand why he did it. When you turn thirty, I will loan you money as an advance on your inheritance. You won't have to wait until you're fifty."

"You'd do that for me?"

"Of course, I will. You know you're like a son to me."

"Thanks."

We both got up to leave the office, but I paused in front of the wet bar. Gazing at the top shelf, I admired my father's collection of fine liquors. None of the bottles looked like the liquor I'd bought at the convenience store; these bottles looked worthy of collection and display with their chiseled crystal-like appearance. Reading the labels, I didn't see anything aged less than twenty years. And only a few of the bottles were even opened.

"Which of these bottles do you think is the most expensive," I asked.

Uncle Bob turned and perused the offerings. He scratched his chin. "That Old Stone Bridge Whiskey is about $500 a bottle."

I grabbed the bottle by the neck, lifted it from its place amongst the other bottles, and then we strolled casually out of the law firm. Along the way, I made no effort to conceal the bottle.

Chapter Twenty-Five

A fter my father died, I continued to bounce from job to job, just as he'd predicted. For a year or so, I worked as a bartender at a little dive bar in the downtown area called Down & Out. Below street level in the basement of an old hotel, it was a hard to place to find. As a result, I usually poured for a group of regulars who'd made the joint their second home. The owner also owned a catering business and gave me extra work on the side tending bar at his events. One spring night, I worked a charity benefit for a doctors' organization that my Uncle Bob was involved in. He came by my station early in the evening when I was still setting up.

"I always like seeing you in a tuxedo shirt and bow tie," he said, ribbing me. "You clean up good."

"Are you giving a speech tonight?" I asked him.

"No, I'm just making an appearance. I've got to get home. I've had a benefit or fundraiser every night this week."

It wasn't unusual for me to see him at the events I worked. Uncle Bob was very active in the community.

Later that evening, a man who stood out from the crowd of mostly doctors approached my bar. He looked like a man of substance, sharply attired in a silver sport coat, black turtleneck sweater, black slacks, and Italian shoes, but he didn't seem like the doctor type. He was cooler than the average doctor, and his self-assuredness didn't include a whiff of arrogance. I'd never seen him before, but he had an ease about him that made me feel comfortable around him right away.

"Do you have Old Stone Bridge Whiskey?" the man asked.

"I do not, but you've got great taste."

"Have you ever tried it?"

"I haven't, but I've got a bottle at home I'm saving for a special occasion."

"There must be a good story behind such a great bottle of whiskey."

The well-stocked bar in my father's office from which I'd stolen it flashed in my memory, and then I spoke.

"My father gave it to me before he died."

"Were you close?"

I hesitated. "Very close."

"Well, give me your best whiskey neat."

"You got it."

I grabbed a bottle from the shelf behind me and placed a tumbler on the bar. With a slow flick of my wrist, I gave the gentleman with the wavy brown hair and hefty Rolex watch a heavy-handed pour. I didn't know why, but I liked him already.

"When I was a boy," he said, "I spent a lot of hours with my father in his workshop behind our house. He taught me to appreciate the beauty of wood and to respect power tools."

"Is he still alive?"

"No, he died about five years ago."

"My dad died three years ago."

"What kind of things did your dad teach you?"

I hesitated. "He taught me to love books and respect the law."

"It sounds like he was a good man?"

I reached for a towel. "Yes, he was."

"How often do you work these events?"

"Only a couple of days a week if I'm lucky."

He looked me up and down like he was making an assessment. "Are you looking for work?" he asked.

"Are you hiring?"

"I'm about to start building a home near Crescent Ridge. It might take me as long as two years to complete it."

"Are you going to build it yourself?"

"Most of it, but I need to find some help. What do you say? I'll pay you more than you're making here."

"We just met."

The man reached into the inner pocket of his sport coat and retrieved a business card. The plain white card identified him as the Founder and CEO of a group of boutique hotels called "Simpatico," along with a handful of other successful entrepreneurial ventures. When I did an internet search later that night, I learned that he'd been heralded as the "The Quintessential Entrepreneur" on the cover of Portfolio Magazine a year earlier, and his estimated net worth was over $300 million. He'd certainly accomplished a lot and didn't even look forty years old yet.

"Here's my card," the Entrepreneur said. "Call me if you're interested, and we'll talk some more."

He threw back the rest of the whiskey in his glass. As he lowered his tumbler, he looked me straight in the eyes. He smiled like he'd read me.

"You lied about your father, didn't you?" he said.

"What do you mean?"

"He didn't give you that bottle before he died, and you weren't close."

"You're right on both counts, but how did you know?"

"You have a tell. You diverted your eyes and hesitated before you spoke."

"Remind me never to play poker with you."

"Give me a call tomorrow."

* * *

Two days later, I met the Entrepreneur at an old white brick building on the southside that once served as a Texaco gas station back when attendants still pumped gas. He'd converted it to a workshop with stacks of lumber on one side of what were formerly the service bays and an assortment of power tools on the other side. Waiting for me outside the open doors, he looked like a man in his element, quite different from the other night when we met. He wore black jeans, a red T-shirt with Cherry Creek High School scrolled on the front, a gray baseball cap sans logo, and Wayfarer sunglasses with light blue lenses. As I approached, he greeted me with an easy smile that I came to recognize as his calling card. We stepped inside the shop and began walking around the crowded space.

"I rented this old gas station six months ago to prepare for my project," he said, glancing about with a proud look on his face. "About half of these power tools belonged to my father."

"What did he do for a living?" I asked.

"He worked for the City of Denver on a crew that maintained public parks and other facilities. He barely made enough to feed our family, but he loved his job."

"When we met the other night, l thought you came from a wealthy family."

He shook his head. "Not at all," the Entrepreneur said emphatically. "The only things my father ever owned that had any value at all, he made with his own two hands in his workshop."

"My dad was a lawyer who spent all his time reading books."

"Well, I think we're all drawn to the things in life that make us feel good about ourselves."

"I never thought about it that way."

"That's why I want to build my own house. My father taught me the value of accomplishing something on my own. There is no better feeling in life than standing back and marveling at what you've done, most particularly when you weren't sure you could do it."

"I don't have any experience at this sort of work."

"Do you listen well?"

"I do."

"Can you follow instructions?"

"I can."

"Can you learn new things?"

"I can."

"Can you clean up a mess?"

"I can."

"Can you run and get stuff for me?"

"I can."

"Then you're just the guy I'm looking for. What do you say? Do you want to build a house with me?"

"Definitely."

Along with my decision to marry Abby, my decision to work with the Entrepreneur on that house was one of the best decisions I ever made. My twenty months working alongside him changed my life and gave me my first exposure to what would eventually become my life's work. My time with him transformed me from a guy with no plan to a man with a purpose. Sometimes in life, the right word at the right moment can make all the difference. Definitely.

Chapter Twenty-Six

It was an unfortunate mathematical result that no one foresaw. Wyatt and his kids came to our home on Saturday afternoon, and we all gathered around the table for dinner in early evening. Abby prepared fried chicken, mashed potatoes, and biscuits because she knew the Dawson family loved her fried chicken. Anyone could see those little girls were in dreary states of mind, so we tried any little things we could to raise their spirits, even temporarily. At our dining room table, which seats ten, our family occupied five chairs, as we always did, and Wyatt and his three daughters occupied four chairs, leaving one chair unoccupied. While I didn't think the young girls understood the symbolism, I noticed that all the adults at the table glanced at the empty chair periodically, all seeing it as the chair where Jessica should be seated. Her place at our table. Until recently, we filled that table perfectly.

The Dawson girls' clothing was rumpled and disheveled, and Amelia was wearing two different socks. The colors and patterns of their outfits made it clear that they wore whatever was handy and clean or closest to it. Earlier in the day, I'd seen Christi seated on the sofa in the living room with her hairbrush in hand, brushing each of the little girls' hair. Before dinner, Nate took the girls on a short hike to a small lake near our home. After my mother and sister died, when I was barely in elementary school, I spent a lot of time alone in the great room of my childhood home, so I was happy to see our families merged and active. I knew for a fact it was better this way.

"How are the girls doing?" I asked Wyatt as we shot pool after dinner.

"Not good," he said while chalking his cue. "Their world will never be right again."

"It's going to take time."

"When did you get over the loss of your mother and sister?"

Fifteen feet from the pool table was a grandfather clock that my mother gave my father as a gift after he'd won an important case. The clock was seven feet tall, made of beautiful, dark mahogany wood, and had a silver face with Roman numerals. In my father's home office, it had occupied a place between two bookcases, one with law books on the shelves and the other with the leatherbound classics that I loved. As a child, I enjoyed the sweet sound of the clock's chimes, most particularly in the late morning hours, at ten, eleven, and twelve o'clock, when it rang out the many hours. The sound was beautiful and always reminded me of my mother. During its time in my home, I'd cherished that grand clock and had moments when I wanted to take a sledgehammer to it. The truth was that the pain of losing my mother and sister had taken up residence in my being and never left. I'd never gotten over it. At times, I'd felt so cheated by their loss that I'd almost lashed out at that clock. When marking time seemed neither noble nor beautiful to me, I'd wanted to take an ax (or at least a pool cue) to it. On my worst days, the chimes were simply reminders of another hour without my mother and sister. Gazing at the clock in the corner of room, still tall and marking time, the fact that it hadn't been reduced to splinters must've meant I'd learned to live with the pain.

I looked at Wyatt. "I never got over it," I said, "but I've learned to live with it."

He sighed. "I don't like what my kids are learning these days."

"I know. It's hard."

"They're just so lost without Jessica."

"How are you doing?"

"I'm lost, too. I feel so empty and broken."

"We're here for you."

"I know, and I appreciate it."

"Keep bringing your kids here. I think being together helps."

He put the pool cue over his shoulder. "It does, but right now, I can't imagine feeling good again, enjoying something again."

"You will."

"Like this game of pool," he said. "We've played pool after dinner a hundred times, and I always enjoyed it. I'm not enjoying this game at all."

His comment caught me off guard. He looked at me with a sad, "what can I do" look on his face. I didn't have an answer for him. Eventually, I placed my pool stick on the pool table and Wyatt did the same. I walked over to him and put my hand on his shoulder.

"Let's just watch a little TV," I said. "Maybe there's a rodeo on."

"Very funny."

Chapter Twenty-Seven

When we returned from Huntsville, Matt got a job as a bagger at a grocery store. The pay was good, and the hours were flexible, so I felt good about this outcome. I knew Matt needed something to occupy his mind and provide him with a feeling of productivity. As an added benefit, I thought it would be good for Matt to work in a public setting that would help him come out of his shell. After only about twenty shifts at the store, Matt came home with an announcement. As he walked in the front door, he called out to Abby and me as we relaxed in the living room.

"I quit my job today," he said.

"What?" Abby asked as he walked toward us.

"Why?" I added.

"I want to go back to Huntsville. Donny's execution is a month away."

"Why do you want to go back?" I asked, my original question expanded.

As I spoke, I did my best to keep my tone casual and nonchalant to hide my true feelings. The truth was, a month ago, when we returned from Huntsville, I hoped I'd never hear the name Donny Reed again. In my mind, I'd done the right thing—I'd told Matt about his birth father, he'd met him, and we could move on. That was all behind us. Now, with

Donny's name being bandied about the living room and the prospect of seeing Donny again suddenly a possibility, my stomach churned.

"I met Donny on my first trip," Matt explained, "but I didn't get to know him. I feel like I have to get to know him before it's too late."

"Is this something you feel strongly about?" Abby asked.

"I do, Mom. I feel like I'll never truly understand myself if I don't get to know him."

Oh crap, I thought.

I mustered my fatherly resolve. "I thought we'd closed the book on this saga," I said, "but I'm willing to go back." The words tasted sour and rotten as they'd left my mouth, but I'd said them.

"I want to go for the whole month," Matt said.

Holy crap, I thought. *This just keeps getting worse.*

"A month?" Abby said. "Are you serious?"

"That's how long he has left. I want to spend that time with him."

I searched my mind for an innocent objection. "That's a long time in Huntsville," I said. "We're not built for that kind of heat."

Matt looked at me. That was rare. "I need to do this."

I'm screwed, I thought. "What the Hell," I said, turning towards Abby, "I'm in between projects, so I can go with him."

"I can go alone," Matt said.

"You're not going alone," his mother said sternly.

At that moment, I knew I was going to Huntsville, so I started telling myself this could be a good thing. We'd spend a lot of time together, which could bring us closer to one another. I wanted that.

"I think we need to do this together anyway," I said, "Matt and me."

"Well, okay then," Abby said. "Pack your bags. You're going back to Huntsville."

Chapter Twenty-Eight

In the five weeks we'd been away, the heat in Huntsville had progressed from simmering to stifling and reduced daily life to quick trips between air-conditioned spaces. It wasn't until after sundown each day that the town cooled down enough for outdoor activities. On our first night back, we pulled into our hotel parking lot around 8 p.m. as the townsfolk began to emerge from their lairs. It was still in the mid-80s, but the sidewalks were coming to life. Switching drivers intermittently, we'd made the entire fifteen-hour drive in one day.

"Are you sure we can survive for a whole month in this town?" I asked as I grabbed my suitcase.

"Oh my God," Matt said, his tone sharp, his eyes red from the drive. "Don't start complaining the moment we arrive."

His patience clearly tested, he grabbed his backpack and marched toward the hotel entrance.

I called out to him. "We may survive the heat but kill each other."

Matt glanced over his shoulder, more irked than ever. "Keep whining like a little girl, and you won't make it through the first night."

I chuckled. "Fine. Let's check-in and get some rest."

* * *

By midday in Huntsville, zapped of all my energy and fluids, each day felt like my last day, which was appropriate for the "Execution Capital" of the U.S. Relaxing in the hotel room, remembering our little dustup from the night before, I imagined a conversation that probably took place in many television newsrooms across the country between old, gruff station managers and wet-behind-the-ears reporters.

"I need you to go to Huntsville to cover the Reed execution," barked the station manager.

"Can't you send someone else?" asked the reporter.

"No one else is available."

"I went to Huntsville last August to cover the Smith execution, and it almost killed me."

"Save your hard luck story."

"The town's specialty is killing people. Please don't make me go back."

"Pack your bags."

* * *

Normal visiting hours at the penitentiary were on weekends, but with the execution date looming, we were told we'd be allowed additional access. Three or four days a week was doable. That was very good news because waiting the whole workweek for visits would have been hard. Bright and early the next morning, we set off for the penitentiary.

On arrival, once again, we parked in its massive parking lot and marveled at the impenetrable nature of the sprawling complex. Though we'd been there before, it wasn't any less intimidating. Inside, we passed through a metal detector, received a pat down, were buzzed through six steel doors, presented our IDs to a man in a booth, and were escorted by an armed officer the whole way. After thirty minutes, we reached the visitation building and waited in the room until we heard inmates being escorted into the booths. Whether it was a coincidence or not, I didn't know, but we were led to the same booth as last time to see Donny waiting on the other side of the glass.

I took a different approach during this visit and spent a lot of time at one of the tables near the vending machines. I wanted to give them space so they could get to know one another. Let them talk freely. Instead of standing behind Matt the whole visit, I moved in and out of the booth sporadically so I could casually monitor their conversation. I wanted to give them space, but I also wanted a sense of how the visit was progressing.

At one point, I heard Donny tell Matt about his mother. Paula Reed was a by-the-book Catholic who regarded the Bible as an instruction manual for life and quoted verses from it often. He said his mother dragged him to St. Peter's Church at least three times a week for masses and made him go to confession regularly. He told Matt that sitting in those pews felt the same as sitting in his cell; he wanted to be anyplace else. Donny's voice lagged when he talked about his mother, and it didn't seem like they had a good relationship.

"Every night when I went to bed, my mother told me, 'Say your prayers, Donny, or you'll go straight to Hell when you die.'"

"She sounds like a scary woman," Matt said.

"Oh, she scared the hell out of me. She told me that the devil was inside a lot of people, so I had to be careful. She told me to watch for signs like swear words, smoking, and alcohol use."

"So, if people cussed, they had the devil in them?"

"That's what she told me. I was a kid. I believed her."

"You must've been one frightened kid."

"An old man in our building drank and cussed. I ran away and hid every time I saw him. I believed the devil was inside him."

Another time, I heard Matt tell Donny about his one season on the varsity football team. He told him that he started every game and received a varsity letter for his play that season. He said he didn't return the next season because he thought his coach was too hard on a couple of his teammates. He said it bordered on abuse, and he wasn't comfortable watching it. He'd never told me that.

"I played tight end in high school," Donny told Matt, "but I think I dropped as many passes as I caught."

At another point, Donny's tone turned sentimental as he recounted the afternoon he met Abby at a Fourth of July party held at the home of a mutual friend. He even described her outfit and said she was the most beautiful woman he'd ever met.

"Plenty of women have physical beauty like your mother," Donny told Matt, "but, within ten minutes of meeting her, I knew she was beautiful on the inside too."

"How long were you together?" Matt asked.

"About a year. My memories of our time together are like night and day."

"How so?"

"I have some great memories, but some really bad ones too."

"Were the drugs the reason for the bad memories?"

"Mostly," Donny said, a pained look on his face. "It sure wasn't Abby."

Matt told Donny that he worked for twenty days at the grocery store after his last visit. He said he quit so he could return to Huntsville.

"Be careful," Donny said in response, "your work history is starting to sound a lot like mine."

They both laughed, and it wasn't the only time.

Laughter floated from within the booth occasionally and, several times, I heard Donny choke up. Quite different from our first visit, Matt and Donny had serious conversations about real subject matter and even seemed to be forming a bond. By the end of our third visit, it was safe to say that they'd become friends. At the very least, they liked one another. Originally, I hated Donny Reed, but with each successive visit, I started to believe this experience would be good for Matt in the long run. He needed this time with Donny before he died. As for me, I felt more on the outside of my son's life looking in than I ever had. It seemed like the distance between us was expanding, not shrinking as I'd hoped. Watching them smiling and laughing as they exchanged stories, I could only hope that feeling would pass.

The screen of my cell phone lit up with the name "Abigail" on it, so I touched the screen to accept the call.

"Hi, Abby," I said.

"Hi, honey," she said. "How are my boys doing?"

"Mostly bored. Now that we've seen the statue of Sam Houston, there isn't much to do in this town."

"How was that?"

"He was a stately dude with mutton chops and a cane. He reminded me of your mother."

She chuckled. "You leave my mother out of this."

"I'm just kidding."

"Wish I'd been there."

"No, you don't."

"How is Matt? Is he hanging out with the coffee shop girl again?"

"Yeah, we drink a lot of iced coffee when we're here."

"Is it anything serious?"

"Hell, if I know. Matt doesn't tell me much."

"Do you like her?"

"I do. She's a sweet girl and very smart, just like her mother."

"Well, talk to her mother. She'll be able to tell you what's going on."

"I will. We're going to have dinner at their home this weekend."

"Have you seen Donny yet?

"We did. They had a much more personal conversation this time. Matt's getting to know him. Donny told him about his mother."

"She was something else."

"I gathered."

"I always referred to her as Saint Paula."

"I get it."

"I sure hope this goes well."

"Me, too."

"Ask Donny where he hocked my mother's silverware?"

"He stole your silverware?"

"He did."

"Well, I'd better get ready. We're going to the penitentiary again in an hour."

"I love you."

"I love you, too."

Chapter Twenty-Nine

During my time in Huntsville, I'd had moments when I considered the appropriateness of the death penalty and found myself sympathetic with both sides of the issue. On the one hand, I understood the viewpoint that it was not our place, as human beings, to cast judgment and take lives. To those people, a death sentence was a barbaric act that made society as cruel as the offender. In their opinion, taking a life was basically sinking to the level of violent criminals. On the other hand, I also understood the viewpoint that some crimes were so heinous that the only proper punishment was the death penalty. Some crimes were such sins against humanity that the perpetrators basically forfeited their right to live amongst us, and revoking their membership cards in the human race was reasonable. In the biblical interpretation, it was simply a case of an eye for an eye.

Coming and going amongst the forty thousand residents of this town, I'd seen protesters in front of the execution site with signs that supported and denounced executions. Reading the signs, one thing was always clear to me: The political implications of this execution didn't matter to me. I'd come for much more personal reasons. More than a decade ago, Donny's legal team had exhausted his appeals so there was little doubt that his execution would happen on August 23rd. With his crime captured on video, the truth was his execution order was essentially carved into stone the moment he was sentenced. Public opinion and the fact that he was incarcerated in Texas made a stay of execution unlikely. Personally, I wasn't waiting for a stay or some other miraculous, though unlikely, turn of events, I was here so my son could get to know his father before he was put to death. It was as simple and unpolitical as that.

* * *

Like many small towns in America, the Huntsville downtown area consisted of simple, three-story brick buildings in row house formation that had been converted into shops and businesses to serve the townsfolk. The basic necessities, and even a few luxury items, were available for reasonable amounts and provided by shopkeepers who included a smile and a chat with every purchase at no extra charge. A stroll along the town's main street was an enjoyable way to spend an afternoon (or early evening in the summer), but only for a short while and only once, as its length and offerings were limited. Also common in small towns was the sinking feeling that the downtown area was an endangered species that wasn't thriving in its natural habitat anymore. Despite all efforts to protect it, the internet and rapidly changing world were challenging the downtown's survival and creating the notion that it should be appreciated and enjoyed for as long as it survives.

In the cool of late evening, as the shopkeepers turned out the lights and locked the front doors, I walked the downtown to get out of my hotel room for a while. I felt far from home, isolated in this small East Texas town, and alone. As I walked, I thought about the accident that killed my mother and sister, and I wondered if it had anything to do with my mad dashes up my hill in the wrong lane. Was it possible that I'd so lost touch with reality that I wanted to die the same way they did? Had I convinced myself that if I died that way, I'd join them in the special corner of heaven reserved for accident victims? At the time, I was distraught about my uncle's death and Abby's affair, and I wasn't thinking straight. For the last three months of 2016, I was out of control. Devastated by the loss and the betrayal, I rushed up my hill twelve or thirteen times in the wrong lane, and I somehow managed to do it without causing a collision. In the final analysis, I didn't know why I did what I did, but I was glad I stopped my antics before something terrible happened.

As I walked, I also thought about my father and the distance that had existed between us. There were three things I'd always wanted to hear my father say to me: "I love you," "I'm proud of you," and "You're a good son." He never said any of those things. Over the years, those unsaid words echoed loudly in my heart and mind. Though we were never close, he was still my father, and I longed for those very important words of approval and acceptance. In fact, I wanted to hear those words so badly it physically hurt me at times.

After years of reflection, I realized I wasn't totally without blame. I recalled how I called him "Father" far more often than I called him "Dad." Somewhere in my teens, I made it even more formal when I started calling him by his first name, Ray. The first time I said it he didn't even flinch; if anything, he acted like I was finally getting with the program. In retrospect, we both made our efforts to remain apart and at a distance. We never came together as father and son.

Alone on the sidewalk, beneath the streetlights, I realized it was all connected: my failed relationship with my father and my lack of connection with my son. My father and I had never gotten it right, never connected as we should have, but I felt I had an opportunity with Matt to fix that. If I could create a healthy relationship with my son, maybe I could heal the wounds left over from my youth. Ironically, this journey that I didn't want to take might be my salvation; this journey to meet his birth father may turn out to be the catalyst for our healthy relationship. Matt was at the most critical crossroads of his young life, and, unlike my father with me, I wanted to walk that road with him. I wanted to be by his side. Whatever it required, I needed to be a father to him.

Instinctively, in our complicated, flawed, and inconsistent stepfather/son relationship, I sensed my redemption.

Chapter Thirty

S ince his sophomore year, Matt had done all he could to avoid conversations with Abby and me. He acted bothered whenever we tried to learn about his friends, school work, after-school activities, general interests, or interactions with others. If we cornered him and forced him to talk to us, he typically responded with one-word answers and avoided anything that resembled a real conversation. On many occasions in the past, I'd watched my son as he yakked away with his buddies on school grounds, only to clam up as soon as he climbed into the vehicle beside me. When talking with his parents, Matt conserved his words like they were as precious as oxygen.

While in Huntsville, I'd noticed something about Matt that I could take advantage of—he was much more talkative after a couple of iced coffees than at any other time of the day. Hyped up on caffeine, Matt participated in conversations with me and went well beyond his usual one-word answers. In fact, he really opened up and told me about what was going on in his life and how he felt about things. With the Garcia Girls as my trusted accomplices, I used his caffeine highs to help me cultivate a better relationship with him during carefully orchestrated, mid-afternoon, caffeine-fueled hotel room chats.

"Here's your iced coffee," Matt said as he entered our room one day.

"Thanks," I said, accepting the tall cup with the "GG" logo on it.

"I meant to tell you that I picked up my diploma before we left for Huntsville." Matt smiled. He seemed uncharacteristically proud of himself.

"Good," I said. "I want to see it when we get home."

"Sure."

"Did they spell your name right?"

"They did."

"Did I ever tell you that my name is misspelled on my high school diploma?"

His head jerked. "No way."

"It's A-l-a instead of A-l-e."

"That's crazy. Why didn't you get another?"

"I kind of enjoyed the mistake."

"Why?"

"Because, back then, I always felt judged by my father and my teachers."

Matt grinned. "I know *that* feeling."

"And I never felt I lived up to their expectations."

"I get that, too."

"For some reason, I felt some kind of vindication in their error."

I could see in his eyes that he understood. "It's your proof that they're not perfect."

"Exactly. Do you know what we have in common?" I asked.

"What?"

"Neither of us attended our high school graduation."

"You didn't go either. How come?"

"I didn't want to attend."

"What did your dad say?"

"He didn't care. I told him I wasn't going, and he said okay. That was that."

"I think I'm glad I never met him."

"He wasn't a warm man."

"So, you've said."

"I really regret not going now."

"Why?"

161

"Because Uncle Bob wanted to see me graduate. I should have gone to the ceremony for his sake."

"You should've. He was a good guy."

"He sure was."

My eyes teared up, and I looked away for a moment. Uncle Bob had died eleven months earlier, but it was still raw. All my life, he'd always been there for me. It was still hard for me to accept that he wasn't in my life anymore.

"What are you going to do when we get back to Boulder?" I finally asked when I got my emotions in check.

"I don't know," Matt replied, "maybe I'll take my bagging skills to another grocery store."

"You only bagged for a month."

"I know, but you'd be surprised how quickly you can master it."

"I guess so," I said with a chuckle.

Matt's expression turned serious. His tone changed also. "Heck, I don't know if I'll ever do more than bag groceries," he said. "I'm not smart like Christi and Nate."

"You know, Matt, when I was your age, I couldn't have even imagined being married, having children, or being successful at what I did. None of that happened for me until I was in my thirties."

"Really?"

"Yeah. Do the math, I'm fifty-one now."

"Well, that's good to hear because I can't imagine any of that either."

"A smart guy once told me to have faith in myself, to know that I'd find my path in life as long as I continued to make the effort."

"Was that Uncle Bob?"

"No, it was the guy who taught me to build houses. He believed in me, and that meant a lot to me."

"I'll bet."

"I believe in you, Matt. I know you're going to do great things with your life. Have faith in yourself, okay?"

His face brightened a little. "Okay."

Slurp! Matt's straw made a sound as he reached the end of his beverage. He gyrated the straw in the lid to get it all. Slurp! It sounded again.

"I'm gonna need another," Matt said. "Do you want one?"

"No, I'm good."

"I'll be right back."

When the door slammed behind Matt, I was left alone in the room, still contemplating the misspelled name on my diploma. Remembering my younger days, I was amazed by how little thought or consideration went into many of the decisions of my young life. At the age of fourteen, while hanging out with four guys I barely knew, I smoked my first joint because the oldest lit one up and passed it to me. I didn't want to be uncool, so I puffed it. Two years later, under similar circumstances, I dropped my first tab of ecstasy at a party with a girl I wanted to impress. At twenty, I quit junior college because a friend of mine moved to Seattle, and I went to visit him. When I returned from the trip, I never went back to class. Looking back, I had a good mind, but the truth was I didn't use it all that much.

About ten minutes later, Matt returned with his new beverage in hand. By my count, that was his fifth iced coffee of the day, so I knew I could count on continued conversation with him. He was high on caffeine, or as I liked to think of it, brimming with truth serum. My methods felt unscrupulous, but I really enjoyed being able to have meaningful conversations with my son. Anyway, it was in the mid-nineties and overcast outside, as usual, so we had no other options but to hang out in the room and talk.

"Do you think I look like Donny?" Matt asked once he'd settled down on his bed.

"I do," I said. "I see some resemblance."

We were both quiet for a moment. I waited to hear what he had to say about Donny, but he remained silent. Finally, I asked.

"What are your thoughts about Donny?"

"We had a good talk the other day," he said, "but I'm having a hard time getting past the fact that he shot that old lady in the face."

"I know what you mean. It was such a cruel act. She'd already given him the money, so it was that much more senseless."

"Do you think I have that in me?"

"I don't know. Maybe we all have it inside us. I do know that we all make our own choices in life."

"I worry that I could do something bad," Matt said. "After all, I'm his son."

"I'm pretty sure that Donny will have the exact opposite effect on you."

"What do you mean?"

"Some people in our lives," I told him, "show us good examples to follow while others show us mistakes to avoid. If we're smart, we learn the lessons that other people offer us."

"What's that got to do with Donny?"

"Let me tell you a story. When I first started high school, I knew a kid who was a few years ahead of me. He wasn't a friend of mine, but I knew him through other kids. This kid got into heroin and really messed up his life. He became a junkie, got arrested several times, messed up his family, his parents divorced, and he ended up in a psychiatric hospital. At the time, I wasn't the smartest kid, and I'd experimented with pot and some other party drugs, but this kid showed me to never mess with heroin or any other hard-core drugs. When I saw what happened to him, I drew a line in the sand that I knew I'd never cross. If not for him, who knows what stupid things I might've done? I may very well have become a heroin addict myself and wrecked my whole life."

"So, you think that having Donny as a father will keep me from doing bad things."

"I do. I'd be willing to bet you'll leave this whole experience with Donny an even kinder person than before. Personally, I think that's the effect Donny will have on you."

Chapter Thirty-One

F or more than a century, stockholders of Coca-Cola have known that investments in addictive products were very lucrative. Turning our SUV into the driveway of the Garcia home, it was evident that Rosalita Garcia also understood that Coca-Cola's sales advantage applied to the business of coffee as well. Her proprietary roasting process and freshly ground beans produced an aromatic and flavorful gourmet cup of coffee, as well as lots of profits. It wasn't unusual for her customers to return to her stores for as many as three or four cups in a single day. After fifteen years of hard work, Rosie had five Garcia Girls locations in the Huntsville area that were basically an institution.

The Garcia home was a beautiful Spanish-style house with an orange terra-cotta roof, a large wooden front door with an arched top, and decorative wrought iron all around the property. A courtyard with a stone fountain, wood benches, clay pots, and ivy on the red brick walls preceded the front door and seemed to transport visitors to a bygone era. The house was built before the founding of Coca-Cola in 1886 but had been cared for and restored with meticulous regard for its history. It was easily the most beautiful home on the block, and from what I'd seen during my visits, maybe the entire town.

On one of Matt's many trips to their coffee store, Rosie and Angie invited Matt and me to come to their home for dinner. We were promised the best steak fajitas this side of the Rio Grande.

"In our family," Rosie said as we passed bowls around the table, "young girls learn the family recipes as soon as they make their first communion. Long ago, somewhere in our family tree, someone decided that was the proper time for the recipes to be handed down. As soon as this one received communion, I taught her the family secrets in the kitchen beside me."

"These fajitas are delicious," I said. "Did you ever consider opening a restaurant?"

"Had I not found my way into the coffee business I may very well have opened a restaurant."

"You would've been a success."

Rosie smiled. "Ahh. You're so kind."

"I think you would've been a success at whatever you did, Rosie," Matt added.

"Like father, like son," Rosie said.

"Where is Angie's father?" I asked.

"He abandoned us when Angie was four and returned to his hometown in Mexico."

"I'm sorry to hear that."

"I believe most women, and a lot of men, have a yearning to be parents, but, unfortunately, there are also a lot of men who don't. That's why so many men leave their children. It's not uncommon. You're lucky to have this good man for your father, Matt."

Thank you, Rosie, I thought. *All things considered, I really appreciated her endorsement. It was timely.*

"Have you met your father?" Matt asked Angie.

"I haven't," Angie replied. "I have only seen pictures of him."

"Do you want to meet him?" Matt followed up.

"It doesn't matter to me. I have a very strong mother who taught me how to make my way in this world. I am grateful for the one who stayed."

This dinner couldn't be going better if I scripted it myself, I thought. *The Garcia girls are a Godsend.*

166

"Matt tells me you build beautiful homes in the mountains of Colorado," Angie said to me.

"Next spring," I said, "I will break ground on my largest and most beautiful home yet. It will be almost 9,000 square feet when completed."

"That sounds like a mansion to me," Angie said. "I would love to see the Rocky Mountains one day."

"We'd love to have you come visit us."

"Definitely," Matt said, "you should come to Boulder. If you do, I'll show you the Flatirons."

"What are Flatirons? I've never heard of them."

"Red rocks on the west side of Boulder that rise from the ground in slanted formations."

"They are surrounded by pine trees," I added, "and really beautiful."

"I would love to see them."

At the large wood plank table in their dining room, beneath an ornate copper ceiling, we all ate a wonderful meal, drank strawberry margaritas, talked about family and life's work, and laughed an awful lot. All the while, I marveled at the harmonious relationship between mother and daughter and hoped that one day, Matt and I would be as close. Rosie and Angie were one of those mother and daughter pairs who were sometimes mistaken for sisters. Angie was born when Rosie was only seventeen, and nineteen years later, they both had a youthful glow that caused the confusion. Both mother and daughter were strikingly beautiful with sculpted features, mesmerizing brown eyes, full, pouty lips, and curves with all the right measures. Suffice it to say, the Garcia girls never entered a room unnoticed.

Late that night, Rosie told me that she always prepared a special meal every Sunday evening. It was a Garcia family tradition and one that she did not want to see fade away. She said her Sunday meal featured both family recipes and ones she'd acquired over the years, with appetizers and main courses, and she always made enough food for ten people. On many nights, they invited family and friends to join them, but, on some nights, it was just Rosie and Angie.

"For as long as the Bryant boys are in Huntsville," she said in a no-

nonsense tone, "I will expect you both at my dinner table at 7 on Sunday nights, and I won't take no for an answer."

"After that delicious meal tonight," I said, "we'd have to be fools not to come."

It was well after midnight when we finally thanked our gracious hosts, departed their home, and went back to our hotel.

* * *

Wyatt called just after noon.

"Hey, Wyatt," I said.

"Hello, Alex. How are things in my home state?"

"Hot."

"Welcome to Texas in August."

"How are the girls?"

"Oh, you know, they're struggling. A good day is any day I can make them forget and have some fun for just a while."

"I'll bet."

"Your wife has been over here almost every day. You've got a good one in Abby."

"Don't I know it."

"Whenever I tell her she is doing too much, she tells me her problem children are in Texas, so she has time."

"That sounds like Abby."

"She is so good for the girls I can't even tell you."

"That's great to hear. We're going to get past this tragedy together."

"How is Matt?"

"He is an eighteen-year-old in a situation few forty-year-olds could handle, but he's doing okay. He's getting to know his father."

"How are you doing?"

"I'm a fifty-one-year-old in a situation few fathers could handle, but I'm doing okay."

"We've sure got our hands full."

"We sure do. If I learned anything from my father, it's that being a parent isn't easy."

"It's a good thing we've got the Mayfield house behind us. Can you imagine?"

"No, I can't."

"We really need this time for our families."

"We do."

"I'll see you in late August."

"Hang in there, buddy."

Chapter Thirty-Two

E very time we visited Donny at the penitentiary, he wore white prison uniforms that resembled hospital scrubs. The shirts were short-sleeved, buttoned in the front, and hung loosely on his frame; the pants were the same material and loose as well. Looking at him through the glass, I almost expected him to be called away at any moment to perform an emergency C-section or appendectomy. The image through the glass never seemed quite right to me. In old movies, convicts usually had thick stripes on their garments that made it clear they were incarcerated. I would've been more comfortable with stripes.

On our fifth visit with Donny, he was relaxed with Matt and even introspective as they talked. Rather than going in and out of the booth as I'd been doing, I sat on the other side of the cinderblock wall on a plastic chair to hear the conversation. After an hour together and without Matt even asking, Donny started talking about his crime. As he did, I moved my chair to the edge of the cinderblock wall so I could see Donny.

"I did so much meth in those days," Donny said, wiping sweat from his brow, "that people believed me when I said I didn't remember that night or shooting her."

"Was it true?" Matt asked. "Did you remember?"

Donny grimaced. "I remember it like it was yesterday. I relive it all the time in my mind."

"Why did you pick that convenience store?"

"A week earlier, I bought a pack of cigarettes at the store, and I noticed the old lady behind the counter. I knew she wasn't going to put up a fight. It'd be easy."

"Tell me about the robbery."

"I waited on the side of the store until there was no one around, and then I rushed in the front door with my gun in the air."

Our side of the glass was air-conditioned; the inmate's side wasn't. Donny took a deep breath. Once again, he wiped the sweat off his brow. His expression was pained. He shifted uncomfortably in his chair.

"I shouted at her, 'Open the damn register and give me the money.' I was a little unnerved by the way she responded. She didn't seem afraid. She was calm."

At that point, Donny's eyes filled with tears. He was nearing the part of the story that had put him on death row, the instant when his life had changed irreversibly. In his eyes, along with the tears, I saw remorse.

"She grabbed a paper bag from beside the register, pulled the bills from the tray, and slipped them into the bag. I remember thinking that there was more money than I expected."

"Do you remember how much you got?"

"Two hundred seventy-three dollars."

"What did you plan to do with it?"

"Buy meth. That's what I did with all my money."

Matt paused. He took on a pensive look. When he spoke, I understood why. "So, why did you shoot her?"

That question had remained unanswered since the bullet exited the gun.

Donny shook his head. "As she handed me the bag, we locked eyes for a moment. She said, 'Without that gun in your hand, you're nothin' but a loser methhead. You got nothin' good inside ya and nothin' good going for ya.'"

Donny broke down. He dropped his head, and his shoulders heaved as he sobbed. He wept like a man who regretted his birth, one who'd forfeit all of his days to undo one. It took him more than a minute to regain his composure and continue recounting the events of that fateful night.

"I shot her because every word she said was true. I couldn't stand hearing the truth. I was nothin' but a loser methhead."

Matt put his palm against the glass. Donny placed his palm in the same spot. Matt spoke. "Do you realize you told me all about the crime but never said her name?"

"Mary Jo Donovan," Donny whimpered. "I'm so sorry, Mary Jo."

"Are you a better man today than back then?"

Donny wiped tears from his cheek. "I am."

"I don't believe this Donny Reed would pull the trigger. Do you?"

"I'm clean today, and I am a good person. There is no way I'd hurt anyone now."

Watching Matt lead Donny through his confession and act of contrition of sorts, it felt like Matt was trying to help Donny forgive himself. After all this time with Donny, I believe Matt sensed that he indeed had influence in the matter. He'd come to understand his father and his crime, and he wanted to help him. After all, Donny had less than twenty days to live. It was a level of maturity I'd never seen in Matt.

"In all these years," Donny said, "I've never told my story to anyone."

"It's good that you told me," Matt said.

"I know."

As we drove back to the hotel that afternoon, Matt remarked, "Donny's drug use sure derailed his life."

Without his meth addiction, Matt believed Donny wouldn't be in prison; in fact, he probably would've lived a normal life. He told me that talking with Donny made him question his own experimentation with drugs. He said he didn't want to make the same mistakes.

"It's obvious to me," Matt said, in a reflective tone unusual for him, "that Donny isn't an evil man who was destined to murder someone. But his decision to use meth was a really bad choice that ruined his life."

In several ways, those words that afternoon made meeting Donny Reed and all our time in Huntsville worthwhile. A smile appeared on my face as I drove.

* * *

My cell phone lit up with Abigail's name on it.

"Hello, Abigail," I said.

"Hi, hon," Abby said.

"How are you?"

"Mostly busy with Wyatt's kids."

"I've heard."

"How are the visits going?"

"Donny told us about the murder today."

"No way. What did he say?"

"He said he shot her because she called him a 'good for nothin' methhead.'"

"He said that?"

"He said he couldn't stand to hear the truth."

"Well, I'll be."

"He seems remorseful. I can't believe I'm saying this, but I don't hate the guy."

"Maybe he's changed, maybe not," she said, sounding skeptical. "Most death row inmates are probably remorseful when their execution is imminent."

"He cried, Abby. It was quite a session."

"Has Matt said anything about going to the execution? I read that only family members of the victims and the condemned are allowed. They have two separate rooms."

"It hasn't come up. I never considered the idea of us going. Hell, I don't want to be there."

"I don't think you should go either. Don't bring it up, and hopefully we won't have to decide."

"Do you think Matt would want to be there?"

"I have no idea."

"Sleep well."

"You, too."

Chapter Thirty-Three

Less than two weeks before Donny's execution, we had an abbreviated visit with him. That morning, he marched into the booth in an agitated and angry mood. Donny looked like a man who hadn't been allowed to make a single decision for himself in more than seventeen years. He looked like he'd finally had enough of all the constraints and degradation that came with prison life. Once seated, he practically ripped the phone off the wall. Standing beside Matt, I reached over and turned the speaker on.

"Well," Donny said, "my support group has returned. I've got bad news, guys. You're not helping me."

"Good morning to you, too," Matt said, miffed by Donny's tone.

"Aren't you getting a little tired of these monotonous sessions?" Donny asked, smirking at us. "I know I am."

Matt scratched his chin. "More monotonous than staring at the gray block wall in your cell all day?" he asked.

"My cell wall is white."

"Gray. White. What the hell difference does it make?"

"I've got eleven miserable days left. If I bought a dozen eggs today and ate one every day, I wouldn't even finish the carton."

"I didn't come here for a math lesson," Matt said, his brow furrowed. "I learned subtraction in the third grade."

"Did you?"

"If you hadn't abandoned us for your fucked up, meth-fueled life, you'd know that."

"I think it's time for you to go back to your damn life in the mountains and get the hell out of mine."

Matt's cheeks reddened. "Fuck you, Donny."

Donny grinned, cocky-like. "I didn't want you around back then, and I don't want you around now. Hit the road, kid."

"Let's go." Matt rose and grabbed my arm at the elbow. "I've had enough of this asshole."

As we made our way through the secure hallways of the penitentiary, I couldn't help but notice the grimace on Matt's face, and the anger in his eyes. He looked ready to punch something, and I could only hope it'd be a wall and not a prison guard. After we reached our vehicle, we drove in silence while Matt steamed in the passenger seat like an overheated radiator on a Texas highway. Halfway back to the hotel, I finally broke the silence.

"We can go home tomorrow," I said. "You'll be back in your own bed tomorrow night."

"I don't see any reason to stay in Huntsville," he said. "Certainly not for that dickhead."

I could've left it alone and gone home, but I knew that wouldn't be good for Matt. He couldn't part ways with his father like that, each hurling obscenities at the other. Each saying hurtful things. I'd parted with my father in that manner, and I'd always regretted it. The image of my dead father at my feet was permanently etched into my memory. Better than most, I knew the value of a proper goodbye. Whatever their last words, Donny would be dead soon, and Matt would have to live with those words. Like most fathers, I wanted better for my son.

"He's afraid, Matt," I said. "They're going to put that needle in his arm real soon, and he's afraid."

"Do you think that's why he acted like that?"

"I do. It wasn't meant for you. He's just lashing out at the world. Hell, he might've even tried to push you away for your protection. To spare you."

"I think you're giving him too much credit."

"Maybe. But more importantly, I don't think you should leave on that note. I think you need to see it through."

"Well, we're not scheduled to see him again for three days. Let's see if he shows up at the visitation."

"How about we grab an iced coffee?"

"The Garcia Girls?"

"Of course."

Chapter Thirty-Four

When we arrived at the Garcia home on Sunday, Angie met us at the front door with two mai tais in tall glasses in her hands. Swirled shades of red and orange resembling a tropical sunset made the concoction a welcome sight on a sultry Huntsville evening. And the slice of chilled pineapple dangling on the rim—sunny, succulent, and enticing—made it more appealing. As she handed us the glasses, Angie gave each of us a peck on the cheek, said, "Aloha," and smiled the joyful smile of vacationers arriving on Maui. Gleefully, I accepted my glass.

"Tonight's meal has an island theme," Angie informed us. "The main course is lomi lomi salmon."

"Aloha," I said, hoisting my glass in a toasting motion. "An island getaway sounds wonderful right now."

"Aloha," Rosie called out from the kitchen. "Come and taste some poi."

Once again, we gathered around the wood plank table beneath the ornate copper ceiling to enjoy another meal as new friends. Rosie and Angie wore white orchids in their shiny, black hair and Hawaiian blouses with colorful flowers, so our luau felt authentic. Their bright smiles were also replete with the Aloha spirit. Both mother and daughter seemed to revel in the enterprise of entertaining.

"I'm fortunate to have a lot of family in Huntsville," Rosie said, halfway through dinner, "because half of the employees at my stores are family. Most businesses have to worry about employee theft, but that's never been a concern for me."

"How many siblings do you have?" I asked.

"I have seven brothers, and five of them live in Huntsville."

"Are you the only girl?"

"I am. I was the last of eight children."

"Speaking of family," Angie said, looking at Matt, "how are your visits with Donny going?"

"For the most part," Matt said, "good." He hesitated. "As we're getting closer to the execution, Donny's had moments when he's been stressed or angry, but that's understandable."

"Now that you've spent a lot of time with him," Rosie asked, "how do you feel about him?"

"Well," Matt returned, "I don't see him as a monster anymore. I've gotten past that concern."

"That's good," Angie said. "It would be horrible if you thought that."

"He has become a cautionary tale for me," Matt said. "He had a drug habit that simply owned him, and he did some really bad things. He wasn't a good person back then."

"Do you think he has changed?" Angie asked.

"I believe so," Matt said.

"Do you see yourself in him?" Angie followed up.

"Yeah," Matt said, "we're a lot alike."

"How would you feel if I went to meet Hector one day?" Angie asked her mother.

"Just stick a knife in my heart before you go, mijita," Rosie answered. "That man is a good-for-nothing low-life."

"He's my father," Angie objected.

"We're better off without him," Rosie said. "Just leave well enough alone."

"People can change, Mom."

"Not Hector Garcia. He cheated on me with two women and then ran off to Mexico and abandoned us."

"He didn't kill anyone," Angie said.

"Angie!" her mother exclaimed.

"That's okay, Rosie," Matt said. "It's the truth. My father murdered a woman. I can't ever forget that."

"Do you know where Hector is now?" I asked.

"He lives in the town of Cordonero, and he is a police officer," Rosie said.

"How bad can he be if he's a police officer?" Matt asked.

"In Mexico," Rosie said," there are many corrupt police officers and lawless towns. Some places are downright unsafe."

"I've never been outside the U.S.," I volunteered. "Not even Mexico or Canada. I was traumatized by a plane crash I watched on TV when I was young, so I don't fly. Our little luau tonight is as close as I'll ever get to a tropical island."

"Well then," Rosie said, "you should have another mai tai. I'm going to make another round."

"With extra pineapple on mine," Matt requested.

"Of course, mi amor."

Everyone was in good spirits that night, and we sipped mai tais and talked and laughed until almost midnight. Just before we departed, Matt and Angie made plans to see a movie the following evening. Our dinners with the Garcia girls had become a pleasant distraction from the serious visitations and monotonous waiting that characterized our days in Huntsville. Driving back to our hotel, I was already looking forward to our next meal with them.

Chapter Thirty-Five

Working with the Entrepreneur, we knocked off every Friday at 2 p.m. and went to town for a good meal and a couple of beers or glasses of wine. He said it was important to celebrate accomplishments, and, after five days of hard work each week, he said we had plenty to celebrate. Sometimes, we went to pubs for sandwiches, and other times, we went to fine restaurants for steaks. Either way, I always looked forward to Friday afternoons. At the job site, I learned a lot about the art and craft of homebuilding. At lunch each Friday, I learned a lot about life.

During our meals together, the Entrepreneur told me stories about when he opened his first hotel and the many mistakes he'd made along the way. He told me about the challenges he'd faced and the obstacles he'd surmounted. Within a few months, he said he knew he'd either go broke before his third year, or he'd have many hotels and be successful. Any middle ground was simply unacceptable to him. He told me he liked the hotel business because people were in good spirits at hotels: seeking relaxation, attending a special event, or out on an adventure. Early on, he realized that the key to his success was creating an environment and experience that people would talk about for years to come. He said his hotels were in the "memories business."

One afternoon, at a four-star restaurant called The Haberdashery, over thick cuts of New York steak, the Entrepreneur spoke words I knew I'd always remember, which wasn't unusual because he was a noteworthy individual.

"From my experience," he said as he buttered a slice of bread, "there are two kinds of decisions in life, and it's important to handle each in the proper manner. The first kind pertains to matters that you decide with your heart, issues of right and wrong."

At that moment, I remember putting my knife and fork down on my napkin. We were a couple of months into the project, and, by that time, I'd learned to pay attention whenever the Entrepreneur spoke about his philosophies on life. Heck, I'd learned to pay attention whenever he spoke. He was concise and soft-spoken, so I always made the extra effort to listen carefully. I wanted to hear what he had to say. I admired him and found him inspirational.

"When it comes to this kind of decision, you need to be careful about your inner dialogue. You see, most people know immediately what the right thing is, but given enough time to convince themselves otherwise, they'll rationalize and find reasons to do what's in their best interest and not necessarily what's right."

I nodded. "I've done that before."

"In those circumstances, you need to hold yourself accountable. You'll be better off in the long run if you just do the right thing."

"I know what you mean."

"Now, the second kind of decision pertains to matters you decide with your mind. Business decisions are a good example. These decisions require you to collect all the information and data you can and determine the most likely outcomes. Unlike decisions you make with your heart, these decisions require a lot of thought and a good inner dialogue. You need to think them through."

"That makes a lot of sense."

"I believe that one of the keys to success in life is handling each kind of decision in the proper manner. Reversing the methodologies will mess you up every time."

"My problems usually come from talking myself out of doing the right thing."

"Unfortunately, most people are much better at rationalizing than facing the truth."

"I know I need to do a better job at holding myself accountable."

"We all do."

"I'm going to try."

"Good. It may come as a surprise to you, but I would much rather make a bad business decision than betray my heart and not do the right thing."

"Really?"

"Absolutely. It's the dings to my character that I've found I regret most in life."

"But bad business decisions cost you money."

The Entrepreneur smiled. He seemed nostalgic when he continued. "That's okay. Much like life, business is a process where you learn as you go. Whatever the cost of a bad business decision, you simply accept the lesson and move on."

* * *

Another day with the Entrepreneur I'd never forget happened about four months into the project when we'd completed the framing of the house and the structure was starting to take shape on the mountain. It was one of those magical days in the mountains when the wonder of it all was simply overwhelming, when the jagged peaks and millions of pine trees formed a panorama that took my breath away. Looking out on it all, I felt both awe and wonder—awe for the beauty around me and wonder about my place in it. In mid-morning, while I was busy carrying a load of materials from the truck to the worksite, I noticed that the Entrepreneur was gone. He'd left the site. After a while, and several more loads of materials, I realized he'd hiked up the mountain and taken up a position on a large boulder overlooking the home. When I finished moving the materials, I hiked up to where he sat.

"Isn't that a beautiful sight?" he asked me when I reached him.

"It looks great," I said. "We're making progress."

"Five months ago, it was just an idea in our heads," he said, "and soon, it'll be a beautiful home. Making our thoughts and dreams into reality is one of the noblest things we can do in life."

"You've got a great way of looking at things," I said.

He smiled. "The right perspective can take you a long way."

"It has worked for you."

The Entrepreneur's gaze shifted from the structure beneath us to me. "Thank you for all your hard work," he told me. "I've really enjoyed working with you."

"I'm enjoying this project, too. Thank you for hiring me."

"You've got a lot of potential. I know you're going to do great things in life."

His vote of confidence meant a lot to me. "Thanks for saying that," I said.

"I really mean it," he added. "When we finish the home, I want you to know you can always come work for me at one of my hotels if you want."

"Really?"

"Sure, I'd be happy if you did."

"Maybe I will." His job offer told me he meant it.

"Well, whether you work for me or do something on your own, I know you're going to do well. Have faith in yourself, okay?"

"I will."

He looked at the framed structure beneath us. "Do you know what the difference is between most other people and me?"

I chuckled. "You're rich, and they're poor."

"Be serious."

"I don't know. What?"

"I was willing to bet on myself. I wanted that bet. Most people are unwilling to risk losing when the stakes are that high."

"I see that all around me."

"When the time comes for you, I hope you'll have faith in yourself and make the bet. It'll happen if you do."

"What makes you think I'm not one of those other people?"

He shook his head. "Because you're not. I see it in you. You're a lot like me. I know you're going to go your own road; I just want to encourage you to go confidently down that road."

Years later, I sometimes wondered if my father's absence from my life was so apparent in my person that the Entrepreneur was attempting to fill the void with his encouragement.

* * *

A month before we completed the Entrepreneur's house, I asked Uncle Bob to join me for lunch at The Haberdashery. I'd grown fond of the place. Wearing my only suit—a blue double-breasted number with white pinstripes and wide lapels—I waited at a table beneath a display of hats from early in the twentieth century. Gazing at a black bowler, I felt it would've gone well with my ridiculous suit.

Who am I trying to impress anyway? I asked myself.

I was twenty-eight years and ten months old, and somehow, I'd made it to this stage of adulthood without any inkling of purpose. Clearly, it was time for me to get serious about my life; time for me to lay claim to that pitiful designation of "late bloomer" and get off my ass and do something. I had to find a purpose for my life, something more meaningful than minimum wage jobs. Like most pitiful people, I had a plan.

"How's my favorite nephew?" my uncle said as he joined me at the table.

"I'm your only nephew."

"Well, that fact only adds corroboration."

"What can I get you to drink, Dr. Bryant?" the waiter asked.

"I'll have whatever he's having," my uncle answered, pointing to my beer.

For the next twenty minutes, I told my uncle about my project with the Entrepreneur and the fact that we'd be done with the house soon. I told him about the many things I'd learned about the homebuilding process and how much I enjoyed doing it. I told him how much I admired and respected the Entrepreneur, and how much he'd taught me about life. I even told him about some of our conversations at that restaurant.

My words that afternoon were the most passionate that I had ever spoken. For the first time in my life, I felt the possibility of purpose, the sensation of meaning. I'd heard a voice from deep within my being speak to me, and I knew the direction I wanted to go. I felt energized. I felt alive. I even felt reborn. After all my rambling, I finally got to why I'd asked my uncle to have lunch with me.

"I want to build rural houses on my own," I said. "I plan to start by building a few small, second homes and A-frame homes and then gradually move up to luxury homes like the one we're about to complete. I think I've found my calling in life."

"Well, that sounds great," my uncle said. "You've obviously given this a lot of thought. So, why did you ask me here today?"

My Uncle Bob was both a smart and polite man. I was pretty sure he knew the answer to his question, but he wanted to give me a chance to speak my mind.

"I've compiled a list of the tools and equipment I'll need to get started, and it totals $27,500. And I'll need at least another $25,000 for start-up expenses. I know I'm only twenty-nine, but I'm hoping you'll loan me $75,000 against my inheritance."

He stopped mid-sip. He smiled. "You'll be twenty-nine in two months, Alex."

"Okay, almost twenty-nine."

"On your way here today," he asked, pausing to finish the sip of his beer, "what percentage chance did you think you had that I'd loan you the money?"

I thought for a second. "About seventy percent. I also thought you might tell me I had to wait until I was thirty."

"Well, I want you to know that I have no hesitation whatsoever about making the loan. I believe in you."

"So, you'll loan me the money?"

"Come by the house on Friday, and I'll have a check for you."

"Thanks."

"Now, let's order some steaks and celebrate your new venture."

Chapter Thirty-Six

In 2009, when Matt was in the fifth grade, he was interested in trains. He built model trains on the desk in his room, painted them different colors—though mostly black—and displayed them on a shelf when completed. He was fascinated with anything railroad related, and so, on his tenth birthday, we gave him a Lionel train set. As an added bonus, that afternoon, Abby, Matt, and I drove to downtown Denver to visit Union Station so Matt could see a real station with real trains. For the entire drive to Denver, he had a smile on his face as wide as train tracks.

Union Station was a beautiful building that harkened visitors back to the time when train travel was the most desirable way to move about the country. The building had terra-cotta floors, beautiful marble walls, tall, arched windows, and a curved, white ceiling that was seventy feet above the hustle and bustle beneath it. As we wandered around the station, I noticed a beautiful clock with a white face on one of the walls as well as a bronze statue of a stately gentleman. Within the walls of Union Station, the Industrial Revolution was alive and well.

"This place feels familiar," I remarked to Abby as we passed the ticket booth.

A ticket agent with epaulets on her shoulder and a pill box hat waved at Matt as he gawked at her.

"Did you take a train trip when you were young?" Abby asked as we walked on.

"I don't remember ever being on a train."

"My mother took my sister and me on a train to Sacramento to visit our grandparents once."

"Was it fun?"

She beamed. "I loved it."

"Maybe we should take the family on a train trip. I hear the northbound route is quite beautiful."

"We could go to Yellowstone."

"We should do that."

"Matt would go ballistic."

We walked out of the station to one of the platforms where a train bound for Topeka, Kansas, was currently boarding. The sleek, silver train cars were lined up on the track for as far as the eye could see. Looking at the amazement in Matt's eyes, I believed he thought that train was about one thousand cars long. Passengers with suitcases on wheels moved alongside the train as they prepared to board. A conductor wearing a black hat, black vest, and white gloves extended his hand to Matt as we approached.

"Let me help you board, young man," the conductor said.

"We're not traveling today," Abby told him. "We came to the station so our son could see the trains."

"He loves trains," I added.

"We've got a little time before we leave. How about I give you a quick tour, young man?"

"Can I, Mom?"

"Of course you can," Abby answered.

We followed the conductor, a pinch-eyed man with Sam on his nameplate, into the sleeper car where he led us up the isle to a nook with his supplies. Sam retrieved a plastic locomotive pin with the words "Junior Engineer" on it from a cardboard box. He pinned it on Matt's shirt and told him that he was now an official railroad employee. Then, we crossed between two cars so Matt could see the dining car and its seating for about 100 passengers. He was impressed by the fact that riders could eat a full meal while the train was rolling. Finally, we passed through another car that served as a lounge, and then we emerged from the train with Matt glowing like he'd just ridden his favorite ride at Disneyland.

"Thanks, Sam," Matt told the kind conductor.

When we reentered the station, I continued to have the feeling that I'd been there before. As we walked through the aisles of benches, I searched my memory once again, but I didn't remember ever being on a train. A train trip seemed like something I'd remember. Once again, I looked at the terra-cotta floors, beautiful marble walls, tall arched windows, and curved, white ceiling and wondered why I had this feeling of familiarity.

"Come back here," Abby called out to Matt, who'd ventured on ahead of us.

Fifty feet from us, Matt was standing before the bronze statue with his head arched backward staring up at the dignified man. A little miffed, Abby approached Matt and took him by the hand.

"You need to stay with us," she told him.

The sight of Matt standing before that statue and then being led away by his mother caused a flash of recognition in my memory. I spun around and saw the wood bench where my mother and I sat all those years ago and waited. I recognized it immediately. It was the very spot where she'd promised me ice cream when we left and where she'd mussed my hair and told me I was her little man. The words, "I love you to the moon and back," began echoing in my mind like "Ave Maria" sung by a choir. This train station was the site of my most cherished memory of my mother, the one that I wasn't sure whether it actually happened or not. Staring at that bench, I remembered the tight, loving clasp of my mother's hand. In a sense, I suddenly felt like I'd gone to heaven and reunited with my mother. In that grand and beautiful building, I felt her presence once again. My one memory of her, the one that I'd clung to through the storms of my childhood and adolescence like a life preserver, was, indeed, real.

"Wow," Matt said, his eyes wide. "This is the most beautiful place I ever saw."

"It makes me think of Heaven," I told him.

"Does it?"

"Yes. It definitely does."

It was Matt's birthday, but our excursion to the train station had turned into a wonderful gift for me.

Chapter Thirty-Seven

I'd met death at a much younger age than most, but I'd met him when I was too young to fully understand how he operated. How he swooped into the lives of unsuspecting people and decimated their worlds. I'm not referring to the ones he took with him, but rather the ones he left behind. That's where he inflicted the real damage. I'd already lost significant people—my mother, my father, my sister—but I didn't fully understand his diabolical ways until a death that truly devastated me, one that hit me harder than my previous losses, even though it wasn't totally unforeseen; the deceased was eighty-three years old.

Over the years, cellular service at my worksites had been a rare luxury, but my site at that time had it. It was late in the afternoon, and I was alone at the site when the screen on my phone lit up with "Maggie" on it. Though my aunt called me at least once a week, a chill went down my spine when I saw her name so I answered it apprehensively. Beset with a premonition, my voice quivered as I spoke.

"Hello Aunt Maggie," I said. "What's up?"

"Where are you, Alex?"

I swallowed hard. Her question and tone reinforced my fear. "I'm at my worksite. Why?"

"I've got bad news for you, honey. Your uncle died this morning."

"Oh, no," I said softly. "Not Uncle Bob."

"He loved you very much."

I couldn't speak or even hold myself up. My knees weakened, and I allowed myself to crumple to the floor. In the middle of what would be the great room of my latest project, I laid on the bare wood floor and sobbed.

"Are you there, Alex?" my aunt repeated several times.

Finally, after a minute or two, I managed to speak. "I'll be there in an hour," I said.

"Be careful driving," she warned me. Apparently, she'd heard my sobs, which caused her concern.

My uncle had always been my source of stability, encouragement, guidance, and love. During my hard times, he'd been the person with a kind word and tight hug when I needed it most. He was the one who told me everything would be all right, and I believed him. In many ways, when my father abdicated his role, my uncle stepped in and watched over me. My uncle was the best man I'd ever known and the one I respected most. His passing would leave a gaping hole the size of a mountain canyon in my life.

On August 31, 2016, the funeral for Dr. Robert Thomas Bryant was held at Mountain View Memorial Park with more than 300 mourners in attendance. The day before, on page three of *The Denver Post*, the beloved pediatrician and his more than thirty-year career were the subject of a full-page tribute article that honored his service to the Boulder community. In the article, the writer calculated that Uncle Bob had provided care and counsel to more than 25,000 families. In the days after his death, the outpouring of condolences and support—from some we knew, many we didn't—was overwhelming for Aunt Maggie, my cousins, and me. Beneath a bright blue sky on a cool summer morning, we stood beside the oak casket while a priest and three family friends delivered eulogies.

"Bob was our family's pediatrician for two decades," a middle-aged woman with silver hair and maroon fingernails said as she began her eulogy," but that's not what I'll cherish most when I think about Bob. What I'll cherish most is that Bob was a great man and a great friend. When our sixteen-year-old daughter was in a serious automobile accident, Bob rushed to the hospital at eleven o'clock at night. His medical skills weren't needed; he'd rushed to the hospital as our friend."

When the eulogies ended and the crowd started to drift away from the casket, I noticed a man out of the corner of my eye who was moving against the stream. From my quick glance, I recognized his wavy brown hair and confident stride as belonging to the Entrepreneur, and he was coming my way. I hadn't seen him in five years and wondered why he'd come to the service. Even from a distance, the sight of him comforted me.

"I'm sorry for your loss," he said when he reached me. "I know how much your uncle meant to you."

"Did you know my uncle?"

"I knew your uncle for more than twenty years. He was my wife's family's pediatrician even longer."

"How come you never mentioned that to me?"

"Your uncle and I kept a secret from you all these years. Way back when, I'd asked Bob if he knew someone who could help me build my house. He sent me to meet you that night at the benefit."

"It wasn't a chance meeting?"

"Not at all. Bob even told me to mention that whiskey I asked you about."

"Old Stone Bridge Whiskey?"

"Yeah, he suggested I order it."

Tears welled in my eyes. "Uncle Bob arranged that meeting?"

"He sure did. We met because of your uncle. He truly loved you, Alex."

I'd cried so much since my uncle's death that I didn't think I could cry any more, but the Entrepreneur's revelation caused tears to stream down my cheeks. That meeting led me to my chosen profession and my life's work. That meeting changed my life. The fact that Uncle Bob had arranged it was overwhelming for me.

"My uncle always looked out for me," I said. "He must've known that my time with you would profoundly effect my life."

"I ran into Bob about a year ago and he rambled on and on about your family and the beautiful homes you'd built. He showed me some photos on his phone and beamed so proudly while he spoke about you."

Hearing that my uncle was proud of me, my emotions intensified, and I didn't know if I could speak the next words I wanted to say. I swallowed hard and tried to regain my composure. During my choked-up moment, the Entrepreneur waited patiently, smiling that easy smile of his until I finally spoke.

"My uncle gave me the love, support, and guidance my father wasn't able to give me. In many ways, he was my father."

Of all the life lessons and words of encouragement that the Entrepreneur had said to me, his words that day meant the most. Learning that about my Uncle Bob surpassed everything else.

Later that night, Abby and I stood beneath a bright, full moon on the deck in front of our home as about twenty mourners remained inside. The sky was clear, and a billion stars twinkled above us like celestial candles lit in my uncle's honor. All the heavens were aglow to welcome him. For both of us, the day had been a long, emotionally draining one. Beside me, Abby looked exhausted. Alone with our sorrow, Abby reached over and gently clasped my hand, perhaps sensing the disoriented condition of my soul. Abby knew my uncle was my most trusted counselor, my North Star and source of guidance when I was lost, and the man who'd steadied my world when it wobbled. Beyond my own needs, my uncle was a remarkable man and one who'd made a real difference in many people's lives. Standing in silence beneath all those flickering candles, I knew my life would never be the same without him.

"I never told him I loved him," I said.

"He knew," Abby said. "He loved you like he loved his sons. You were his third son."

"I know he did," I said, struggling against emotion to speak the words, "but I should've told him."

Chapter Thirty-Eight

"Seven days from today," Donny said, "they're going to give me the cocktail, and it'll be over. Just like that."

Donny looked like he hadn't slept since our last visit four days ago. He had dark circles under his eyes, and he blinked regularly. He described a tug-of-war battle that waged within him where his body pulled him toward sleep, but his mind pulled him back. He spoke in rambling sentences and often stared blankly ahead while he did. Before me, on the other side of the glass, I saw a frightened man coming to terms with his wasted life.

"What was the point?" Donny asked. "Why was I even here?"

"I'm eighteen," Matt said, shrugging his shoulders. "I don't have that answer for you."

Standing at the edge of the booth, watching from the cheap seats, I realized two things: This visit was going to be different from all the others, and I was right when I told Matt we shouldn't leave Huntsville. It would've been a mistake to go home. Donny needed us now.

"In my cell the other day, I counted the really great days of my life, and I didn't even run out of fingers. How pathetic is that?"

"You've spent a lot of years in here."

"Yeah, but I still should've run out of fingers."

"Maybe."

"You know what the best day of my life was?"

"The day I was born?"

"I wish I could say that was true, kid, but I didn't even know you'd arrived until weeks later."

"What was it then?"

"When I was nineteen, I worked at a gas station so I could save enough money to buy my dream car."

"What car?"

"A 1967 Camaro with a 275 horsepower, V8 engine and mag wheels."

"That's a nice car."

Donny's face brightened. "Mine was cherry red with two thick, white racing stripes across the hood, roof, and trunk. I was so happy the night I drove it home. It felt like the whole world was laid out in front of me."

"I know what you mean. My first car was my mom's old Land Rover. I felt independent and grown up when she gave it to me."

"A car can be magical thing to a young man. That was the best day of my life."

"What happened to the car?"

"I totaled it two years later."

"That's too bad."

"Story of my life."

It's rare that a person knows in advance the exact moment of their death, I thought. *We're going to witness a brutal review of a man's life in the next few days.*

Donny stared at the wall to his right. It was hard to gauge whether he was reflecting or simply exhausted. As he did, he rested his chin in his palm with his elbow on the counter. At times, his head wavered like a bobblehead.

"Tell me about a time when you were really happy," Donny said to Matt.

Matt raised his eyes in thought.

"Well," he said, "I met a girl here in Huntsville."

"What's her name?" Donny asked, smiling as he did, his interest piqued.

"Angelica."

"So, you came to your father's execution and met an angel. That's poetic."

"She goes by Angie."

"Is she the one?"

"Oh geez, I don't know. We've only known one another for a few weeks."

"Are you happy when you're with her?"

"I am."

"Well, that's a start."

"It is."

"I never really had great love in my life. I regret that. I had my chance with your mother, and I blew it."

"Why did that happen?"

"I loved Abby very much, more than any other women I'd ever met, but I loved meth more. I ruined our love and our chance at a great life together by getting into meth."

"That's too bad."

"It really is. Learn from my mistakes, Matt. Life doesn't always allow second chances. You've got to take advantage of the opportunities you get."

"I'll try."

Though Donny was exhausted, this visitation was a marathon session with subject matter that was emotionally taxing. He spoke about his life in a thoughtful and examining way that delved into the very heart and guts of his time on this earth. He took responsibility for his mistakes and shortcomings and spoke the words of a man who had nothing left to hide. The good and bad of his life were laid bare, and he seemed at peace with it. The upcoming execution found its way into the conversation several times.

"Do you think death by lethal injection is a painful death?" he asked.

"It's not," Matt said. "I read about it."

"What did you read?"

"The process is designed so that the first dose of drugs puts the person out, and the second dose ends their life."

"That doesn't sound so bad. Will you be there that night?"

Damn it, I thought. *Please say no.*

"I don't know if I can," Matt answered. "I don't know if I should see that."

"I understand, but think about, okay? Seeing your face before I die would mean a lot to me."

"I'll think about it, but I can't promise I will."

"That's all I ask."

* * *

I called Abby after dinner that night.

"Hello, Alex," she said.

"Hi, Abby," I said. "How are you?"

"I laughed so hard today I was in tears."

"What about?" I asked.

"I remembered our time in We're Fucked, Texas."

"Oh, God. It's still too early for me. I won't be able to laugh about that fiasco for a long time to come."

We both laughed.

"I thought about arriving at the motel and how the kids were so appalled by our predicament," Abby said. "We've spoiled them."

"I told Christi it was just for the night," I said. "What a lie that turned out to be."

We both laughed again.

"How is Matt? Has he said anything about attending the execution?"

"Donny brought it up today. He asked Matt to be there."

"Oh no."

"He did."

"What did Matt say?"

"He didn't commit to attending but said he'd think about it."

"Oh no."

"I think he's going to want to be there for Donny.

"My son is not attending an execution without me. I'll fly to Huntsville on Monday."

"I think you'd better come. I don't know whether we'll be at the execution or not, but you should come."

"I'll book a flight."

"Okay."

"See you then."

"Love you."

"I love you, too."

* * *

Hearing Abby laughing on the phone reminded me of how much her place at the center of my universe meant to me. Like the sun, my whole world revolved around her; her aura was like a gravitational pull for me, irresistible. Abby provided warmth and light to my world that I'd never been able to generate on my own. Since her affair, my world had darkened, and my orbit had loosened, but I still couldn't imagine my life without Abby at the center. Without her, I knew my world would be a cold and dark place; it would be a constant state of winter in my soul. From a young age, the thing we're taught about the sun is that we must look away during an eclipse and know that the sun will still be there when we look back. We must have faith in powers that are greater than us. I had loved Abby since the day we met, and I knew I'd love her until the sun stopped shining. After many months of soul searching, I'd finally found clarity and a sense of peace. I had to let the eclipse pass. Abby was my sun.

Chapter Thirty-Nine

When Matt and I arrived for the next visitation, Donny surprised me by telling Matt he wanted to have some time alone with his "Dad." He was referring to me, of course, and it was the first time that year I'd heard the word in relation to my oldest son; Matt hadn't called me Dad since Abby and I had told him about Donny. It felt intentional on Donny's part, and if that was the case, it was the most fatherly act Donny had ever done for his son. As we spoke, his words convinced me that was true.

After Matt wandered to another part of the visitation center, our conversation began.

"You look exhausted," I told Donny once I'd taken a seat before him.

"I haven't slept in a week. Waiting to be executed is the worst thing you could ever imagine."

"I'll bet."

"My life will be over in four days, and I'm both afraid to die and afraid of what comes next. My mother always warned me about Hell."

"If it's any consolation to you, I don't believe in Heaven or Hell."

"You don't?"

"No, I think the truth is that we, as human beings, have no idea what's next. Personally, I like to think there is a big, wonderful reveal when we die. We learn about God and what's next."

"Go on."

Donny's posture perked up as I spoke. His eyes were wide as he stared right at me. Looking at him, I realized I had the most captive audience of my life. He hung on my every word.

"I'm not a religious man," I told him, "but I have an examining mind, and, as I got older, I concluded that no one truly knows anything about God. Everything we're taught when we're young is simply made up. No one knows. As human beings, we simply can't imagine or comprehend that being.

"How so?"

"Close your eyes. Try to imagine what a being that could create this endless universe and spectacular planet is like."

Donny closed his eyes. He was silent for a full minute and then he spoke.

"I got nothing."

"Exactly. We can't even imagine what God is like. We're human and knowing and understanding God is simply beyond us."

"I get your point."

"Just to emphasize my point, now consider the fact that this being created it all from nothing."

"Wow. That blows my mind."

"Exactly, it's incomprehensible. And there's nothing wrong with acknowledging that. We simply don't know."

Donny had a slight grin on his face as he seemed to ponder my ideas on God. I'd never thought of myself as someone who could do missionary work, but under the circumstances, I tried to do my best.

"So, for me," I said, "when I die, I believe I'm either going to meet God and learn what's next or go nowhere; I'll just be dead, and there's no afterlife. I like to hope it's the first option because it allows me to be comfortable with dying."

"Your version is better than my mother's."

"It's just my thoughts on the matter. No one knows."

"Do you think God will punish me for what I did?"

"I don't know, Donny, but I don't believe it's about judgment. I'd like to believe it's about love."

"I really messed up my life."

"You did."

"I asked Matt to leave us alone because I wanted to thank you for stepping up when I'd abandoned them. I really let Abby and Matt down."

"Your loss was my gain."

"I know, but I see what a great job you did with Matt, and I feel I need to say it."

"You're welcome. I was happy to do it."

"I missed out on so much."

"You did. Abby adds beauty to my life. She places flowers on the counter, and while I'd never do that for myself, it reminds me that she is the color and beauty in my world. If I hadn't met her and Matt, I would've continued my days in a black-and-white world."

"My whole life has been black and white, and sometimes not even white."

"I understand. For your sake, I hope I'm right about God."

"Me, too. I'm a little less afraid right now. The God you describe is one I want to meet. Maybe I'll even get an hour or two of sleep tonight."

"Good."

Throughout 2017, on both ends of the spectrum, both good and bad, my life continued to dumbfound me. It seemed like this year was determined to challenge and test me. When Abby told me about Donny eight months ago, I never would have imagined that I'd help him as he made his walk toward the gurney, that I'd comfort him in his final days and provide spiritual counsel. The idea that I'd even like the guy would have seemed ridiculous. On the contrary, I would have thought I'd be looking forward to the day they strapped him down, the day the State of Texas ended his life. I would have thought I'd be relieved and glad when he was out of my world for good. But, in actuality, nothing was further from the truth. With the day fast approaching, I felt only sadness.

* * *

When gunslingers roamed the Old West, a judge's decree that the convicted "will hang by the neck until dead" would often produce unexpected results. Too short of a rope meant the condemned would struggle and writhe for several minutes until asphyxiation finally caused death. Too long of a rope decapitated the condemned and caused instant death, along with a horrible, stomach-turning mess. After years of torturous or violent hangings, a proper rope length was calculated based on the height and weight of the condemned so that the drop would break the neck but not decapitate, causing instant death without the carnage. As a result, the science of death by hanging was improved but never perfected, as inefficient and messy hangings still occurred.

The electric chair was invented in the 1880s as a more humane method for carrying out the death penalty. In practice, a first charge of electricity was administered to stop the heart, and then a second charge of electricity was administered to damage the internal organs and cause death. Much like hangings, electric chair executions weren't always reliable. Sometimes, the shocks didn't produce the desired result and heartbeats were detected later. In particularly horrible instances, the condemned was brought back to the chair, strapped in a second time, reattached to the electrodes, and administered additional charges once the chair was restarted and operational again. Some electrocutions took up to twenty minutes, and some produced bleeding and singed skin. After witnessing an execution in 1890, George Westinghouse, the founder of the Westinghouse Electric Company, was quoted as saying, "They would've done better with an ax."

Since the 1980s, lethal injection has been the primary method for executions in the United States. Lethal injection was accomplished by a series of drugs that produced unconsciousness first and then death by stopping the heart. When administered correctly, executions were uneventful and sanitary, while the issue of the actual suffering endured by the paralyzed and dying man remained a point of contention. Witnesses only saw the condemned strapped to a gurney with intravenous lines inserted and a heart monitor attached. Once the flow of drugs began, the condemned slipped into unconsciousness and was usually pronounced dead in seven minutes or so. No flailing or writhing in pain occurred, and no severing of body parts or bloody execution scenes resulted. From the witnesses' perspective, lethal injection removed the aspect of visually dramatic deaths from executions and left only the termination of a life.

In my spare time (and I had plenty of spare time in Huntsville), I'd read a lot about executions because I wanted to know what to expect if Matt decided to attend this one. While I was relieved to read that the process wasn't overly dramatic or grisly, I knew not to underestimate the trauma of watching another human being's life taken, particularly when that human being was Matt's biological father. In my research, I'd seen photos of the execution chamber and witness rooms, which were, at best, stark and bleak. The brightly lit chamber with block walls, white gurney on center stage behind a viewing window, and medical devices in the wings were sure to be fodder for sleepless and nightmare-filled nights. In many ways, the chamber reminded me of the laboratories of mad scientists from horror movies of the 1940s and 50s. A macabre sense of theater hinted that the production that night would be one we'd never forget, no matter how hard we tried.

* * *

"I actually got a little sleep last night," Donny said as we arrived at the visitation booth. As he did, he glanced in my direction and smiled ever so slightly.

"I'm glad to hear that," I said.

Despite his rest, Donny still looked haggard and hopeless, with dark circles under his red eyes and a gaunt and emaciated frame. He'd lost a lot of weight since the first day we'd met him. Given a little more time, it seemed like Donny was willing to save the state the drugs and the trouble of executing him and waste away on his own, but his appointment with the executioner was less than sixty hours away, so the state would do the deed. In his weakened state, sitting with us was an effort on his part. We all sat in silence for long periods as he mostly wanted our company at this point. At least, that's how it seemed to me.

"I committed other crimes, you know," he said at one point. "I robbed a lot of homes."

"I figured as much," Matt said. "The convenience store didn't seem like a one-time event."

"It wasn't," he said, almost in a whisper.

"Did you ever hurt anyone else?" Matt asked.

"I saw a woman in a business suit outside a supermarket one evening, so I followed her home. I figured she'd have expensive jewelry that I could hock. I watched her house for a couple days to learn her routine. It was obvious she worked a nine-to-five job somewhere. I didn't care where."

Donny hung his head like he needed a break from his tale. I looked over at Matt. He shrugged.

"Did you rob her house?" Matt asked.

Donny raised his head and continued. "I broke in early one morning after she'd left. When I'd watched her, I never saw a husband or kids, so I thought it'd be an easy job. After I'd been in the house for about ten minutes, an old lady came out of a back bedroom. Her mother lived with her."

"How old?" Matt asked.

"About eighty."

"You didn't hurt her, did you?"

"No, but I regret what I did."

"Did you rape her?"

"Oh, God no, Matt."

"What did you do?"

"I got some shoestrings from a closet, and I tied her up. I left her there on the floor in the hall."

"Well, at least you didn't hurt her."

"She was old. I never should've done that to her."

Once again, Donny hung his head, and we all sat in silence. As the time approached 4 p.m., I told Donny we had to leave to pick up Abby at the airport.

"Is she coming to see me tomorrow?" he asked.

"I don't know," I said. "She is coming to Huntsville in case Matt decides to attend the execution."

"Ask her to come tomorrow, Alex. I would love to see her one last time."

Chapter Forty

During the time we'd been in Huntsville, the sky had been a constant, unchanging gray. Every day, almost all day, gray clouds overlaid the town with a dull and dispirited aura that seemed to slow the passage of time. As we left the penitentiary that day, those same gray clouds opened up for a downpour that quickly flooded the gutters and roadsides. Seemingly out of nowhere, currents of water swept across the blacktop of the highway and made the driving treacherous. When the wipers could no longer hold back the deluge, I had to pull our vehicle to the side of the road, and Matt and I watched as raindrops struck the hood of our SUV like bullets fired from a Tommy gun. From past downpours, I'd learned not to challenge an intense East Texas rainstorm, so we waited it out instead.

"What did you say to Donny that helped him sleep?" Matt asked while we waited.

"We talked about God and what comes next," I told him.

"Whatever you said, helped him. He seemed more relaxed."

"I hope so."

"I didn't expect you to get along with Donny."

"Me neither."

"Do you think Mom will meet with him?"

"I honestly don't know."

With the ring of a school bell, Abby's classes started and ended at precise times. Whether at school or elsewhere, she was a stickler about promptness and always grew impatient and snippy whenever we were running late for anything. With her carry-on at her side, Abby stood beneath a bold, red sign that read, "Arrivals," with her arms crossed and lips pursed. As we pulled up to the curb, she glared at me.

"We're in trouble," I said to Matt, as he opened his door to help his mother with her luggage.

"We had to pull over because of the rain," I heard Matt tell her without even saying hello.

"You're forty minutes late," Abby said, ignoring his explanation.

"How was your flight?" I asked as she climbed into the backseat.

"On time," she answered.

Abby ranted against our tardiness until we cleared the boundary of the airport, and then she finally changed the subject.

"Our youngest isn't speaking to me," she said, "because I wouldn't let him come to Huntsville and witness the execution."

"Are you serious?" Matt said. "Nate wanted to witness the execution?"

"He did."

"It's not surprising when you think about it," I said. "His curiosity is limitless."

"Was it his curiosity or his interest in the macabre that motivated him?" Abby asked. "It fits in nicely with his fascination with serial killers."

"Either way," I said, "we'd better sleep with one eye open when we get home."

Abby chuckled. "I did last night."

"Donny wants you to come with us tomorrow," Matt said. "He wants to see you one last time."

"Damn it," Abby exclaimed. "I don't want to talk with him."

"How can you say no?" I asked her. "He's being executed the next day. It's like a last request."

"I know," Abby said. "I'll go with you tomorrow."

I'd always felt like my past stalked me every day of my life. Everywhere I went, I dreaded the unpleasant memories and cruel reminders that might lurk around the next corner, hidden in the shadows. I looked over my shoulder often; I watched my back. With the specter of a face-to-face meeting with Donny looming, this was the first time I'd seen it happen in Abby's life. Better than anyone, I knew her unease.

* * *

"You can only bring your ID," I advised Abby as we arrived at the penitentiary. "Nothing else."

"I can't even bring my purse?" she shot back in an agitated tone.

"It's a maximum-security prison," I said. "Be glad they let you wear your clothes in."

"Mom," Matt said, from the backseat, "we've got a half-hour of security checks to clear before we see Donny. You need to relax."

"I am relaxed," Abby said.

"I've got to agree with Matt," I said. "You seem rather tense this morning."

"Well," Abby said, "I don't want to see Donny, but I don't feel like I have a choice."

"Why don't you want to see him?" Matt asked.

"Because that son of a bitch abandoned me when I was six months pregnant, Matt, and I can't say what I want to say to him because his execution is tomorrow."

"Why not?" Matt followed up.

"If I say what I want to say, I'll only regret it after the execution. He'll be dead, and I'll have to live with the harsh words I said. What's the point?"

"Whatever scores you have to settle," I said, "now's the time to do it."

"I'd like to slap him across the face, but the guards won't let me do that, will they?"

"No, they won't."

"Give him a chance, Mom," Matt said. "I think you'll be surprised. He knows he let us down, and he regrets it."

"We'll see," Abby replied.

"You're right about one thing," I said.

"What's that?"

"You don't have a choice. You have to see him."

"I know."

The time was a few minutes before noon on Tuesday, the day before the execution. As we walked toward the penitentiary, it was still another stifling hot, cloud-covered day in Huntsville. According to what I'd read, the standard procedure was for the prisoner to be transferred to the site on the eve of the execution, so this would be the last time we'd see Donny unless Matt decided to attend the execution. While Matt had said he didn't want to witness the execution, I sensed we'd be there because he didn't want to let Donny down either. As far as I knew, no one from the Reed family was in town to support Donny during his final moments. Many times, as we'd come and gone from the penitentiary, I'd asked the guards if he'd had any other visitors.

"Not a soul," the guard usually responded. To me, that seemed like an apt death row response.

Without us in attendance, the room reserved for his family members would be empty. I didn't want that, but I didn't want to go either.

Crossing the parking lot, Abby's tight expression and flushed cheeks made me wonder if this meeting with Donny was more essential for her own well-being than she realized. Over the years, I'd often sensed that Abby had unfinished business with Donny because she'd always gotten miffed and annoyed whenever we spoke of him. Pregnant with her first child, I couldn't begin to imagine what she must have experienced when Donny deserted her at that most vulnerable time. I could imagine that Abby must have lain awake in her bed every night and wondered if she could take care of her child on her own. Could she provide for him? Could she keep him safe? Little would have been more painful for Abby than the thought of her child's needs not being met, her failing as a mother. From my time with Abby, I didn't believe she'd ever gotten over that betrayal. She never forgave Donny. Hopefully, she'd find some measure of peace and closure today.

When we arrived at the visitation booth, Donny was already seated behind the glass with the telephone in his hand. His face brightened, his eyes widened, and his back straightened when he saw Abby turn the corner, like he'd spotted a long-lost friend or family member. Without acknowledging him, Abby took a seat in the chair in front of Donny while Matt and I stood behind each of her shoulders. I was content to simply watch the exchange, hoping they'd provide one another closure but not sure what to expect. Personally, I was glad there was a plexiglass barrier between them.

Sitting there, Abby's face didn't mirror Donny's elated expression. Her uneasy stare reminded me of someone in a police station who was identifying the culprit in a lineup. All she needed to do to complete the scene was point at him and exclaim, "That's the guy." For more than a minute, her eyes remained locked on him, without so much as a smile or a wink. Two feet apart, Donny had to notice Abby's disdain, but he never showed it. He was the most upright and alert we'd seen him in days.

"Oh my God, Abby," Donny finally said in an almost gushing manner. "It's so good to see you."

Abby nodded her head slightly, but her steadfast stare remained constant. While he beamed at her, she never even blinked.

"I wasn't sure you'd come," he added. "I wouldn't have blamed you if you didn't."

"I came for Matt."

"I know," Donny said, unfazed by her rejection. "I'm just glad you're here."

Abby nodded again.

"More than anything else," Donny said, his glow and smile vanished from his face, "I needed to see you again. I needed to tell you that I'm sorry for what I did."

"You left me pregnant and alone in that crappy apartment on Burton Street. Do you remember how unsafe that neighborhood was?"

While Abby spoke, Donny's eyes welled with tears. His elation from moments earlier was replaced by anguish, and his body and spirit seemed to deflate. It had seemed as if Abby's arrival had lifted him off death row momentarily, but the reality of her presence had just replanted him there. This was not a joyful reunion; this was a reckoning.

Matt stepped forward as if he wanted to intercede, but I grabbed his wrist and held him back.

I leaned over and whispered in his ear. "Let them be, Matt. This might get difficult at times, but we need to stay out of it."

He hesitated, looked my way, and then conceded.

"What I did to you was horrible," Donny said, tears streaming down his cheeks. "I have no excuses."

"My mother and sister were two hundred miles away," Abby returned. "I had no one."

"I know," Donny said. "I'm sorry."

"I was so afraid I wouldn't be able to take care of Matt on my own. I was so afraid I'd lose him."

"I was wrong to leave you."

"Do you have any idea how hard it is to care for a baby on your own?"

"I should've been there for you and Matt. I'm so sorry."

Abby began crying too. It seemed to me that this reunion was taking her back to the most vulnerable and difficult time of her life. Angered, she lashed out.

"It's a little late for sorry."

"It is," Donny replied. "I know that all too well. It's all over for me tomorrow."

Abby paused. "I know," she said, her tone softened by his reminder about the execution. For the first time since their exchange began, her look conveyed more sadness than anger. After all, Donny had done a lot of stupid things in his life, but it's not like they were without consequence. The fact that he was scheduled to die the very next day must have made it hard for her to stay angry after his apologies.

"I just want you to know," Donny said, "that I've thought about you and our child and regretted my actions every day since. I so wished I could undo what I'd done."

At that point, both Donny and Abby wiped tears from their faces. Watching them, awash in emotions, I could only hope that they were releasing more than just water and saline with those tears.

"Meeting Matt and Alex," Donny continued, "only confirmed for me how stupid I'd been, how much I'd lost."

Donny hung his head. As he did, I saw teardrops splat on the counter in front of him. In a whispered tone, he added, "I missed so much."

"I'm lucky to have them," Abby said.

"I know," Donny said, lifting his head once again. "I'm grateful that I got to meet them."

"Matt is a good man. You'd be proud of him."

"I am proud of him," Donny returned. "He's the only good thing I ever did in my life."

A long silence ensued as Donny and Abby seemed drained by the exchange. Unable to talk to one another for so many years, their words had rattled around inside them without any means or opportunity to seep out or be expelled. Clearly, there were words that needed to be said and words that needed to be heard. In the silence, both seemed relieved and unburdened. Both seemed content with the result.

"Tell me you forgive me," Donny said, a hopeful look in his eyes.

To me, it seemed like Abby had forgiven him, but I guess he needed to hear the actual words. Sometimes, three little words can mean everything.

"I need your forgiveness," he added.

"I forgive you," she said, smiling for the first time that day.

Chapter Forty-One

I n my early fifties, the one thing I could say with certainty was that I'd led a reluctant life. Never, ever had I charged forward with unwavering confidence in my abilities, convinced that I was up to the task at hand. Even at work, while considering a new project for a prospective client, even ones with a work scope similar to other homes I'd built, I'd have to gradually convince myself that I could do it. You see, belief in myself never came easily; it was always a maddening process. Somehow, this uncertainty was rooted in me at an early age. I'd been reluctant for as long as I could remember. My father never believed in me; my Uncle Bob and the Entrepreneur did, so I guess disparagement at a young age overrides encouragement and votes of confidence that come later.

Despite its unattractive nature, reluctance had also served a purpose in my life by making me hesitate before doing stupid things. Typically, whenever I did anything, I proceeded in a herky-jerky manner, allowing myself many pauses to question the prudence of my plan. On many occasions in the past, I'd caught myself during ill-advised moments and reined myself in. These moments of hesitation saved me from embarrassment and trouble. My reluctance was never more evident than the afternoon of August 23, 2017, as I prepared to be a reluctant witness at the execution of Donny Reed. I knew that attending the execution was a really bad idea for Matt, Abby, and me, but I also knew that decision belonged to Matt. It would be his father on the gurney that evening. When I was only a few years older than Matt, I'd watched my father die in front of me; I knew his father's death would be a moment he'd never forget. He'd carry it with him for the rest of his days, no matter how hard he tried to put it aside. Somehow, I hoped we'd miss that moment.

By 4 p.m., we were all dressed and waiting in the hotel room while the minutes passed in an onerous manner. Matt sat in a chair by the desk and tapped his foot nervously. At times, I noticed that the pace of his tapping sped up or slowed momentarily as if it was registering the level of anxiety in his body. On her flight, Abby had brought a blue suit for me and a gray sport coat for Matt. Matt wore the sport coat with a pair of faded blue jeans. Abby wore a bright yellow dress with white polka dots because she said she refused to dress for a funeral while the man was still alive. I didn't know what the proper attire for an execution was, but amongst the three of us, we'd certainly covered all the options. All dressed and ready to go, we sat quietly, avoiding eye contact. I'd never been more reluctant and uncertain about anything in my life. I couldn't even imagine what Matt and Abby were thinking.

Looking up from the floor, Matt said, "What do you think Donny is thinking about right now?"

"I have no idea," I answered.

"He's probably thinking about you," Abby said. "He said you were the only good thing he ever did."

"I think he's remembering his time with you, Mom," Matt said. "He talked about your early days together like they were the best days of his life."

Abby only smiled, and a sad smile at that. Her eyes pooled with tears, and it was obvious she couldn't speak. She shook her head slowly in a regretful sort of way.

I'd been to plenty of funerals, more than most. I understood the pall of gloom that descended upon those days, the sadness that held my heart and mind hostage, and the pain of a loss that could never be reversed. Many times, I'd carried caskets weighted by much more than the remains of the deceased. But this feeling was entirely different. This wasn't mourning or gloom or sadness—this was dread. We weren't there for the dead; we were there for the actual death. And an unnatural death at that. This was much worse!

"Are you sure you want to attend?" I asked Matt in a tone that conveyed my apprehension.

His eyes narrowed. "I don't want to be there," Matt said. "I've got to be there. He's my father."

"Maybe you shouldn't go," Abby said, looking my way. "I'll be there with Matt."

I knew Abby was only trying to protect me, but her words stung, nonetheless. I felt like she'd highlighted the fact that I didn't have a connection to Donny, not legally or biologically. My role at this execution was merely that of unrelated onlooker. I knew she didn't mean it, but I felt that way.

"It's all of us or none of us," I shot back.

"Okay," she said, rebuffed, her look confused. "All of us," she added.

Matt's foot tapping accelerated. "I've got to be there," he repeated.

"We're all going," I told him.

* * *

Commotion was not the norm in Huntsville. In summer especially, and mostly due to the heat, the streets and sidewalks were often still and without passersby. The stillness in town surpassed the normal sleepiness of other small towns and brought the term "ghost town" to mind. But, on the night of the execution, as we exited the hotel and walked toward the penitentiary, the streets were full of protesters, curiosity seekers, and camera crews, so much so that a noticeable police presence was also on hand.

As we walked, we passed many protestors with signs in hand, some against the death penalty, some in favor of it. The signs supporting the execution were blunt with messages like "Death to Donny" and "Kill the Murderer." The signs against the execution were more subdued and politically motivated like "Protect Life." As they chanted, those in favor of the execution seemed bloodthirsty and mob-like, like they had a personal stake in the proceedings that evening. For those of us who actually had a personal stake in the execution, the scene was unexpected and unnerving, at least for me. Confounded by the chaotic atmosphere around us, we walked slowly along the sidewalk toward the penitentiary.

Across the street, a man with a megaphone blasted his message to all on the block.

"The Bible says an eye for an eye," he declared, "so it is time for this murderer to meet his Maker."

Fifty yards in front of us, a skinny man emerged from the doorway of a dingy bar and turned in our direction. He was dressed as the Grim Reaper, head to toe in black garments with a long cape draped over his shoulders, a skeletal mask, and a large scythe in his right hand. At once, we all stopped walking and stared at the dark figure as he strode briskly down the sidewalk in our direction. He lurched as he walked, and the scythe flailed about beside him. The whole scene felt surreal to me, like one of the many dreams I'd had about Donny.

"A soul will be mine tonight," the man said as he strolled past us, our mouths agape.

We watched as he walked another fifty yards up the sidewalk and then paused at a folding table where an old woman in a black veil was selling churros for five dollars. From within his cape, he produced a bill and handed it to the woman. She made the sign of the cross above the table and then handed a wiry pastry to him. After examining it, the man in the Grim Reaper outfit took one vigorous bite and walked off.

"I don't know what to say about that," Abby said.

Pained, Matt scanned the street. "A man is going to die," he said, "and they're turning it into a sideshow."

When we reached the entrance of the red brick building, we stopped briefly while a newswoman reported live for a local television station. On the front of the building, the large white clock atop black iron windows served as the backdrop while the cameraman stood ten feet away and filmed her report.

"In less than an hour," the young reporter began, holding a microphone with a large "5" on it, "convicted killer Donny Reed will be put to death inside these penitentiary walls for the murder he committed at an Abilene mini-mart almost seventeen years ago. It is considered one of most brutal crimes in the state's history because Reed shot the elderly cashier in the face after she'd already given him the money. Unfortunately for Reed, his entire crime was captured on the store's security camera, and its graphic nature created a public outcry for the ultimate penalty. At his trial, the jury deliberated for only three hours before handing down their guilty verdict."

Matt cringed as he listened. His eyes continued to scan the unsettling scene around us.

For the last hour, I'd kept a close eye on Matt because, in my mind, I questioned whether he had the maturity to witness the execution of his father. Would he be able to handle that memory, or would it torment him for the rest of his days? While I'd watched Matt, I'd seen him stare off into oblivion like he was almost comatose. I'd seen his cheeks redden and eyes fill with rage. I'd seen his head hung and his shoulders hunched like he'd collapsed on the inside. I'd seen his eyes look hollow and empty like he had no will left. We still had an hour to go before the actual proceedings and Matt had already been through an emotional wringer. Even more than before, I knew our presence at the execution would be a huge mistake. But what could I do?

Chapter Forty-Two

At exactly 5:50 p.m., I stood with Matt and Abby outside a secure door in a short hallway on well-worn Saltillo tile. Above us, only three of the five lights in the ceiling worked and dimly lit the hallway like an Italian restaurant. In this hallway, in a building that dated back to 1849, nothing looked updated or modern except the card reader beside the locked door. A painting on the wall depicted the scene at the Alamo as the hopeless battle waged. Leaning against a solid concrete wall, I felt like I was standing amongst history and spirits.

Accompanying us were three prison guards and two representatives of the media, one from the Associated Press and one from the local paper, *The Huntsville Item*. No one said a word while we waited. No one even looked at one another. On the other side of the door was a small viewing room for family members that was attached to the execution chamber. I'd seen pictures of the room previously but didn't feel like I had any sense of what it would feel like on the other side of the door. I assumed the reporters had been there before.

Earlier in the day, we'd been briefed on the process. At exactly 6 p.m., the warden receives two phone calls, one from the governor's office and one from the attorney general's office, each telling him to proceed with the execution. With those go-aheads received, the warden makes the short walk from his office to the cell where the prisoner is being held and speaks just two words on arrival, "It's time." Without handcuffs or restraints of any kind, the prisoner is escorted to the execution chamber. Upon arrival, five officers, all part of a group known as the "strap down team" and each with very specific assignments, strap the prisoner to the gurney in less than thirty seconds. Once the prisoner is strapped onto the gurney, the medical team enters the room and inserts two IVs into the prisoner, one in each arm. Only one is used during the execution, but the second is inserted as a backup. With the preparation complete, the warden takes his position beside the prisoner's head, and the chaplain takes his position near the prisoner's knees. At exactly 6:09 p.m., family members and the media are escorted into the viewing room.

After what felt like an eternity in the crowded and somewhat claustrophobic hallway, the largest of the guards squeezed past us on his way to the door. He placed a card in front of the sensor, his free hand on the knob, and slowly opened the door. Without looking any of us in the eyes, he said, "It's time to go into the viewing room," in a monotone voice. It was the kind of invitation that would cause anyone to pause.

I glanced at my watch. It was exactly 6:09 p.m. A lump formed in my throat. I'd been dreading this moment ever since it became a possibility about a month ago.

As I entered the viewing room, I was struck by just how small it was, no more than ten feet wide by fifteen feet long, with a large picture window on the far side. On the other side of the glass, the execution chamber glowed like an incubator; only its purpose wasn't nurturing life but rather ending it. In the center of the chamber, the gurney occupied most of the floor space with its silver frame, white cushions, and big, brown leather straps. A few medical devices lined one wall, but the rest of the space was empty. As I stepped up to the window, Donny was already strapped down on the gurney, and the sight of him immobilized and helpless brought tears to my eyes immediately. I looked over at Abby and Matt and tears were already streaming down their cheeks as well. We stood together in the front of the room, in the center of the large window, with Matt in the middle. Abby whispered, "I love you," to her son and simultaneously took his hand. I so wished I could grab both their hands and drag them out of there. I was afraid for all of us.

The warden was an older man, past retirement age, with gray hair and glasses and deep creases in his forehead and beside his eyes. In my mind, I imagined it was time in that chamber that had formed those deep creases and grayed his hair. During our briefing earlier that day, we'd been told that when the warden removes his glasses, that's the signal to the medical team to start the flow of chemicals. The warden looked down at Donny on the gurney and asked, "Do you have any last words you'd like to say?"

"I do," Donny answered in an almost whispered tone. Then, he cleared his throat as a microphone was lowered from the ceiling.

"If I could go back in time," Donny said, "I would do everything much different. I'd be a better man. But I can't go back, so I just want to say I'm sorry to those I hurt or let down. May God forgive me."

With that said, Donny closed his eyes, the microphone slowly ascended to its position near the ceiling, and the warden removed his glasses. Though silent and undetectable, we all knew the chemicals were flowing in the IV.

"I can taste it," Donny said in a barely audible tone.

Then, Donny coughed and gasped.

Matt sobbed. His shoulders and upper body heaved. Abby pulled him into her embrace.

I looked at my family clutching one another beside me, and then I looked back at Donny, who was motionless on the gurney. A portly man in a white coat had taken a position beside Donny and begun placing a stethoscope in different spots on Donny's chest. Next, he placed two fingers on the side of Donny's neck, and then he grasped Donny's wrist momentarily. This went on for a minute or two at most, but it seemed endless.

Finally, the man examining Donny looked at the warden and said, "Time of death, 6:17 p.m."

Like a proclamation, the warden then repeated the statement, a little louder and with more finality. "Time of death, 6:17 p.m."

"No," Matt cried out. "No."

Matt crumbled to his knees, pulling Abby down to the floor with him.

At that moment, I swear I heard something break within my son. It was a snapping sound like you'd hear if you bent a twig beyond its limits. Maybe I imagined it; I don't know for certain, but, when I looked at Matt's face, I saw despair and hopelessness like I'd never seen in any of my children. I'd seen it on my own face before, at times when I felt absolutely lost, but never on the face of one of my children. It was far more devastating that way.

Abby's face had dark, black mascara lines running down her cheeks as if she'd been marked by her time in the room. Her face looked despairing and hopeless, a very foreign look for such an optimistic woman. On her knees, her arms wrapped around her son, she looked up at me with an expression on her face that clearly said, "Oh my God, what have we done?" Feeling hollow and sick, I wondered the same.

Less than a minute after the warden's proclamation, prison guards swept through the room in a coordinated manner, helped Matt and Abby to their feet, and directed us out of the room. Dazed and confused, I walked the short hallway on the well-worn Saltillo tile and several longer hallways after that. We were escorted to a larger room on the other side of the prison with only three chairs in it. I guess they figured we needed more space for all the silence and sadness. If that was the case, we would have needed a room as big as the prison itself. There were not words to express the feeling that came after watching a man be put to death, after watching a condemned man unwillingly breathe his last breath. Suffice it to say, it was an experience I wanted to forget, one I wanted to erase from my memory...but I couldn't.

Chapter Forty-Three

J ust as I feared, the execution had an overwhelming effect on me. I'd watched a man take his last breath in the most unnatural of manners. Worse still, I'd watched someone I'd come to regard as my friend take his last breath in the most unnatural of manners. I felt hollow inside, like the price of admission had been my humanity. I felt diminished, a lesser version of myself than before those chemicals flowed in his veins. At the very least, I felt changed. I wondered how long it would take for this hollowed-out feeling to go away. Like someone who'd suffered a trauma, I could only hope it wasn't permanent. As I sat in the large room with Abby and Matt, I could still hear Donny's last words, his final plea, "May God forgive me." In my mind, his last gasp for air echoed like a call for help in a canyon.

A beautiful mosaic cross, crafted with blue, crimson, and gold tiles, and bearing the words, "Votum Fecit Gratiam Accepit" (Vow made, Graces received), adorned the wall opposite the folding chairs where Abby, Matt, and I sat. It was dated beneath the Latin inscription with the Roman numerals MDCCCLXXVII.

Looking over at Abby and Matt, I barely recognized them. They were not the same people I'd left the hotel with two hours earlier. In much the same way that I felt changed, they looked different. Their faces looked empty and depressed and dispirited; their postures looked worn and depleted and defeated like even the slightest wind gust could blow away the remnants of their previous selves. Together, we filled the room with anguish.

We were alone in the large room. When they left us, the guards had given us instructions, but I hadn't paid attention. They might've said they'd wait in the hallway, but I didn't know. My only concern was how Abby, Matt, and I would process this ordeal and move forward, but I knew that wouldn't be easy. It was, after all, a truly devastating experience. Could we move past it? What could possibly restore our now hollow beings? Though I felt gutted, I was most concerned about Matt.

As we sat there, tears slipped from our eyes and rolled down our cheeks, and I wondered if Abby and Matt, like me, questioned the reason for their tears. In my case, I didn't know if I was crying for Donny or myself. Was I crying because Donny was dead or because I'd witnessed it? I didn't know, but either way, it didn't matter. That information wouldn't change anything.

We sat there for more than an hour without exchanging any words, only subtle glances at one another when we thought they'd go undetected. Finally, Matt raised his head and broke the silence.

"I can't believe I just met him, and now he's dead."

"He was happy he got to know you," I said. "You made his final days much better."

"I tallied it up the other day," Matt said. "You first told me about Donny ninety-three days ago. I met with him fourteen times for a total of about 100 hours. That's all I'll ever get with my father."

"This is a lot to deal with," Abby said, her mascara now raccoon-like. "Take it easy for a while."

"I will."

"Let's go back to the hotel," Abby said.

"I'm going to stay with the Garcia's tonight," Matt said.

"Okay," I said quickly before Abby could object.

Her head tilted, Abby looked my way, a puzzled look on her face. Turning to Matt she said, "We're here for you if you want to talk."

"I know."

"We're going to get through this together," I added.

Matt nodded.

An hour later, at the hotel, I explained my thinking to Abby as we prepared for bed.

"I think Matt will be more comforted by Angie than here with us," I told her. "Trust me on this one; the Garcia's are good people."

I was exhausted and hoped I could sleep. As she turned out the light, Abby expressed the same concern.

Chapter Forty-Four

On Thursday morning, after a not so satisfying night's sleep for both of us, Abby changed her flight home from later that night to Friday afternoon. Together, we decided we were mentally, physically, and emotionally drained and not up for travel. As I drank my coffee, I knew I couldn't set out on a fifteen-hour road trip back to Boulder; the prospect of the journey through the nothingness of West Texas seemed absolutely daunting. As much as we wanted to leave Huntsville, we knew we had to decompress first.

At 8 p.m. that night, Abby and I arrived at 1836, a steakhouse in a beautiful, white Italianate country villa that looked more like a governor's mansion than a restaurant. We'd invited Matt and the Garcia girls, but they'd declined, saying they weren't up to a fancy restaurant that night. On the contrary, Abby and I hadn't eaten anything substantial in over forty-eight hours, so we eagerly perused the menu. Once we ordered, we nibbled on warm bread while toasting with good wine, but our spirits were still disconsolate.

"Matt's had a horrible senior year," Abby remarked with a pained expression on her face. "No kid should have to deal with his father's execution."

"It's hard to imagine a worse year," I said. "There was Jessica's death also."

"I have such fond memories of my senior year," she said. "I feel so bad for Matt."

"He'll be okay."

"Do you have fond memories of your senior year?"

"Not really."

"What's your best memory?"

"The day after graduation, I went to Uncle Bob's house, and he greeted me so proudly saying, 'Way to go, kiddo. You're a high school graduate.' When he reached me, he wrapped his arms around me in a tight embrace and whispered to me, 'That's my Alexander the Great.'"

"He was such a good man."

"I miss him."

I'd slept that afternoon and well into early evening, so I felt refreshed and renewed. I also felt like the hollowed-out condition I'd experienced the day before was refilling with a new appreciation for how fragile and precious life truly is. I found myself thinking about my mother, my sister, and Jessica—people in my life whose lives had been cut short. I would have given anything for more time with them. And that's the thing about time: We don't know how much we've been allotted. Twenty-four hours later, it seemed like watching a man die had given me a new perspective on life. I couldn't waste a single second of it.

"Are we okay?" Abby asked timidly, a tone and demeanor she seldom used.

Having just attended an execution twenty-four hours ago, her question could have had so many meanings, but I knew exactly what she meant. If I'd had any doubts, her follow-up statement would've removed them.

"It's almost been a year."

"We are good," I assured her. "The fact that we survived this year says a lot."

"I know we survived the year, but are we good?"

"Abby, we've never been better."

"Why do you say that?"

I looked into her beautiful blue eyes.

"I know I've always loved you. I also know I would never give you up. That was never in question. What I struggled with this last year was the fact that I'd let you down. Yeah, you cheated on me, but I let you down as your husband."

"How so?"

"I worked too much. I wasn't there for you. But more important than my absence was my distance. Like my father, I kept you and the kids at a distance. I didn't open up and share myself with you."

"You tend to keep it all inside."

"You're always in everyone's face, just being yourself. I so admire that in you. I never wonder what you're thinking or who you are."

"Lately, I've noticed you're more expressive with the kids and me."

"I want to be. I'm trying. Going through this ordeal with Matt has taught me a lot."

"What have you learned?"

"I think I'm arriving at a part of the maturing process much later than most. My father wasn't the best example, and I learned some of the ways I interact with people from him."

"He certainly wasn't the best role model."

"He wasn't. But what I've come to realize is that, as part of maturing, we have to acknowledge the fact that our lives and who we are will be whatever we make of them. I realized I needed to stop using my father as an excuse in my life and simply make myself a better man, make myself the man I want to be."

"That's profound, honey. I'm proud of you."

Usually, when dining out, Abby and I had a custom of sharing a dessert. On this occasion, both so hungry from not eating, we each ordered our own selection. Abby ordered a slice of chocolate cake while I chose the cheesecake. After ten minutes with our desserts in front of us, Abby asked me, "Why aren't you eating your cheesecake? Why are you watching me?"

"I just love that face," I said, in a tone that told her I was serious. "I have always loved watching you. Even doing the most mundane things, you affect me."

* * *

That night at the hotel, Abby and I made love with passion and sensitivity reminiscent of our early days. Like our first night together, there was tenderness in our touches, reverence in our stroking, and joy in our kisses. Sex is the most intimate expression of love that exists between two people—a physical, mental, and spiritual melding of hearts, minds, and bodies—and our sexual activity that night served to reestablish true intimacy between us. Moving in unison atop the sheets, we pressed naked skin against naked skin: hers soft and beckoning, mine firm and wanting. Our bodies entwined, we moved in a natural rhythm that was both familiar and exhilarating to us. Gradually, our movement turned into a beautiful dance that floated and fluttered like a ballet one moment and then pressed and gyrated like a tango the next. Near the end of our blissful dance, Abby and I stared into one another's eyes and watched as our pleasure escalated and reached an inspired crescendo.

"It's always been you," Abby said when we finished. "From the first day we met, I knew I'd always love you."

Our night of lovemaking reminded Abby and me of the deep love we felt for one another and the significant roles we played in one another's life: lover, spouse, partner, and friend. In that hotel room, after what had been a difficult year, we rechristened our love and reaffirmed our life partnership. We put our mistakes behind us and embraced our future. Once again, we felt the connection that had brought us together all those years ago, and we both realized that it had only grown stronger with the passage of time.

Chapter Forty-Five

L ike a kick in the ass from the town of Huntsville to send me on my merry way, the temperature was 109 degrees when we dropped Abby at the airport early that afternoon. On the way, we'd stopped at the Garcia Girls coffee store for iced coffees, as well as to thank them for their gracious hospitality while we'd been in town. At that point, I considered them good friends. While I was happy to be leaving Huntsville, this court-sanctioned detacher of earthly coils, I hoped that our friendship with Rosie and Angie would continue. From the look in Matt's and Angie's eyes when they kissed goodbye, I sensed it would. They were clearly a couple now and would have to figure out the long-distance aspect of their relationship. Many times, I'd invited Rosie and Angie to Boulder, and I hoped they'd take me up on it.

"Take a few days with the drive," Abby said as she kissed me goodbye outside the terminal. "Be safe."

"I will," I said. "We'll be home on Sunday."

"Goodbye, Matt," she called out as he'd remained in the backseat.

"Bye, Mom," he responded.

"Keep your eyes on him," Abby said to me.

"Oh, you can count on that."

"I love you."

"I love you, too."

We were getting a late start that day, so I decided to go as far as Abilene, about a four-hour drive. If I timed it right, we could arrive just before dinner and take care of something else I wanted to do, one final act in what had been a long, emotional journey for Matt and me. At the edge of Abilene, I stopped at a grocery store and bought a summer bouquet of flowers, their biggest one. As I did, Matt was unaware of my plan and slept soundly in the backseat of our SUV. The dark circles under his eyes had told me he had a lot of sleep to catch up on.

As I drove through the tall, black gates at the Abilene Cemetery, the sun was setting into a Creamsicle sky. It was two days after the execution of the perpetrator of one of the town's worst crimes, so I suspected the victim's grave would be easy to spot. Almost immediately, I saw a grave blanketed by wilting bouquets, deflated balloons, and even a few stuffed animals. I was pretty sure I'd found it.

"Wake up, Matt," I said. "We're in Abilene."

Groggy, he said, "Are we stopping here?"

"We're at Mary Jo Donovan's grave. I thought we'd pay our respects."

He wiped his eyes. "My father was just executed for her murder. Do you really think I need more reminders of the crime?"

"I think it will help you in the long run."

"You do whatever you want. I'm not getting out of the car."

"This might provide some closure."

"Again," Matt said, his tone sharper this time, "you do whatever you want."

I shrugged. "Alright." I was disappointed.

Just as I thought, when I walked up to the marble marker, it read, "Mary Jo Donovan, Beloved and Missed, 1923-2001." Standing amongst more than fifty items left in memory of Mary Jo, it was clear to me that many, many lives had been affected by Donny's crime.

"If not for Donny Reed," I began, looking down at her name, the bouquet in my hands in front of me, "our lives would never have inter- sected. Two days ago, I witnessed his execution in Huntsville because he is the biological father of my oldest son, Matt. All those years ago, Donny Reed committed a horrendous act when he shot you. He was convicted of murder and sentenced to death, but I suspect, Mary Jo, that none of that truly matters to you. What matters to you is the time you lost with your loved ones. I came here today to simply tell you I am sorry for all you lost."

Over the past week, I'd seen pictures of Mary Jo Donovan in the newspaper coverage of the execution, and I thought she had a kind face. I'd had the feeling that I would've liked her; standing amongst the items left at her gravesite, it seemed like a lot of people did. In the still and quiet of early evening, I bent over and added my bouquet to the sea of flowers.

"Goodbye, Mary Jo," I said. "Rest in peace."

* * *

After a good night of rest and a leisurely breakfast, I drove down the entrance ramp for I-25 onto the open highway to continue our journey home. Matt had reclaimed his reclined position in the backseat and made it clear that he intended to sleep the whole way to Boulder.

"You're driving," he told me. "I'm too tired to take a shift."

It was late morning, and already, the shimmer of the heat rising from the road blurred the horizon and had a mesmerizing effect on me. As I passed a road sign that read (in my mind, at least), "We're Fucked, 215 Miles," I thought about my hill in Boulder, the one I'd raced up in the wrong lane on many occasions. I hadn't done it in more than eight months, since mid-December of last year, and now, my behavior back then seemed absurd to me. For the first time, I thought about the other lane, the oncoming traffic, the passengers in the vehicle, the innocent victims, the Mary Jos in my life. In a selfish, irrational moment, I could've taken out a young mother and her two children; or maybe some high school kids who'd ditched classes for a day in the mountains; or a husband and wife who'd been married for thirty years and cherished their golden years and their golden retrievers. It could've been anyone, but they all had one thing in common—they didn't deserve to die that way. Mary Jo didn't deserve to die that way.

Cruising over the blacktop, I thought more about the act of pressing the accelerator to the floor and rushing up that hill. The more I thought about it, the more I came to believe that it wasn't about dying at all. I didn't want to die. I had never wanted to die. I was unsatisfied with my daily routine and the man I'd become, and I wanted to feel different. I wanted to be different. That exhilarating rush up that hill in the wrong lane provided a temporary escape from my unsatisfying life, an escape from the full-of-excuses man I'd become. Now, with the turmoil in my life from my Uncle Bob's death, Abby's affair, the death of one of our closest friends, and the execution of Matt's biological father in the rearview mirror, I could see my foolhardy actions for what they were—a cry for help. Most importantly, I could see that I was crying out to myself. I was pleading with myself to be a better man, to live a more authentic life, to stop being a victim of my childhood and my distant father, to take responsibility for the man I'd become. Just as I'd told Abby two nights earlier, I needed to acknowledge that my life and the man I am would be whatever I made of them. It was all in my control. I could change who I was, and the way I interacted with others. I could be a better man. I wasn't seeking a fiery crash and death atop that hill; it was, instead, a cathartic act; I was seeking rebirth.

After what had been an arduous and transformative year, I was sure of a handful of things. First, lifetimes are not nearly as long as we think. I was already fifty-one, and so my remaining days were, most likely, less than I'd lived. Simply put, I needed to make better use of my days. Second, my life would be what I made of it, the product of my own choices and actions. Third, I was determined to be a better man: a better father, husband, friend, neighbor, and citizen. To do that, I needed to demand more of myself. Fourth, if I allowed myself to live in the past or fall back on excuses, I would never be that better man. And finally, when I lay on my deathbed and my final breath nears, I will be the only one accountable for what I did with my life. No one else.

Along the roadside, I saw another sign that read, (again, in my mind) "We're Fucked, 27 Miles." Though I'd planned to stop there and revisit the site where my family had been stranded, I knew I couldn't. I'd be going backward, and I was unwilling to do that. I couldn't allow my past to dictate my future any longer. When I reached the turnoff, I accelerated rather than slowing down, and I blew past that exit with the same determination that I wanted to muster to move forward in my life. I wasn't stopping anywhere else on this journey. I was going home.

When I pulled into our driveway around 10 p.m., I felt relieved to be home and ebullient that I'd reached the end of this long and difficult year. Our home, still well-lit for the evening, with yellow windows that promised warmth and comfort within, beckoned me like an old friend. I looked at Matt in the rearview mirror—sound asleep in the backseat—and hoped our arrival marked a new beginning for him. I didn't know it at the time, but Matt and I still had one segment remaining in our current journey together...

Chapter Forty-Six

T he week after our return to Boulder, Matt was even less responsive than normal. He spent most of the time in his room and only ventured out of our home once for a late night with one of his friends. On rare occasions when he joined the family for a meal, he said very little and barely made eye contact with anyone. Matt only spoke when annoyed, but even then, he mostly relied on sneers and dirty looks to convey his displeasure. Whenever prodded, he was as irritable as a high school senior with a ten o'clock curfew on prom night. And, if all that wasn't bad enough, Matt's personal hygiene was deteriorating because he hadn't showered, changed his clothes, or combed his hair in days. With a scrunched nose, Nate had commented about his "feral scent" on more than a few occasions.

One evening during dinner, Christi, reacting to the overarching gloom in her older brother, said she wanted to treat Matt and Nate to pizza and a movie on Saturday afternoon.

"What movie?" Nate asked enthusiastically.

"How about Revenge of the Nerd," Matt said in a snippy tone as he got up from the table. "Count me out," he added as he walked away.

"I thought it might do him some good," Christi said once he'd left the room.

Abby shrugged. "He's not himself these days."

"Actually," Nate said, "I'd say he is acting just like himself but even more so."

"Give Matt some space, kids," I suggested. "He's got a lot on his mind."

Each evening, Abby and I practically wore a path in the wood floors between the kitchen and Matt's room. When we weren't in his room talking with him, we were downstairs talking about him. Together, we were concerned that Matt wasn't processing the time he'd spent in Texas in a positive way. We believed he was stuck in that horrific moment when he'd witnessed the execution of his birth father. But, despite our best efforts, Matt remained obstinate and unreachable. He wouldn't talk to either of us and seemed angered and put off by our efforts. Since we weren't making progress, we told Matt we wanted him to talk to a therapist. As his parents, we believed he needed a professional to help him sort through his feelings about his birth father and all the issues that came with him, which, at their core, were issues that had to do with his identity, self-worth, and well-being. Issues clearly vital to his future. Together, Abby and I researched the credentials of several local therapists and sought referrals from social workers and people we knew. One therapist we spoke with said that she considered parent/child relationships her forte. When we hung up from the call, Abby shook her head and said, "She's never had a case like this one." After several hours of research, we finally selected a therapist and scheduled a first appointment. When we told him, Matt hung his head and mumbled, "I can't believe my parents think I need a shrink."

* * *

Two weeks after our return, Matt started spending little time at our home, either staying out until the wee hours of the morning or disappearing entirely for days at a time. His presence in our home became as rare as Sasquatch sightings, and family members reported their encounters with him with a similar sense of wonderment and disbelief. Since his junior year, Matt had been pulling away from us, distancing himself from us, but his time in Texas seemed to have exacerbated this process. In the wake of the execution, matters clearly went from bad to worse.

Abby and I were asleep when my phone rang around 2 a.m.

"Hello," I said reluctantly. As a general rule, parents don't want the phone to ring in the middle of the night.

"Is this Alex Bryant, the father of Matt Bryant?"

"Yes," I responded, even more reluctantly.

"This is Officer Carson at the Boulder Police Department," he said.

"Is Matt okay?" I asked.

"Who is it?" Abby asked.

"The police department."

"Matt is okay, Mr. Bryant," the officer informed me, "but he was taken into custody when our officers broke up a fight."

"Put him on speaker," Abby whispered in my ear.

I placed my phone on speaker so Abby could hear the conversation. She leaned on my shoulder, and we huddled over the light from my phone.

"He's being held on the charge of disturbing the peace," Officer Carson said.

"Not again," Abby blurted.

"That's his mother, Abby," I informed the officer, "I've got you on speaker."

"Hello Abby, this is Richard Carson. My daughter was in your class two years ago."

"Ally Carson, of course, I remember her."

"You were her favorite teacher. I can't tell how many Mrs. Bryant stories I heard at night."

"That's so sweet."

We all paused for a moment as if the light tone was inappropriate for this phone call. Then, Abby brought us back to reality by asking, "Has he been drinking, Richard?"

"Yes, Abby. He's intoxicated."

"Oh geez," Abby said.

"I'm sorry to call so late with such bad news," Officer Carson said.

"We'll pick him up tomorrow afternoon," I told the officer. From his previous arrest six months ago, I was already familiar with Abby's "no nighttime pick-up" policy pertaining to incarcerated children. He'd have to spend the night in jail again.

"I can't believe he did it again," Abby said once I'd disconnected the call.

"I can't believe you taught this cop's child too. Do you specialize in the children of police officers?"

Abby smiled. "I guess I shouldn't be surprised by this call. He's been in a bad place since the execution."

* * *

After Matt was released from jail, he disappeared entirely. Though Abby had grounded him indefinitely, he left late on the first night and never returned. On the fifth day of his absence, we started calling friends to find out where he was staying. Much to our dismay, no one had seen or heard from him. When we talked to the friend he was with the night he got arrested, we finally learned what had happened.

Matt and his friend, Theo, arrived at a college party held at a small bungalow on the north side of Boulder around midnight. The house was packed with about 100 partiers and difficult to move around in, so they remained on the lawn. Earlier that night, Matt and Theo had purchased a case of Coors beer at a liquor store, and Matt had already consumed most of it.

"He was wasted," Theo said.

It wasn't until after 1 a.m. when the party had thinned that Matt and Theo made their way into the kitchen where the keg was located. Beside the keg stood a guy they knew from high school who Theo described as an "unprecedented asshole." His nickname during high school was "Tweaker." Like Matt, Tweaker was very drunk and slurring his words when he spoke. Though Theo didn't think Matt and Tweaker were friends, Tweaker called out to Matt as soon as he saw him.

"Matt Bryant," Tweaker shouted, "I saw an article that mentioned you on the internet last week."

"What the hell are you talking about?" Matt asked.

"The article said you went to your father's execution in Texas."

"Where'd you see that?"

"It said your father murdered a woman during a robbery at a gas station."

"Back off, Tweaker," Matt said.

"Is it true, Bryant?" Tweaker taunted Matt. "Are you some kind of evil seed?"

"I told you to back off."

According to Theo, Matt was enraged at that point. His face turned crimson, and he glared at Tweaker.

Tweaker grinned. "So, it's true," he said. "You've got a murderer's blood running through your veins."

Matt lunged at Tweaker, and a violent brawl ensued wherein both assailants were bloodied and bruised within the first minute. Their arms flailed furiously as each battered the other with serial blows. Fortunately, the police were already outside the residence and broke the brawl up quickly; otherwise, someone would've been seriously hurt.

"He tried to kill me," Tweaker yelled at the cops as they separated them. "His father was a murderer who was executed in Texas."

Set off again, Matt tried to break free and re-engage with Tweaker.

"That's enough," the police officer told Matt as he restrained him. "You're both under arrest."

Before he hung up, Theo left us with an unnerving comment. He said, "Mr. and Mrs. Bryant, I'm very concerned about Matt. He wasn't the Matt I knew that night. He was different."

* * *

With each day that passed, Abby and I were more concerned by Matt's absence. Our son had witnessed a traumatic event, emerged distraught and unstable, and we had no idea where he was. We'd contacted everyone we thought Matt might seek refuge with, but we'd come up empty. Thinking Matt might not even be in Colorado anymore, we even called Rosie Garcia, but neither Rosie nor Angie had heard from him. After ten days without news, we went to the Boulder Police Department to report Matt as missing, but we were told that, because he was an adult, the police couldn't get involved unless we had reason to believe foul play was involved. We didn't.

"Do you think Matt would commit suicide?" Abby asked me one night in bed when we couldn't sleep.

"Don't go there," I said. "We've got to stay positive."

"He's been struggling for so long, even before the execution."

"I know, but I've never thought he was suicidal."

"I just wish he'd call. This isn't like him. He knows we must be going crazy with worry."

"We'll find him, Abby. I promise."

Chapter Forty-Seven

Twenty days into Matt's absence, Abby and I were anxious and exhausted. On many nights, we sat together on the sofa in our living room and simply hoped for word. We'd already chased down every lead and explored every avenue, so it had basically become a waiting game. Sitting there, trying to keep Abby's hope alive, I also tried to will my phone to ring with news, but it simply wouldn't comply. Night after night, Abby and I stared out the front window at the twinkling lights of Boulder in the distance and worried about our son. Finally, around 6 p.m. one evening, my phone rang and lit up with "Rosalita Garcia" on the screen.

"Hello, Rosie," I said. "I've got you on speaker. Abby is here beside me."

"Hi, Alex," Rosie said. "Hi, Abby."

Abby's eyes widened. Her face seemed to fill with hopefulness. "Hello, Rosie," she called out.

I so hoped Rosie had good news for us.

"How are things in Huntsville?" I asked.

"Well," Rosie said, "I just walked in the door a minute ago, and I found a note on the table from Angie."

"What does it say?" Abby asked, her voice tilted by concern.

"I'll read it to you," Rosie said.

There was a brief pause, and we could hear Rosie handling a sheet of paper. Then, she spoke...

"Mom, I'm going on a road trip with Matt for a few days. When he called, he seemed to really need me, so I couldn't say no. Tell the Bryants that I'm with Matt, and I'll take good care of him. I'll be in touch when I can. Love, Angie."

"Oh my God," Abby exclaimed, "at least we know he's alive."

"Rosie," I said, "I'm going straight to the airport, and I'll be in Huntsville tonight."

"You're going to fly?" Rosie asked, her voice rising as she said it.

"Say what?" Abby said, equally surprised.

"That's right," I said. "I'm getting on a flight for Huntsville tonight."

"You'll have to take two flights," Abby informed me.

"Okay," I said, a little less sure now with that new information. "I'm going to pack a bag."

In the midst of our conversation, I left Rosie and Abby and set off for our bedroom. Five minutes later, Abby walked into the room and found me with a suitcase on the bed with a small clump of clothes in it. She went into our closet, emerged with a carry-on, placed it on the bed beside mine, and moved my small clump to the new bag.

"Take this carry-on," she said. "You're not leaving the continent, and, besides, you can carry this one on the plane with you."

"All right," I said, zipping the bag closed. "I've got to go."

She put her hand on my shoulder. "Are you sure you can do this?" she asked. "You've never flown before."

"I'll be okay."

"I'll book your flights while you drive and text you the details."

At the airport, after dodging other travelers who were hustling in all directions, I arrived at the ticket counter and handed my identification to a man in a blue vest. Accepting it, he said, "Let me find your reservation, Mr. Bryant." After a few taps on his keyboard and the whirring sound of a printer, he handed me a little packet and said, "Have a good flight." Frozen in place, I was unsure of what to do next.

"You probably don't hear this from many men in their fifties," I said hesitantly, "but I've never flown before. Can you give me a few more details?"

"Of course, Mr. Bryant. Follow the signs to Gate 19," the man said, pointing across the terminal to indicate the direction, "and then present your boarding pass to the agent when it's time to board."

"That's it."

"Yes, sir. That's all there is to it."

"Thank you."

"Are you alright, Mr. Bryant? You look a little pale."

"I'm okay. I feel a little flustered."

"There are thirty thousand flights in the U.S. every single day," the man said, flashing a reassuring smile. "You've got nothing to worry about."

"Thank you."

The flight had just started boarding when I arrived at the gate. Unaware that Abby had purchased a first-class ticket for me, I was surprised that my boarding group was the first to board. Along with about fifteen other passengers, I walked the jetway to the point where the airplane's door came into view, about thirty feet away. Taken aback by the sight of the open door, I stepped out of the flow of foot traffic and watched as the other passengers boarded the plane.

With my back against the wall of the jetway, I remembered the plane crash I'd watched on television as a child. In my mind, I saw the wing dip as the plane descended, the fuselage flip when the wing clipped the ground, and a fireball of flames erupt all around it as it cartwheeled off the runway. In that jetway, the image of the fireball was as clear to me as it was forty years earlier in our great room. Suddenly eleven years old again, I was horrified by the thought of boarding the plane. My legs felt immobile, sweat broke out on my brow, and my hands were suddenly clammy.

With my carry-on at my side, I let passenger after passenger go ahead of me and board the plane. Like a frightened child, I squeezed as far as I could into my little corner of the jetway. In my mind, the fireball continued to blaze. I watched as the flight attendant, a bubbly woman in her early twenties, smiled and greeted each passenger as they paraded past her.

"Welcome aboard," she said over and over again.

After sixty or seventy people had passed me and I was alone in the jetway, the young woman looked my way.

"Are you flying with us tonight, sir?" she asked me. "We have to close the door."

I thought about Matt. As I did, the fireball fizzled out, and thoughts of my son moved to the forefront of my mind. I knew he needed me. It was as simple as that.

"I am," I said nervously as I walked slowly towards her and boarded the airplane.

* * *

In the middle of the night, in a nearly empty airport terminal, Rosie was waiting for me as I emerged from the jetway in Huntsville. She sprang to her feet, rushed across the white linoleum floor, and wrapped her arms around me in a much-needed hug. Wiped out from the journey, I felt both dazed and exhausted.

"Are you okay?" she asked. "You must be tired."

"I am," I responded. "It was very stressful."

"I can imagine. It was your first flight."

"It took everything I had to walk onto that plane in Denver."

"Would you fly again?"

"Only if one of my kids needed me."

"You're a good father, Alex."

"I want to be."

Originally, I'd planned to grab an Uber to the hotel and rent a car the next morning, but Rosie objected.

"I won't hear that kind of talk," she told me as we made our way through the quiet corridors. "You'll stay with me. I've got plenty of room. And, if you need a car, Angie's car is parked in the driveway."

"Okay. Thank you."

Until that day, I'd never even been in an airport. I'd never experienced the thrust and roar of a jet aircraft as it rumbled down a runway and lifted skyward. I'd never looked down at the earth from 30,000 feet or felt the wobble of an aircraft as it passed through turbulence. All of that had been terrifying for me on my flights that night. Now in Huntsville, with my feet on the ground again, I was able to relax. I was able to breathe.

Never again, I told myself.

"I've already talked with my friends at the police department," Rosie said, "and they've put out a bulletin on Matt and Angie."

"Really. The Boulder Police wouldn't get involved."

"Here in East Texas, we look out for one another."

"Well, that's great."

"When I tell you they're looking for them, believe me, they're looking. I got Matt's vehicle information and license plate number from Abby. I'd be surprised if we don't hear something today."

"I sure hope so."

As we walked, I noticed a glint at belt level on Rosie whenever the flap of her red leather jacket opened. Whatever it was on her belt, it was metallic in nature and about the size of my hand. Every few steps, I continued to catch little flashes out of the corner of my eye until, eventually, I realized the true purpose of her hidden accessory.

As we reached the parking lot, I stopped and looked at Rosie. "Are you carrying a gun?" I whispered.

"I knew the airport would be empty at this time of night," she said nonchalantly, "so I brought my pistola with me."

My eyes narrowed. Rosie must've sensed my concern because she casually opened her jacket flap to reveal the shiny gun, and then she consoled me.

"Mi abuelo taught me how to shoot a gun in the desert when I was seven. Don't worry, Alex. I'm quite capable."

"I believe you."

Chapter Forty-Eight

A parent's worst nightmare, I spent the first hour of my day creating a "Missing" poster for Matt. Without a doubt, copying and pasting his picture into that poster was one of the most soul-crushing things I'd ever done. No parent wants to see their child's photo beneath the word "Missing" in big, bold type. Working on my laptop, weary from Matt's long absence and my two flights, tears pooled in my eyes, but I persisted, nonetheless, because I needed something to hand out with his picture and my phone number on it when I began searching for Matt and Angie later that morning. They might not even be in the Huntsville area anymore, but I had to keep myself busy while we waited for word from the police.

"I'll be at the downtown store all day," Rosie told me as she left the house that morning. "I'll call you if I hear anything."

At about 9 a.m., driving Angie's Honda Accord, I began searching parking lots for Matt's Land Rover. For five hours, I scoured the lots of hotels, big box stores, fast food restaurants, supermarkets, and strip malls, and even made several passes through the downtown around lunch time. Along the way, I showed Matt's photo to the people I encountered, but no one had seen him.

"He's got a really sweet face," one elderly woman told me in front of a drug store. "He reminds me of my grandson. I hope you find him soon."

I passed the execution site twice during my travels, which only battered my already downtrodden morale even more. The site served as a dramatic reminder of the traumatized and fragile state of my son. While I took some comfort in the fact that Matt was with Angie, I knew I had to find him quickly. In these types of circumstances, time was rarely an ally.

It was after 4 p.m. when I arrived at Garcia Girls Coffee. As I entered, Rosie and I locked eyes in a tortured stare, one that only the parents of missing children would fully understand. The look was a mixture of despair and hope, with despair being the more plentiful component. From the moment of their child's birth, parents dread the possibility of seeing that look in the mirror.

"No word yet," she said immediately, saving me from asking the question.

I nodded and took a seat near the counter.

"I thought we'd hear something by now," she added.

"I didn't have any luck either," I said, exasperated. "I think I searched every corner of this town."

"Let's drive to Dallas tonight and search there," Rosie suggested. "We'll take two cars so we can cover more ground."

"That's a good idea," I said. "There's more chance they're in Dallas than here."

"I think so, too."

Near the southern tip of Dallas, beside the gas pumps at a Chevron station, Rosie marked up two identical maps we'd just purchased in the minimart with a red flair pen. On each map, she made circles and placed either an "R" or an "A" within them. Rosie knew the city of Dallas well, and her circles divvied up the areas where she thought Matt and Angie would most likely hang out. When she was done, she handed one of the maps to me and climbed back into her Escalade. From her open window, she gave me one last instruction.

"The large X on the map is the Hilton," she said. "I'll book two rooms so we can stay over tonight."

"I feel really good about this," I said, mustering my optimism. "We're going to find them."

"I hope so," Rosie said somewhat sadly just before driving away.

Much like Huntsville, I spent the next five hours scouring the parking lots of hotels, big box stores, fast food restaurants, supermarkets, and strip malls. Following the arrows on the pavement, I drove up and down the endless aisles searching for the familiar green and white license plates of my home state. In all, I saw about twenty Colorado license plates, but none of them matched Matt's license plate number and none of them were attached to Matt's Land Rover. Exhausted and unable to search any longer, I headed towards the Hilton around 1 a.m.

At breakfast the next morning, Rosie and I sat quietly with omelets, hash browns, and sides of fruit before us. Most of the business travelers had come and gone already, and we were alone in an alcove of the restaurant with tall, leafy plants that were more awake and alert than us. The night before, we'd covered very little of the Dallas metropolitan area—maybe two percent—and we were both coming to terms with the enormity and futility of our task.

Rosie put her fork down on her napkin and stared blankly across the room. "We're never going to find them driving around parking lots," she said. "We need the police to find them."

"I know it's a long shot," I responded, "but I've got to do something. I've got to look."

"If only we could get their cell phone information."

"They're both adults with their own accounts so we'd need search warrants, which we'll never get."

"I'm just so afraid for them."

"I know. I haven't had a decent night's sleep since Matt left."

Rosie was quiet for a moment. When she spoke again, there was hesitancy in her voice.

"I have to ask you something, Alex. Please forgive me." Then, she looked at me with despair in her eyes and asked, "Do you think Matt would hurt Angie?"

"No, I don't, Rosie," I said. "I really don't. A friend of our family was murdered a couple months back, and his birth father was executed a month ago, so he is lost right now, but I don't think he'd hurt anyone."

"Angie will look out for Matt."

"I know she will."

At that moment, Rosie's phone shook and vibrated on the table with the name "Manny Torres, Police Chief" on the screen. Seeing the word "Police," my heart rate accelerated to an unprecedented pace. Immediately, I knew this call could go either way.

"Oh my God," Rosie exclaimed, "that's the Chief of Police in Huntsville."

"Answer it," I called out, as Rosie seemed paralyzed.

"Hello, Manny," she said after she'd tapped the screen, "I've got you on speaker. I'm in Dallas with my friend, Alex Bryant, the father of the boy who's with Angie."

"Well, that's perfect," Manny said, "because I've got news for both of you."

"Have you found them?" I blurted.

"No, Alex. I wish that was the news, but I do have a sighting."

"Where are they?" Rosie asked.

"I told you I would contact a few agencies in our state and put the word out. Just ten minutes ago, I got a call from the Border Patrol, and their agent advised me that Matt and Angie crossed the border at Los Indios two days ago."

"So, they're in Mexico?" I asked.

"That's right. Los Indios is one of the state's easternmost crossings into Mexico."

"Thank you so much, Manny," Rosie said. "I think I know where they're going."

"Keep me posted," the police chief requested. "I'm here for you, Rosie."

With that said, Manny disconnected the call, and his name disappeared from the screen.

"Where are they?" I asked eagerly.

"Angie's father is a police officer in the town of Cordonero. It's about ninety miles south of that border crossing. I think Angie is going to meet her father."

"I'll bet Matt pushed her to do it," I speculated. "His meeting with his birth father ended with the execution so he might be looking for some kind of do-over with Angie's father. Vicariously, he wants to experience a better ending than the one he got with his father."

Rosie shrugged. "Maybe. The important thing is we know where they're heading. We've got to get there."

"Let's go check out."

"We'll drop my car at home in Huntsville and then drive to Cordonero in Angie's car. The Cadillac is too flashy for Mexico."

"Then that's the plan. Let's go."

Chapter Forty-Nine

I n late afternoon, forty minutes after we'd crossed the border into Mexico, Angie called Rosie. Angie's voice was panicked, she sobbed as she spoke, and the connection was really bad. Since we'd crossed into Mexico, we hadn't seen any populated areas, which probably explained the poor cellular service. A common theme during much of my travels, I felt like I was in the middle of nowhere. Immediately, I was frustrated when I realized our predicament.

"Mom, I'm in Cordonero... arrested...night."

"You're breaking up. What happened?" I asked.

"...horrible...," Angie stammered. "Matt...be so...you."

"We're in Mexico," Rosie called out, trying to calm her daughter. "We'll be in Cordonero in an hour."

"What?" Angie asked.

"We'll be in Cordonero in an hour," Rosie repeated.

"You're coming here?" Angie said, her voice rising with hope.

"We'll be there in an hour," Rosie repeated again.

"Where are you?" I asked.

"Hotel...7."

"Say it again, Angie," I said. "You're breaking up."

"Hotel Fontan, room 277."

"Stay put," Rosie said. "We're coming."

At that moment, Angie's name disappeared from the screen, and I assumed the call was dropped. I called back several times but couldn't get connected again. The phone showed no bars. Whether cell phone technology or my own inability to say the right words, my communication efforts were, once again, inadequate. I sighed. I placed the phone in the cupholder.

"We're almost there," I said as Rosie pressed down on the accelerator, causing the engine to lurch and rev. "This nightmare will end today."

For me, those last five words were a prayer.

* * *

Ninety miles into Mexico, and after a short rise in the terrain, the town of Cordonero suddenly appeared before us, with three prominent church towers as its most noticeable features. On the horizon, the town merged with its natural surroundings in the same way ancient cities did, low in profile like small hills or mountains and built of materials that were once part of the earth. Driving through the town of 205,000 people, the streets were narrow, cobblestone alleyways that wound haphazardly through adobe and brick structures that dated back to the nineteenth century. If not for our mission, I would've enjoyed spending the afternoon in the historic center of town where the beautiful, white stone station with grand copper doors welcomed passenger trains twice a day.

We parked two blocks from the train station when we spotted Matt's Land Rover near a cantina, assuming the Hotel Fontan must be nearby. Rosie asked an old lady selling baskets on the corner for directions to the hotel, and she pointed up the road past the train station. For a brief moment, I wondered why Matt had parked what appeared to be about a quarter mile from his hotel. Then, Rosie and I set off on foot to find the hotel.

We walked past a church with a statue of the Virgin of Guadalupe in a small courtyard, and then we saw Angie sitting on the wall of a large fountain in the center of a square up ahead. Behind her, water rose in elegant streams from several spots in the fountain and rained down upon statues of three women with children. Angie's pose was a dejected one, shoulders hunched, head hung. She didn't see us approach.

"Angie," Rosie said.

"Mom," Angie exclaimed, springing to her feet. She hugged her mother vigorously and advised us, "Matt's in jail."

After Rosie looked Angie up and down and saw she was unharmed, we went to their hotel room so Angie could tell us what had happened. In an emotional rant, Angie provided Rosie and me with a very detailed account of the encounter that had landed Matt in jail.

* * *

Shortly after they arrived in town, Matt and Angie went to the police station to find Hector Garcia. He was out on patrol at the time, so Angie left him a short note:

Hector,

My name is Angelica Garcia, and I am your daughter from Huntsville. I came all this way because I want to meet you. I am staying at the Hotel Fontan in room 277. Please come by when you can. Your daughter, Angie.

According to Angie, Hector was clearly intoxicated when he showed up in an agitated and contentious state at their hotel room just before 9 p.m. He skipped right past greetings and pleasantries and, instead, confronted Angie about her intentions.

"Why did you come to my station?" Hector demanded.

"I wanted to meet you," Angie answered timidly.

"What if I don't want to meet you?"

"I'm your daughter."

Her declaration seemed to anger Hector.

"I have a wife and two daughters," he said, "and you're not one of them."

"I'm sorry you feel that way. I don't want anything from you."

"Just my reputation," Hector shot back, spitting as he did. "You're going to ruin my reputation in this town."

"I'm sorry. I didn't know."

"You're going to destroy my family."

"I am also your family."

"No, you're not."

Those words had brought to life Angie's worst fears about meeting her father. Hector had flat out rejected her. He had his own family and no use for another daughter. Her voice cracked as she continued...

"As soon as the sun comes up tomorrow," Hector told Angie, "you and your gringo boyfriend are going to get the hell out of my town and take your sorry asses back to Texas."

"That's no way to talk to your daughter," Matt said.

Before Hector arrived, Angie had asked Matt to remain silent while she got to know her father, but apparently, in Matt's mind, that part of the reunion was over.

"She's not my daughter," Hector said defiantly. "Her mother slept with so many men that her father could be anyone."

"Don't say that about my mother," Angie shouted.

"This is my town," Hector said. "I'll say whatever I want. Rosalita Garcia no es mas que una puta sucia (is nothing but a dirty whore)."

"Stop it!" Angie screamed as tears began streaming from her eyes. "Stop saying that."

Matt rose from his chair. "You're no father," he said dismissively. "You're a damn drunk."

Hector stepped in front of Matt. The two men were an arm's length apart, locked in a contemptuous face-off. "Watch your mouth, punk," Hector said as he pushed Matt in the chest.

"Don't touch me," Matt said as he pushed him back.

Right away, Hector grabbed Matt's hands and placed handcuffs on them. "You're under arrest," Hector said, grinning, flashing his two gold teeth, "for assaulting a police officer."

"What?" Matt objected. "You pushed me first."

"We'll leave tomorrow," Angie pleaded. "Please, just let him go."

"Too late," Hector said, flashing his gold teeth once more.

* * *

When Angie finished recounting the tale, I looked at Rosie and said, "He baited Matt. He played him."

"Yes, he did," Rosie replied.

"What can we do?" Angie asked.

We both looked at Rosie. She was silent for a full minute. Knowing she was more familiar with Mexican culture than me, I waited to hear what she had to say. I wanted to know her thoughts before I suggested any course of action. Finally, she spoke.

"Angie, I want you to call the police station and tell Hector that Matt's father has come to town. Ask him to come to the room again. Whatever you do, don't tell him that I'm here. He won't come if he knows I'm here."

Chapter Fifty

J ust as night descended on Cordonero, three hard knocks on our hotel room door rattled the room and shook the lampshades. I figured it was force of habit because I knew the man on the other side of the door was a police officer. He'd rapped on the door like he was executing a search warrant or had cornered a suspect. But, when I opened the door, I was surprised to find a short, unimposing figure standing in front of me. Dressed in civilian clothing, the man looked like an accountant or shopkeeper.

Hector was two or three inches shorter than me with a medium frame, balding black hair combed over the top of his head, an unruly black mustache, two gold teeth in the center of his mouth, and a slight limp as he entered the room. He looked like a man who'd tussled a lot in his younger days and usually lost. As he walked past me, the strong odors of alcohol and cigarettes entered the room with him. Once inside, he nodded at Angie, who was seated near the window, and then he sat in the matching chair beside her. A small table provided a yard of separation. He eased back in the chair and crossed his legs.

"I'm sorry I had to arrest your son, Mr. Bryant," he said, "but he assaulted a police officer. I had no choice."

"You pushed him first, Hector," Angie blurted.

"My son is a good kid," I said calmly, "and I know he wouldn't act unless provoked."

"Your son is in a lot of trouble. He could serve three years in prison for his crime."

"Angie tells me Matt only pushed you away after you pushed him. Surely, you can overlook that."

"I can't overlook an assault on a police officer, but I may be able to help you."

"How so?"

"If you were to pay a fine, I might be able to drop the charges."

"How much?"

"Five hundred thousand pesos."

Unfamiliar with the conversion rate, I looked over at Angie.

"About twenty-five thousand dollars," she said.

At that moment, Rosie emerged from the bathroom with her gun at arm's length in front of her, shoulder high, pointed directly at Hector. His eyes widened, and his mouth dropped open as if he was looking at a ghost from his past.

"There'll be no shakedown tonight," Rosie said.

"What are you doing here, Rosie?" Hector said with a stutter.

Hector's demeanor changed. Previously cocky and assured like a man with an advantage, he was now cowering in the chair.

"It's time you know the truth about your father, Angie," Rosie said as she continued to walk slowly toward Hector. "He didn't just abandon us all those years ago. He brutally beat me, and then he fled to Mexico when an arrest warrant was issued for him. He ran away like a coward."

"Please, Rosie," Hector begged, beads of sweat appearing on his forehead, "don't shoot me."

"We'd argued that night," Rosie continued, glancing at her daughter. "Hector hit me across the back of my head with a tequila bottle. I don't remember a lot, but I know I spent nine days in the hospital with a busted jaw, two fractured ribs, a separated shoulder, internal bleeding, and a concussion."

Angie turned to look at Hector. "You son of a bitch."

Rosie finally stopped three feet shy of Hector and aimed her gun directly between his bloodshot eyes. Like he was expecting a bullet at any second, Hector slowly lowered his head.

"But you didn't run because of the arrest warrant," Rosie added with a chuckle. "Did you, Hector?"

Hector said nothing. He kept his head down. It hung from his neck like his bad deeds weighted it.

Rosie continued. "Hector ran because he knew if we were ever in the same room again, I'd kill him."

Not once during the long drive to Cordonero did Rosie mention the beating or her plan to confront her ex-husband. She certainly never mentioned that she might kill him. Her disdain for Hector was evident but nothing more. Watching Rosie threaten Hector with her gun made me uncomfortable, but I remained silent. I wanted my son back.

With her declaration, Hector finally looked up at Rosie again. He looked more afraid than I'd ever seen anyone. His hand trembled on his knee. His lip quivered as he spoke. "Please, Rosie, I'm sorry I beat you and put you in the hospital. I regret it."

"I already had plenty of reason to kill you," Rosie said. "You beat me and abandoned your child. Now, you've added another reason. You've threatened my friend's son."

"I can undo it. I'll get him out of jail."

"Angie," Rosie said, while still glaring at Hector, "go in the bathroom."

"No, Angie," Hector pleaded.

Angie didn't object or even question her mother. She dutifully stood up and went into the bathroom. When the door closed, Hector squirmed in his chair.

"I'll drop the charges," Hector said. "I'll get him out of jail."

"One way or the other," Rosie said, "the charges will be dropped. Either you'll drop them, or the judge will drop them when you don't show up."

"You'll go to jail for the rest of your life," he said. "You'll never see your daughter again."

"If I kill you tonight," Rosie said, "we will bury your body so far out in the desert it'll never be found. No one will ever know what happened to you. And no one will care."

With that said, my role in Rosie's plan was suddenly clear to me. I was going to be the guy who would dig the hole in the middle of the night. I'd shovel sand until my hands were red and blistered. I wouldn't go to jail for murder, just illegally disposing of a corpse. Still, I said nothing. I wanted my son back.

Then, Rosie smiled at Hector. She winked her eye. Her finger tensed as she slowly moved the trigger backward, in the firing motion. First, Hector's eyes got really big, and then he squeezed them shut.

"Click." The hammer tapped the chamber, but the chamber was empty. No bullet fired. Hector's gray pants slowly darkened in the crotch as he pissed his pants. He looked down at his crotch and then up at Rosie.

"The next chamber isn't empty," she said matter-of-factly.

"Oh God, please, let me go."

"You know, Hector," Rosie advised him, "there isn't a statute of limitations for attempted murder in Texas. Fifteen years ago, no one cared about my beating when I was an illegal immigrant without money or power. But now, I am a U.S. citizen with a successful business and friends in the prosecutor's office. I could make that charge happen now. You'll spend the rest of your life in prison."

"Please, Rosie, let me go. Have mercy on me."

"Tomorrow morning, you're going to go to the police station early, and you're going to drop the charges."

"I will. I'll do it first thing."

"We'll be waiting in front of the station at 9 a.m. You make damn sure that Matt walks out of the station at that time. Not one minute later."

"I will. I promise."

"We'll pick up Matt and head north, and you will never see or hear from us again."

"Okay. Thank you."

"If you double-cross me, I'll make sure you regret it." She paused and picked up her phone from atop the coffee table. "I've recorded this conversation."

"I won't. I promise."

Rosie lowered the gun. Hector slowly rose from the chair. He looked uncertain about what he should do.

"Can I leave?" he asked timidly, directed at Rosie.

"Get out of here."

As Hector came my way, I felt a fury rise up in me. I was disgusted by the fact that he'd beaten Rosie severely and almost killed her. On top of that, he'd hurt his daughter and threatened my son. In the most despicable ways, he'd dishonored the roles of husband and father. Over the past year, I'd learned to treat my roles as husband and father with reverence; I'd worked hard to be a better husband and father. This man was an affront to all my growth and change. Rosie may have completed her business with him, but I wasn't done yet.

As he passed me, I said, "Hector, there is one more thing."

"What's that?" he asked as he turned to face me.

With everything I had, I punched Hector in the gut. My fist landed perfectly—right in the flabby part of his belly. He buckled over, gasp for air, and then dropped to his knees. Holding his torso, he rocked back and forth and tried to breathe again. He wasn't having much success.

"That's for Rosie and Angie and Matt," I said.

* * *

That night, I lay awake in bed and didn't sleep at all. All night long, I waited for the Mexican police to break down the door and drag us off to some rat-infested jail, never to be seen or heard from again. Before bed, Rosie had assured me that Hector would keep his end of the bargain. She said he was a coward who beat women and hid behind his badge. She said that cowards always take the easy way out, and that's why she'd given him one. More so than me, she was confident in her plan.

"Matt will walk out of that police station at 9 a.m. tomorrow morning," she said before we turned the lights out. "Don't worry."

Six feet away, I could hear Rosie and Angie sleeping soundly in their bed. Wide awake, staring at the ceiling, I couldn't understand why I was the only one who was concerned.

There are some really bad outcomes here, I thought to myself. *This could all go horribly wrong tomorrow.*

Lying in bed that night, I also thought about my two flights and how I'd wanted them to end so I could stand on solid ground again. Now, lying in bed in a foreign country, I felt unsteady once again and longed for American soil. Up till now, I'd never flown before, and I'd never been out of the country. As it turned out, I didn't like either. The truth was that I didn't even like to be away from home. All I wanted to do was to take Matt home to Abby.

Chapter Fifty-One

As first light appeared on the square beneath our balcony, I sat on a chair at a small bistro table and looked past the grand fountain to the gold building in the distance with "Estacion de Policia" above its riveted steel door. A silver badge with seven points that reminded me of the Old West was painted on the wall beside it. In the quiet of the morning, I thought about Hector and his gold teeth, and I wondered if he planned to double-cross us. Was he inside the station making plans to arrest us right now? Later, as the sun climbed into the morning sky, would Matt walk out of that door, or would we be dragged through it?

At 6 a.m., I'd waited as long as I could, and I called Abby on my cell phone. I wanted to tell her about the events of the prior night as well as our plans for that morning. Most importantly, I wanted to create a contingency plan in case something went wrong.

"We should cross the border by 11," I told her, "and I'll call you as soon as we do. If you don't hear from me by noon, call the Chief of Police in Huntsville, Manny Torres, and ask for his help."

"I've got a bad feeling," Abby said. "Be careful."

An hour later, while Rosie and Angie went to find breakfast and coffee for us, I moved our vehicles to the square. I loaded all of our luggage into Matt's Land Rover and parallel parked them next to one another, near the police station. I even pointed them out of town.

"We need to be outside the police station at 8:45," I told them before they left. "Let's get out of town as soon as Matt is released."

"Relax, Alex," Rosie told me for about the fifth time that morning. "It's going to be fine."

Sure enough, they joined me at the vehicles at 8:45 a.m. with coffee and pastries in hand. Unfortunately, I was too nervous to eat. Leaning against the Land Rover, I sipped my coffee and stared at the steel door.

"He knows not to double-cross me," Rosie said as we waited. "Relax."

Seconds after her remark, a police cruiser appeared on the square with Hector at the wheel. He slowly circled the square and then stopped his cruiser thirty feet behind Angie's car. Through the windshield, I saw him put the car in park and reach for his radio on the dash. Casually, he spoke a few words into the microphone and then returned it to its place. Then, he glanced my way. Hector and I locked eyes and stared at one another for what felt like an eternity.

"Here he comes," Rosie said.

Immediately, I looked back to the steel door and saw Matt coming our way. His stride was rapid like he was anxious to put distance between himself and the station. When he reached us, he hugged Angie, then Rosie, and finally me.

"What are you doing here?" he said to me.

"I came for you," I said.

"Thanks," he whispered.

We quickly climbed into our vehicles, Rosie and Angie in the Honda, Matt and I in the Land Rover. Matt told me to drive because he hadn't slept at all the previous night.

"My cellmates were three unsavory characters," Matt said as we pulled away from the curb. "If I'd fallen asleep, I might not have woken up."

Driving towards the highway, I noticed Hector was trailing us by about ten car lengths. He was keeping his distance while still keeping us in sight.

What's he doing? I thought as I turned onto the highway.

"I'm going to climb in back and get some sleep," Matt said.

"Wait a few minutes," I cautioned him. "We're being followed."

For almost ten miles, Hector trailed us, until, finally, as we passed a sign that read "US / Mexican Border 75," he pulled off onto the side of the road. In the rearview mirror, I watched as Hector made a sharp U-turn and proceeded back towards town. Within a minute, he'd driven over the rise in the terrain and faded from view.

We're going to be okay, I thought.

With my son sleeping in the backseat, I was finally able to relax as I drove. I watched the road ahead of me and thought mostly about Abby and how relieved I was to be returning our son to her. She'd worried so much. Right on schedule, we arrived at the border a little before 11 a.m. At the checkpoint, I took great pleasure from the border agent's parting words, "Welcome home, Mr. Bryant," he said as he handed our passports back to me.

Maybe not home, I thought, *but we're well on our way.*

Back on the road again, I called Abby to let her know we're all right.

"I can breathe again," she said enthusiastically, "for the first time in a month."

After hanging up from my call with Abby, my mind slipped into examination mode. Something about the monotony of driving always sent my mind into overdrive.

Nothing highlights the importance of the people in our lives more than almost losing them, I thought as we rolled along at seventy miles per hour. *And nothing makes us better people than acknowledging and appreciating the importance of those people to our lives. Because of these two hard-earned lessons, I am a better man today than I was a year ago simply because I want to be for Abby and my children. We've got a lot of good years ahead of us.*

I was in the middle of nowhere; still, I was overcome by the feeling that I'd arrived at some place special.

Chapter Fifty-Two

Matt made a beeline for the shower when we arrived at the Garcia home in late afternoon. That was understandable because, south of the border, his accommodations the previous night hadn't included such amenities. His hair was still wet when he joined us at the table, just as our pizza was delivered. Though our food was merely fast food from the local pizza joint, the meal quickly took on a profound tenor and texture. After all, the four of us had been through a lot together. Personally, I felt like I'd completed an arduous journey where I'd been severely tested and emerged with a greater appreciation for life, as well as a real bond with everyone at the table. That simple meal of pizza, salad, and Dos Equis cerveza became a time for appreciation, acknowledgment, apologies, and forgiveness.

"I'm sorry I went to meet him, Mom," Angie said as we started the meal. "You warned me, but I went anyway."

"I'd hoped you'd never meet him," Rosie responded. "He's such a bad man."

"He said horrible things to Angie," Matt said. "He's a cruel man too."

"I'm sorry he hurt you like he did," Angie said.

"When I was recovering in the hospital," Rosie said, "I remember the pain, but I also remember feeling free, like I had to go through that so you and I could have our life."

"You've made a good life for us, Mom."

"At the time, I felt like our lives would be better because of it," Rosie added. "He was gone."

Then, Rosie's mood seemed to brighten as she changed the subject.

"You should've seen your dad punch Hector in the stomach," Rosie said, directed at Matt.

Matt looked shocked. "Say what?" he blurted.

"Alex punched him so hard he dropped to his knees," Rosie added.

"What?" Matt said again. "Did you really?"

"I did."

"Why?" Matt followed up, squinting in a confused manner.

"I don't know exactly," I said. "I think it was because he'd hurt people I loved, and I couldn't just let him walk out of there."

"I didn't know you had that in you," Matt said.

"I do."

"As remarkable as that was, Matt," Angie said, "my mom made Hector pee his pants."

"Say what?" Matt blurted yet again.

For the next five minutes, and in great detail, Angie and I told Matt about our encounter with Hector in the hotel room. Matt listened intently. His lower lip actually dropped when the gun clicked. His astonishment compounded when Hector pleaded for his life. He gasped also when Hector dropped to his knees.

Clearly taken aback, Matt's eyes slowly scanned his dinner companions like he was seeing us anew. "I can't believe you guys did that for me," he finally said, his tone softened. "You could've been arrested or even killed."

"We had to get you out of there," Rosie said.

"I wasn't leaving without you," I added.

A lull occurred in the conversation as we all nibbled on pizza and sipped beer. Rosie smiled at me, a subtle smile that I interpreted as her saying, parent to parent, "Our efforts are getting through to him." Along with a slice of pizza, Matt seemed to have a lot on his plate. He had a lot to digest.

"I'm sorry I put you through that," Matt said. "All of it. What you guys did for me was amazing."

"You put your mother through a lot also," I told him.

"I know."

"If you're going to be in my daughter's life," Rosie said, "I'm going to expect a lot more of you."

"I'll be better," Matt said. "I was so overwhelmed after the execution. I needed some space."

"You can have all the space you need," I told him, "but you can't disappear."

"I know," Matt said. "I'm going to talk with that therapist when we get back to Boulder. I think that will help."

"That's a good idea," I said, nodding at him.

"Are you at the usual hotel?" Matt asked.

"No, I'm staying here in the guest room."

"Where's your SUV? I didn't see it out front."

"I flew to Huntsville."

"Say what?" It was becoming Matt's mantra that evening.

"Two flights," I said. "Denver to Dallas and Dallas to Huntsville."

"Are you kidding me?"

"No. I flew here."

Matt looked directly at me. "Why?"

"You needed me, Matt. I'd fly around the world for you. I'd do anything for you. I love you."

In Matt's face, I saw astonishment. I didn't know if it was what I said or that I'd said it, but it really registered. It was like I'd flipped a switch.

"It's my fault, Matt," I added a moment later, "that you don't already know that, and I'm going to do my best to make sure you always do."

Matt continued to stare at me. Tears spilled from both our eyes. For whatever reason, my two flights made it all real for Matt, the whole ordeal, not just Mexico. Our entire journey together this past year finally registered with him. For the first time since Abby and I told him about Donny, I think Matt realized that we'd been on a journey together as well. He finally realized how this journey had brought us closer to one another. Over the course of these last nine months, we'd closed the gap that had previously existed between us.

"It's been quite a year," Matt said, wiping a tear from his cheek. "I'm glad we had so much time together on our trips to Huntsville. I really enjoyed being with you. I love you, too, Dad."

My head might've actually rolled backward. It was the first time he'd called me "Dad" since Abby and I told him about Donny all those months ago. His words landed in my ears like the sweet sound of church bells in the distance. I smiled at my son.

"Can we stop in Abilene and visit Mary Jo's grave again on the way home?" Matt asked.

"Definitely," I said.

"You were right, Dad. I want to acknowledge her loss and pay my respects. It's the right thing to do."

"I think you'll feel a little better if you do."

"Maybe I'll feel some closure."

"Maybe."

"I feel like Rosie did after Hector beat her," Matt said. "I've been through an awful lot this year, but I know I am going to be stronger because of it. My life will be changed by this journey, and for the better."

* * *

Early that evening, with a couple or three beers in him, Matt made the most astute observation of his young life, one that had us laughing so hard we cried. It started out as a conversation about the atypical relationships Matt and Angie had with their fathers and how parent/child relationships were challenging under even the most ordinary of circumstances. Then, that conversation led to a broader conversation about how the parent/child relationships of the new millennium differed from the previous century, and more specifically, from Rosie's and my childhoods. We were in the middle of what had turned into a deep, philosophical conversation when Matt made his observation.

"I think the relationship between a parent and a child," Matt remarked in a serious tone, "is like a beast whose head is too large for its tiny body, so it always struggles just to hold its head up. The head constantly wants more support, and the body just wants a break. Day in and day out, the beast's head and body can't coexist harmoniously, but they know they're forever bound in life, and that fact only serves to infuriate them even more. There is rarely peace."

After about an hour and another beer, the brilliance of Matt's remarks finally registered with me. For me, the parents were the tiny body that forever struggled to keep their child upright and moving forward in life. The parents had the more difficult task. But, to Matt, the child was the tiny body that forever struggled to manage its parents' weighty expectations. The child carried the heaviest burden. As father and son, we'd interpreted his analogy in two different ways, and our two different interpretations of the same analogy clearly illustrated the nature of the beast.

From that night forward, in the Garcia and Bryant homes, the complicated, challenging, and often frustrating relationship between parent and child was always referred to as "The Beast."

About the Author

A graduate of Georgetown University and recipient of a Master in Business Administration (MBA), Michael Bowe is an accomplished businessman, entrepreneur, investor, and novelist, and a resident of Vashon Island, WA, a short ferry ride from Seattle. In 2020, his second novel, The Weight of a Moment, won the American Fiction Award for Literary Fiction.

Winner
of the
American
Fiction
Award
for
Literary
Fiction
2020

The Weight of a Moment

Michael Bowe